PEARLS OF WINTER
LISA J. JISA

Lisa Jisa
♡
9-17-19

LIAT PUBLISHING
Pardeeville, Wisconsin

For P.
You believe in me.

Book Design: TLC Graphics, *TLCGraphics.com*
Cover: Tamara Dever, Interior: Erin Stark
ISBN: 978-1-7331201-0-4 (Paperback)
ISBN: 978-1-7331201-1-1 (E-book)
First Edition
Printed in the United States
White pearl: ©Depositphotos.com/emaria
Round swiss blue topaz: ©Depositphotos.com/Rozaliya
Diamond snowflake: ©Depositphotos.com/sarininka

ACKNOWLEDGMENTS

Although this book is a work of fiction, parts of some characters were originally based on real people. Names and circumstances have been changed.

Kathy, Amanda, Mom, Pat, Drea, Josh, Jay, David, Shela. My sincere appreciation for taking the time to read all or portions of the book and offer feedback!

Pat, my precious jewel of a friend—I am so grateful that you explained to me how this book truly changed your life. You opened my eyes to see how books can be missionaries.

The many dear friends I made in Uganda, especially David and Concy, Chris and Agnes, Ben, Karim, and Micheal. You shared your families and your lives with me, and I am forever grateful.

Robbie, Jerad, Andrea. Your mom once told me about something that happened to her many years ago, and that was a catalyst for an idea in this book! (I'll tell you what it was after you read it!)

The lovely people of Uganda. You are beautiful and so is your country, the Pearl of Africa. Thank you for welcoming me with open arms.

My fellow Uganda team members who journeyed with me across the ocean—Ben, Gary, Janelle, brother Billy, Rancie, Pastor Brian, David, Rick, Susan, Calen, Carolyn, Joseph, Eric, Gail, Lisa, TJ, Greg, Jay. I hope parts of this book bring you fond memories of our trips to Africa!

The Ugandan children who touched my life in so many ways. Thank you for sharing your lives and your voices. I love you and I miss you.

My Africa-loving sister-friend, Kay. You'll recognize a little bit of our Swaziland adventures here!

Tami, Erin, Dana, and the rest of the TLC Book Design crew. This book has turned out to be more beautiful than I ever imagined it could be! I treasure your expertise, your patience, and your enthusiasm!

The British Airlines employee who upgraded me to first class on a very long flight home simply because my hair looked "so cool" in little braids—what can I say but thanks?!

And finally, a big thank you to my Heavenly Father for opening up my world and taking me to amazing places, for giving me the ability to write, and for bringing me the perfect people at exactly the right times to put all of this together. All the glory goes to You.

When I was a little girl, I used to dream that my bed could fly. Every night I would swoop down and rescue people just before their houses collapsed into dark, watery pits filled with angry alligator-monsters. One morning I woke up and realized that I never saw any other flying beds.

If I crashed, who would rescue me?

CHAPTER ONE

I was peeking out the window at the rapidly increasing snowfall when the timer beeped. I stood there for a minute longer, watching the wind play and swirl the snow around the base of a huge oak tree across the street. The flakes were large and the temperature was just right for packing snowballs and snowmen. And making angels. Any snowfall was perfect for snow angels.

A knock at the door interrupted my momentary enjoyment of this winter dreamland. I knew who it would be—Michael, my fiancé, here to pick me up for Thanksgiving dinner at his brother's house.

Before I could get the door opened all the way, Michael burst into the room, full of smiles and happiness. He loved snow as much as I did, and this current storm brought the promise of at least a foot or more.

"Liv! Look at all this!" Michael stomped his feet on the rug like a child, sending a flurry of flakes to the floor. His blond hair glistened with a light dusting of snowflakes.

I laughed at him as I suddenly remembered the pie still in the oven. I scurried back to the modest kitchen area and picked up stained potholders. Sweet potato pie, a recipe handed down from my grandmother who had gotten it from her neighbor's mother. Mabel Gray lived in the deep south for much of her childhood, and many recipes written in her own unique scrawl filled the red and white checkered recipe collection box that sat on my counter.

"Ooo, I'm going to have to fight Ronnie for the biggest piece of that deliciousness!" exclaimed Michael as he gently brushed aside my auburn ponytail, leaned over my shoulder, and inhaled deeply. Ronnie was Michael's older brother by a few years, and the two of them were closer than any brothers I had ever known. Michael was living in Ronnie's basement until our rapidly approaching wedding date arrived. Five weeks and counting.

I carefully set the pie on a cooling rack. A little bit of the filling was dripping down one side and a small puddle of sweet potato was burning on the bottom of the oven. But it wasn't enough to make the smoke alarm go off like the overflowing apple pie did a few weeks earlier. And the faint burning smell wasn't strong enough to detract from the wonderful cinnamon-infused air.

Michael spun me around and caught me up in a big embrace. He unzipped the front of his well-worn red down coat so I could wrap my arms around him on the inside, then zipped us both in. I stood there for a moment, engulfed in his love and amazed at all the goodness in my life. There had definitely been some rough patches in my 22 years so far, but things were finally turning around for the better. And Michael was a big part of those new changes.

"Oh, my sweet, sweet Olivia!" Michael whispered as he kissed the top of my head and then rested his chin there. "I can't wait for you to be my Mrs.! Thirty-four days til you are all mine!"

I lifted my chin and gave him a quick peck on the cheek, then poked him lightly in the ribs until he pulled down the zipper.

"Hey, is that all I get?" he whined playfully as I slipped my arms out and turned toward the kitchen. If only I had known the anguish that would envelop us later that day, I would have buried my face deep into Michael's chest and held onto him for dear life. But how could I have known? How could anyone?

"That's all for now!" I laughed. "You know Ellen! She will have dinner ready exactly at the time she told us, not a moment sooner or later. Come on, let's go!"

I gathered up the pie and stuffed a few others goodies in a large-handled basket which I handed to Michael, and we made our way out to his silver pickup on the street. Snow continued to fall in big, fluffy flakes, and it was all I could do to keep from smiling for the entire 30 minute drive. I was grateful for the 4-wheel drive, although the roads weren't too slick yet. Michael hummed along to the softly playing radio. There wasn't much traffic.

Ronnie and his wife, Ellen, lived in a modest brick ranch-style home just beyond the far outlying suburbs of Minneapolis. They had a four-year old daughter, Christina. She was an adorable child who loved the doting attention of her Uncle Michael. Christina was born with a rare brittle bone disease that caused her to fracture easily. Due to healing complications, her doctors had recently determined it would be safer for her to use a wheelchair than continue to bump into things and cause more damage to her already weak bones. Ronnie and Michael had built a ramp up to the front steps a few days earlier. I hadn't seen it yet and was anxious to check it out.

As we turned onto Fisher Street, the street lights were just beginning to come on. It was a little early in the day for that, but the low cloud cover had made the sky grow dark much earlier than usual. I craned my neck to watch the swirling snow dance in the light while instinctively reaching my left hand to my neck. I touched the silver pendant that rested there. The special treasure from my father was rarely removed. It had been a gift when I was very young, the last thing he had given me before his untimely and premature death. Reminders of him often caused me to caress the necklace lovingly in remembrance.

The delicate snowflake necklace was the perfect reminder of times when my father and I had played in the snow we both loved so much. Each of the snowflake's branches was encrusted with tiny white diamonds, and a bright blue Swiss topaz rested perfectly in the center.

As Michael pulled up to the curb, he looked at me and nodded knowingly. He understood when I needed a few minutes with my memories. As excited as I was for our upcoming wedding, there were occasional melancholy tears upon the realization that my daddy wouldn't be there to walk me down the aisle. He wouldn't be there to see Michael and me start our life together or be a part of helping raise our future family.

Michael gave me a wink and a smile as he took the pie from my lap. He knew I'd be ready to join the festivities inside in a few minutes. As he stepped away and gently closed my door, I quietly leaned my head down and closed my eyes, trying my best to conjure up an image of my father's endearing smile.

Suddenly there were loud shouts and a commotion that rattled me to alertness. Michael was calling. "Olivia! Take the pie! Quick, take the pie!" As soon as I opened the door and grabbed it from his hands, he went down in a wild commotion of flailing hands and legs.

Ronnie had been waiting. The new ramp up to the front of the house provided good cover and Michael never saw the ambush coming. The two brothers tousled about in the snow, giving face washes and shoving handfuls of powder down each other's backs. I couldn't help but laugh. They reminded me more of playful puppies than they did of grown men.

I carefully made my way past them, admiring the freshly constructed and very sturdy ramp. The house smelled and looked wonderful inside. Ellen was a fantastic cook and a clever decorator, and their house always felt warm and inviting. Ellen was forever finding and lovingly restoring old furniture, and a new wicker rocking chair sat to one side of the red brick fireplace, complete with a dark, floral-patterned needlepoint cushion. A low fire was crackling and a cinnamon-scented candle burned brightly from its resting place upon a dark chocolate-colored antique end table.

Shortly after I entered the house, I was greeted with a kiss on the cheek from Aunt Margaret, an elderly neighbor who was actually the aunt of an old high school friend. Ronnie and Ellen made sure to include Aunt Margaret in family gatherings, especially on holidays when they knew she wouldn't have family in town. I always enjoyed seeing her and catching up on my friend's latest whereabouts.

Aunt Margaret settled herself into an overstuffed green chair where she had a view of the falling snow out the picture window but could also keep an eye on Ellen in the kitchen. By the warmth of the fire, she'd be dozing off before long.

"Olivia!" exclaimed Ellen, rushing to take the pie with one hand and giving me a warm squeeze with the other. Ellen's bouncy blonde curls and petite figure matched her perky personality perfectly. She was always truly happy to see me, and both of us were thrilled that we would soon be sisters-in-law. Neither of us had a sister, so it was a special treat that we genuinely loved each other's company.

I followed Ellen into the kitchen and discovered a feast that was as appealing to the eyes as it was to the nose. Brightly colored dishes mounded with delicious food covered the island, and a juicy turkey rested quietly on top of the stove. She had outdone herself once again.

Within moments the guys burst through the side door, laughing and punching each other playfully. Ronnie tossed his coat on a rack, put his arms around Ellen's waist, and whispered just loud enough for all to hear, "So, did you tell Livvy the news?"

"What news?" I asked slowly.

"Yeah, what news?" sulked Michael. He looked dejected, as though he couldn't believe his big brother would have some important news that had not been shared with him. I watched his eyes search Ellen's face for a clue as he pulled off his boots at the door.

Ellen's eyes grew big and round as she turned to face Ronnie with a look that declared both excitement and fear. As she announced that there was a new little life growing within her belly, I could sense conflicting emotions. Ellen was happy at the anticipation of adding another member to her family, yet apprehensive about its health. Would this baby have the same issues as Christina? And how could she take care of a baby and still be able to provide the level of care that Christina's health demanded?

Without missing a beat, Michael declared his devotion. He and I were scheduled to be leaving for Guatemala shortly after the first of the year, but it was only a three-month commitment. We'd be back at least two months before the baby was due to be born. Michael solemnly pledged to Ronnie and Ellen that he would do whatever was necessary to help his family in any way. He knew I would be on board with that, too. Upon our return to the States, Michael would have to finish med school, so we'd be living relatively close by. I, too, knew that I would do anything in my power to ease the burden on this precious family that would soon be mine.

As laughter and tears spilled over the island in a big tangled group hug, we heard Christina slowly making her way down the hallway to the kitchen. Her wheelchair bumped along the wall a few times, but she was managing quite well as a new driver.

The bewildered look in Ellen's eyes showed that Christina didn't yet know about the prospect of becoming a big sister. I elbowed Michael to make sure he kept his mouth shut. He grabbed my arm and twisted it behind my back in a playful gesture.

"O-Libby!" Christina squealed upon entering the room. I knelt down and embraced her gingerly. I loved that little girl but was scared to death of causing her pain. "When are you gonna do my hair?" Christina asked.

"Oh, sweetie, it's almost time for dinner," said Ellen. But the innocent look on Christina's face as she peered up at her mama was enough to melt any heart.

Ellen relented. "Five minutes!" she conceded as she grabbed foil out of a drawer and began covering up the dishes of food while I followed Christina into the bathroom with a grin. Ellen would give Christina whatever pleasure she could, even if it meant dinner would be a little cooled off.

When Michael and I had asked Christina to be the flower girl in our wedding, she had accepted the proposition with pride. I wasn't sure who was more excited about the upcoming wedding—Christina or me! I had mentioned possible hairstyles a few weeks ago and promised we could try them out on Thanksgiving. Obviously, Christina had not forgotten.

When we emerged into the living room ten minutes later, Ronnie let out an audible gasp. Christina's hair was up in a french braid crown and I had tucked little sprigs of baby's breath along the outer edges. Christina's whole countenance sparkled as she proudly tilted her head to the left and to the right for all to see. Little curly wisps encircled her face. She had blond curls like her mama and was the picture of angelic beauty.

Michael jumped up and kissed Christina on the top of her head. She beamed as he declared, "You better watch out, little beauty! I might have to change my mind on who is the prettiest girl to marry!"

As our group was finally gathering around the dining room table to sit down for Thanksgiving dinner, a loud clicking noise sounded from a box in the living room. Ronnie's scanner. He was on duty for the volunteer fire department in this area tonight and a call was coming in. An address was sputtered out for the Jackson's house, just around the lake and about two miles down the road.

"Old man Jackson was probably having a smoke in bed after turkey dinner," Michael offered kiddingly. But this was no time for jokes with Ronnie. He took every call quite seriously. They didn't need him very often, but he was always prepared to go at a moment's notice.

Ronnie jumped up, grabbed his gear that was always waiting at the ready, and began to head out the door when he realized Michael's truck was blocking the driveway. Without missing a beat, Michael reached into his pocket and tossed him the keys. Ronnie caught the keys with a grateful nod, blew a kiss toward all of us, and headed out into the night as we heard the eerie sound of a siren in the distance, muffled by the falling snow of an early winter storm.

CHAPTER TWO

Dinner was delicious. The turkey was done to golden perfection and the mashed potatoes had just the right hint of garlic. The green bean casserole was as comforting as it was tasty, and every bite of homemade cranberry bread slathered with thick chunks of butter danced with a tangy tartness on our tongues.

Aunt Margaret shared funny stories of Thanksgivings from her childhood. Some were funnier to her than they were to everyone else, but we laughed politely. Michael set Christina into peals of laughter with his winking game. Everything was wonderful and the only thing that was missing to complete the Thanksgiving table was Ronnie's presence. But he'd be home soon. I felt a warm comfort all the way down to my toes. This was the family life I had always dreamed of and it was soon to be my reality.

After dinner, Michael and I cleared the table. Ellen wanted to help, but Michael insisted she put her feet up. He even got a blanket and tucked it around her shoulders. He tucked Aunt Margaret into her chair, too, and then not wanting Christina to feel left out from all the attention, he went to grab a blanket for her from her bed.

"Grrr! Grrr!" came the sounds from underneath a growling blanket that crawled its way down the hall moments later. The menacing sounds did not match very well with the smiling duck pattern that adorned the fleece.

Christina erupted into joyous laughter as Michael peeked out from the blanket with a silly look on his face. "Who needs a blanket?" he asked in his best Daffy Duck voice. He tossed the blanket lightly over Christina's head as her giggles grew even louder.

"Michael! Careful!" muttered Ellen under her breath. She was very protective of Christina. Michael carefully lifted the blanket off of Christina's head and gently tucked it under her chin. He knew better than to upset Ellen. After all, she and Ron had opened their home to Michael for the past year. No sense ruffling feathers now, so soon before we'd be getting married and he'd be moving out. We wanted to be included in these family dinners for years to come.

After putting away the food and making up a plate for Ron to eat later, I sliced up the pie. Ellen had set out some adorable red pie plates with little snowmen standing at attention around the edges. Michael carried in pieces for Ellen and Christina, but Aunt Margaret was already snoozing. She'd have to eat some later.

I carried in a piece of pie for Michael along with a handful of forks and then curled up on the floor next to him by the fire.

"First bite goes to the amazing pie baker!" Michael exclaimed, carefully cutting the point off the slice of pie with his fork and reaching it toward my mouth. He gently cupped his other hand under my chin so none of it would spill. Mmm.

"So Olivia, tell me more about this trip to Guatemala," suggested Ellen. "And the wedding, too! I pump Michael

11

for more information all the time, but he doesn't seem to remember very much!"

I shared the details of the upcoming month. Our wedding was all set for the evening of December 27. It would take place at the chapel on campus where we attended weekly services and had met the others with whom we would be going to Guatemala. We wanted to keep the wedding small and simple, so Ellen, Ronnie, and Christina were the only ones we had asked to be in the wedding. There were 15 other people invited to the ceremony, mostly Michael's family.

I had picked out a deep forest green fabric for the matron of honor and flower girl dresses, but left it up to Ellen as to the style they wanted to wear. She was so handy with a sewing machine and I fully trusted that she'd come up with something lovely. She was also working on my wedding dress and asked if I wanted to try it on so she could check the hemline. I declined because I was so stuffed from dinner, but promised to come back out to the house sometime over the weekend. I had been swamped with projects for school and studying and hadn't made it out to the house in the past two weeks.

Since the chapel would already be decorated with twinkling white lights and greenery for Christmas, there was no need to splurge on extravagant decorations. I preferred simplicity, anyway, and knew that Ellen's decorating expertise could help put the final touches on everything with a few well-placed bows and candles.

"Oh, I'll have to show you the pretty white ribbon I found last week," said Ellen. "It's got a hint of glitter around the edges, but not too much. We can use it for bows on the ends of the pews."

Stanley Greenstar, the pastor at the little chapel on campus, had become a dear friend to both Michael and me. The plan was that he would officiate our wedding and then lead our team to Guatemala on January 12. It was to be mainly a medical mission, and Michael was thrilled at the opportunities he'd have to use his medical training while helping the underserved Indian population in Guatemala. I would be assisting with medical things as well as leading some Bible school activities for children in a nearby orphanage. We'd be back on April 1, about 7 weeks before Ellen's baby was due. The timing would be perfect. It was already promising to be a great upcoming year.

We finished eating the sweet potato pie and Michael gathered up our plates. Aunt Margaret stirred and opened her eyes when he inadvertently dropped a fork that bounced off the braided rug and clattered onto the pine floor. "Oh, pie time!" Aunt Margaret exclaimed when she saw Michael standing there with the stack of plates. That sent Christina into a new fit of giggles.

"Let me get you a piece," offered Michael.

Christina asked if I wanted to play Chinese checkers, and Ellen moved over the lamp so we could set up the game on the end table. Christina scooted over in her wheelchair and parked it like a pro.

About 45 minutes after Ronnie's departure, the phone rang. Michael jumped up to answer it, eagerly awaiting his brother's return home so we could resume more of the Thanksgiving Day celebration. He hadn't flipped on any football games yet, knowing that Ronnie would be a much better companion for that activity than the rest of us.

The grin on Michael's face quickly changed to horror. He turned away from us, whispered something rapidly into the phone, and hung up.

"Ellen, where are Ronnie's keys?" he barked hoarsely.

"Is everything alright?" she asked.

"Just give me the keys!" Michael demanded. Then softening as he caught Christina's inquisitive glance, he softly added, "Please."

Ellen stepped over to the counter to grab the keys to Ronnie's SUV, and as her back was turned, he whispered in my ear, "Ronnie never showed up at the Jackson house."

And with that, he bounded out the door.

CHAPTER THREE

As Michael related details to me on the phone about an hour later, his low-pitched voice conveyed a feeling like wading through molasses. The moment Michael discovered what had happened to Ronnie was surreal. He had left the house in Ronnie's SUV headed in the direction of the Jackson house. The snow was finally letting up, but the streets had a fresh covering of at least 6 more inches. Plows were behind schedule due to the holiday. There were very few cars out on the roads, and the tracks Michael was making were some of the only ones visible.

Michael described that as he rounded the bend by the lake, his headlights reflected off something to the right hand side of the road. That seemed odd because it was just a short drop-off to the lake and there weren't any trees on the west side of the road. He slowed down to glance over his shoulder.

"I saw the back bumper of my truck sticking up from the snow on the lake," Michael whispered hoarsely. "My license plate was facing up and I knew that was my truck bobbing in the water." Michael had recently gotten a personalized plate for his truck, ILUVLIV.

Michael's voice was coming out in choking sobs now, making it hard to understand him. I was hiding in the laundry room at Ron and Ellen's house, and the reception kept cutting in and out making it even more difficult to piece together what Michael was telling me. But I didn't want to walk back out and have this conversation in front of the others.

Michael told me he tried to slow down, but the icy undercoat on the road caused the SUV to skid another 30 feet before he was able to get it under control and bring the vehicle to a halt. He peered over the edge and could see that the thin ice had given way to the weight of the truck. Since the lake was not very deep near the edge, the truck was only partially submerged, cab down.

"I flipped on a flashlight to get a better look. It was so dark and shadowy. Oh, Liv, I plunged right in. I knew Ronnie was still in there. I had to get him out."

Michael explained breathlessly what he had discovered. Ronnie was stuck underwater, pinned between a crushed driver's side door and the steering wheel. Michael felt around in the dark, icy water, trying with all his strength to pry Ronnie loose.

Fortunately, another volunteer had been on the way to the Jackson house and had stopped by the lake to see what was going on. He had dialed 911 and hopped into the lake to help Michael drag Ronnie onto the bank. The two men performed CPR on Ronnie until an ambulance arrived to take him to the hospital. They were hopeful because the water had been so cold, and sometimes people who fell into cold water survived.

Michael was crying even harder now, panting from anxiety and probably shivering with hypothermia as well. He was unable to speak for a few moments, and so was I. Finally Michael choked out, "Can you call John Breely?

That was easier said than done because John was probably still at the Jackson house. He was a volunteer firefighter, too, and the one who was likely in charge that evening. I promised to try. I made Michael promise to call again soon. And then I stood there for a few minutes trying to compose myself. Ellen had been putting Christina to bed when Michael called. She still had no idea where Ronnie was, and I was the one who would have to tell her.

Before leaving the laundry room, I held my breath and dialed John's number. His voice mail came on. That wasn't a message I wanted to leave, so I tried again. Finally, on the third try, John answered. As I explained the few details I had been given, a gnawing sense of dread and fear began to fill me.

When I walked out to the living room, Aunt Margaret was dozing in the green chair again. It seemed easier to leave her there rather than bundle her up and walk her home at this hour, so I tucked an afghan around her shoulders and braced myself for the conversation with Ellen.

CHAPTER FOUR

Michael got back to the house around midnight, helped Aunt Margaret get home, and took Ellen to the hospital. I volunteered to stay at the house with Christina. When Ellen had tucked her into bed hours earlier, she had somehow managed to keep her from knowing anything was wrong.

As investigators would later discover, a large buck had jumped out in front of Ronnie. The icy roads hindered steering capabilities, and they collided head-on. The truck tumbled down the small bank and onto the lake where the ice wasn't yet thick enough to hold the weight of the vehicle. The driver's side window was broken where the body of another deer had made impact. They must have been following each other. Ronnie, who was usually so capable in emergency situations, was probably knocked unconscious by the blow. He was strapped into the truck, upside down and under water, for at least 50 minutes before Michael discovered the crash site.

I sat near the fire for most of the rest of the night, hugging my knees to my chest and huddling in a thick blanket but never quite feeling warm enough. I peeked in at Christina every hour, somehow hoping to wish away the pain that seemed inevitably to be waiting on the horizon of the morning.

My thoughts kept turning back to that fateful day so many years ago when my father and I had been on vacation in Europe. It started out as a fun trip exploring places my mother used to love and then we ended up at a ski resort.

For years afterward, I couldn't remember if we had been in Italy, Austria, or Switzerland that day. My father and I had been enjoying a beautiful day skiing when suddenly he didn't feel well. Everything blurred together from there—the snow, the shouting, the ambulance, the hospital, and nurses trying to communicate in broken English with a frightened 10-year-old girl. My father never regained consciousness.

I preferred to go back in my mind to a few hours earlier on that day. My father and I had been nibbling on biscuits and apricot jam in front of a great big picture window that overlooked the ski slopes on the Alps. The walls of the large room were made of a rich carved wood and the ceiling was similarly beautiful. A hand-painted armoire stood in the corner.

My hot cocoa was a little bit too hot and a lot too strong. I tossed in some marshmallows and they melted within seconds. The sun was shining brightly against a sky of deep cerulean blue. The pine trees lining the ski runs stood tall, majestic, and proud.

My father had looked at me with a funny grin, and I knew he was in one of his playful moods. Suddenly he whipped a little velvet burgundy-colored box out of his pocket and laid it on the table in front of me. His eyes sparkled and danced as I looked up for his approving nod. I carefully lifted the lid. Inside was a brilliant silver chain upon which hung a delicate snowflake pendant. It was inlaid with tiny diamonds, and a deep blue, almost indigo-colored stone rested perfectly in the center. After a minute, I realized I was holding my breath. It was quite possibly the most beautiful necklace I had ever seen.

As my father gently hooked the clasp behind my neck, he told me how much he loved me. He told me how sorry he was that I didn't remember my mother, but that I was starting to look just like her, with her auburn hair and deep green eyes. And then he told me how I reminded him of a snowflake—delicate yet strong, and one-of-a kind. He spoke of the unique qualities that he found special about me and how I sparkled. And then he motioned to a hotel worker who was standing nearby.

The man brought over a guitar and handed it to my father. What a surprise! I hadn't known he could play. He started to strum softly and began to hum a sweet tune. As he began to sing, I felt a rush of exhilaration. It was turning out to be one of the most perfect days in my whole life.

My father sang a song that he had written especially for me. He told me he used to write music many years earlier, but ever since Mom was gone, the words had ceased flowing. He was finally at a place of peace and this was the first song he had composed in nine years. Not sure what to name it, he decided to simply call it "Olivia's Song."

You're unique and special, you're one of a kind
There's nobody like you! I'm glad that you're mine.
You sparkle and shimmer as you dance and twirl
My favorite snowflake in all of the world!
Reflecting the light, such delicate art
It might be cold out, but you warm my heart.
You spread joy all over, an avalanche of love

We'll stick together, no matter the weather.
I'll love you forever
My favorite snowflake.

When the song was over, I cheered. I could barely hear the applause coming from the rest of the room because I was caught up in a loving embrace with my dad. I had never before felt so special and so loved.

⌒

A cough from the bedroom aroused me from my dreamlike memory state. Reality. Christina was waking up, unaware of all that had transpired since the previous evening.

Before I could get out of the chair, my cell phone rang. It was Michael, sounding raspy and exhausted. He instructed me to bring Christina to the hospital. This was surprising, as Ronnie and Ellen were so protective of Christina that they had never let anyone else transport her in the van.

"I've called Jesse to come and help you," Michael explained in a voice I hardly recognized. Jesse was one of our fellow students who was also going on the trip to Guatemala. He had become a good friend to both of us in recent months. "It might take him an hour or more to get to the house in the snow, but sit tight and don't try to get Christina into the van by yourself."

I promised. I went into the kitchen and started the coffee maker, then sat down at the kitchen table. There was a small pink sticky note from Ronnie attached to a date on the calendar that hung next to the sink. "Love ya, babe!" was all it said. Earlier in the month, another sticky note had been attached to a different date and this one said, "You're the best!" in Ronnie's handwriting. I walked over to the calendar and flipped up the notes, curious as to the

21

significance of the dates. Underneath each was listed the time for a doctor's appointment for Christina.

Ronnie must have known how hard it was for Ellen to handle Christina's health difficulties. His encouraging words were so sweet, and I knew he tried to get off work to help Ellen take Christina to her appointments whenever possible. I had no doubt that Michael would be as caring of a husband to me as Ronnie was to Ellen. The brothers seemed to challenge each other in everything, and a competition as to who could be the best, most attentive husband would surely be welcomed by both Ellen and me.

Christina called for her mommy and was surprised when I entered her bedroom.

"O-Libby! You're still here! Where's Mommy?" she asked. I avoided her question and went to open the shade.

"Look at all the pretty, new snow!" I told her. "Want some pancakes for breakfast?" I asked, and she nodded eagerly. The french braid crown was looking fuzzy around the edges, but the baby's breath had stayed secure in her hair.

I helped her slip on a fresh outfit and then placed her in the wheelchair as best as I could. She assured me that her mommy let her use the bathroom safely without assistance. Since the doorbell was ringing right then, I let her wheel off and went to answer the door.

I unlocked the deadbolt and swung open the heavy wooden door. Jesse Cuatro was standing on the front porch in a navy blue parka with the faux fur-lined hood pulled up around his face. He was holding the screen door open in one hand and the thick stack of the day's Black Friday newspaper in the other. I let him in quickly because the wind was picking up and snow was once again beginning to swirl around the yard.

Jesse had more information on Ronnie than I did because he had just hung up from speaking with Michael. Ronnie was taken to the hospital and everyone was remaining cautiously hopeful. Someone had heard about a boy in a nearby town who had been trapped under cold water recently and recovered without any brain damage.

Ronnie was on a ventilator to help him breathe. He had hypothermia, but doctors didn't want to warm up his body too quickly, so his temperature was being cautiously monitored to raise slowly.

"How's Michael?" I asked.

"He's a wreck, plain and simple. And he probably got really cold in that water. I'm sure they're trying to warm him up carefully, but he's more concerned about Ronnie than himself."

"Did Michael say how Ellen is holding up?" I asked. Jesse shook his head. I wondered how stress would affect morning sickness.

Christina came bumping along the hallway to the kitchen and I jumped up to get out the frying pan.

"Hi sweetheart," said Jesse. "You must be the lovely Miss Christina! Your Uncle Michael has told me all about you." Christina beamed.

"Want blueberries or chocolate chips in the pancakes?" I asked. "Chocolate chips!" announced Jesse and Christina at the same time.

After breakfast, we got ready to go to the hospital. I was eager to get there sooner, but it was better to keep Christina calm. Who knew what we could find once we arrived?

As I was hanging up the towel after putting away the last of the breakfast dishes, I overheard Jesse talking to Christina in the living room. He was explaining to her in very easy-to-understand language about Ronnie's accident and what to expect when we arrived at the hospital. He was calm and reassuring as he answered her innocent questions, and I was impressed with the sweet rapport he already seemed to have with Christina. He'd be such a great asset to our team in Guatemala with his easygoing way with children.

I helped Christina into her coat and mouthed "thank you" to Jesse over her head. He was always silly and light-hearted at our Guatemala meetings, but I was grateful to see the more serious side of him take over now. He helped me get Christina into the van and I handed him the keys. Michael was right that I would have had trouble doing this on my own. I remembered the baggie of crackers and snacks I had gotten together for Ellen and ran back inside to get them.

We drove around the bend near the lake, scraps of yellow police tape still marking off some of the accident area and blowing in the chilly breeze. Michael's truck must have been towed away during the night. I could see lots of heavy tire tracks in the snow on the bank out my window.

"Look at that squirrel, sweetie!" said Jesse to Christina. He pointed to a tree on the left side of the car just as we were passing the accident scene. How clever of him to distract her just then. "Looks like he ate too much Thanksgiving dinner!"

She giggled, then replied softly, "Daddy didn't eat his dinner yet."

We got to the hospital about thirty minutes later and parked in the handicapped spot nearest the front door. Michael had already texted me the room number. As Jesse, Christina, and I made our way to the elevator bay, I started to feel a little dizzy. Jesse instinctively put his arm around my shoulder to steady me. I wanted to push Christina's wheelchair to give me something to do with my hands, but she insisted on using her new battery.

We thumped out of the elevator at the fourth floor. Beep, beep, beep. Monitors illuminated dark rooms as strange sounds reached out into the hallway.

We found the ICU family waiting room and sat down until Michael came for us. Another family waited there, too, bedraggled and looking as though they had spent the night on the floor.

CHAPTER FIVE

As I looked out the doorway and down the hall, a gnawing pain kept recurring somewhere in my body. Was it in my stomach? In my head? In my very soul? I couldn't pinpoint the source, but it was uncomfortably familiar.

The thin, tan carpet and pale blue walls in the family waiting room were anything but comforting. The odd, wispy pattern on the wallpaper border pasted about a foot down from the ceiling was a failed attempt to bring positive energy into the room. I sank into a threadbare chair next to Christina and leaned my head back against the wall. Christina's little hand touched me on the knee, and I gently rested my own hand on top of it.

Michael arrived about ten minutes later looking dazed. I knew there were only two visitors allowed in an ICU room at a time, but somehow no one minded that the four of us followed a nurse through the big security doors and over to room 4D. Michael must have been able to pull a few strings because of his residency at this hospital.

I hesitated at the threshold. Did they really want Christina to see whatever waited behind this door? My throat felt so tight. I peeked into the room, hoping to make eye contact with Ellen before Christina did. Ellen was sitting on the edge of a chair that had been pulled up sideways next to the bed. Her head was down and her arm was around Ronnie's waist. She didn't even look up when Christina said, "Mama?"

Michael lifted Christina out of her wheelchair and gently set her next to her mother, carefully pushing Ronnie's tubes and wires aside. The child looked overwhelmed, but she trusted her Uncle Michael and didn't speak a word.

It was hard to find Ronnie underneath all the medical equipment. His matted sandy-colored hair was slightly visible behind the bandages that covered much of his head. That was the same hair Michael had. It sent a shiver up my spine.

Beep. Beep. Beep. A monitor measured out the seconds, one after the other. Green lines on a screen went up and down, up and down. Michael bent his mouth near Christina's ear and softly began to explain to her a tragic story to which I already knew the ending. This was too familiar. It was too much.

I turned to leave the room, suddenly desperate for air, desperate for any excuse to get out of this suffocating madness. I ran right into Jesse, who had been standing beside me. He tried to grab my elbow, but I just wanted out right then.

Jesse graciously escorted me to the waiting room and sat with me there. He was calm and gentle as he tucked a blanket over my knees and brought me a cup of strong coffee. Somewhere in the back of my mind, I knew I would need to thank him someday for his kindness, if I remembered. Oh, what was I supposed to remember? Memories and reality swirled together in a strange mixture of melancholy pain.

It wasn't long before Michael came into the waiting room. He motioned for Jesse and me to follow him back to room 4D. I desperately wanted for Michael to take my hand, to pull me in close and tell me everything was going to be alright. But Michael was so lost in his own pain that it was impossible for him to think of anything but getting back to his beloved brother.

We stumbled awkwardly into the room. Ellen had composed herself somewhat and now held Christina on her lap. The little girl's hair held the broken remains of some bits of baby's breath from the day before. Her braided crown was still holding its own, although flyaway strands stuck out wildly around her temples. Was Thanksgiving really only yesterday?

Ellen and I exchanged a hug through tears, but no words could come from either of us. The heartache in the room was tangible.

Michael's infectious personality and good reputation in med school had allowed him to get some special treatment with friends who were on rotation. But it wasn't long before he knew this couldn't be prolonged any more. When Dr. Parker entered the room, Michael let out a mournful moan.

It wasn't supposed to be this way.

Tubes came out and monitors were unhooked so that the family could get a little closer. Ronnie's face was swollen and he appeared somewhat like a caricature version of himself. There was a deep gash across his forehead that had been stitched up and a bruise was beginning to spread down to his jaw. Christina crawled up close to lay her cheek against his and nuzzled against his whiskers with her chin. "Daddy, Daddy, Daddy…"

Michael wanted to say something but couldn't. Jesse stepped in and offered a prayer as we held hands awkwardly. Ellen collapsed and Michael grabbed her before she fell to the floor. It was all so surreal.

It wasn't long until Ronnie exhaled his last breath.

We sat there together around the end for a long time, not wanting to say goodbye but knowing it was over. After awhile, I offered to take Christina out of the room and Jesse said he'd go with me. Michael and Ellen had some things to discuss with the doctors and the rest of us would only be in the way.

We worked our way to the cafeteria in the basement. Jesse went to look at the food selections and bring back a kid-friendly report. As I sat with Christina at a round, blue table, I felt myself frantically searching for a way to bring some comfort to this precious and now fatherless child. I knew what that felt like all too well.

Christina kept looking at me. Why? Did she think I could offer her hope somehow?

My hand reached to the snowflake pendant that hung around my neck. As I caressed it between my left thumb and forefinger by habit, I knew what I needed to do.

I carefully unclasped the chain behind my neck and set it on my lap. With tears in my eyes, I explained to Christina the story of the snowflake necklace that had been so lovingly given to me by my father. Bit by bit, I relived the memories of that skiing trip with my father for the second time in two days.

As Christina and I solemnly nodded in agreement that daddies are indeed special, she let me place the beautiful charm around her neck. Our hands reached for the snowflake pendant together and they stayed that way for a long time.

CHAPTER SIX

The next few days were a blur with extended family members coming into town for Ronnie's funeral. It was a sad and somber occasion, with Ronnie being recognized multiple times for his big heart and endearing charm. Michael was able to compose himself enough to speak at the service, although he stopped and broke down twice. Ellen had insisted on a closed casket because Ronnie's face had been so beaten up and swollen that it didn't even look like him. Michael had argued with her about that, but in the end he gave in.

I had put out an offer to any of Michael's out of town family who wanted to stay at my apartment, but they all wanted to be together at Ronnie and Ellen's house. A few of them stayed with Aunt Margaret across the street.

I secretly wished I could be closer, too, but I knew I'd never finish my class project and prepare for final exams in a house filled with people. Graduation was only one week away, the wedding was four weeks away, and the trip to Guatemala was fast approaching as well.

Michael was in such a fog that I took it upon myself to contact his professors and beg for an extension in each class. In a strange twist of role-reversal, I now felt like the stronger half of the couple. Michael had always been the life of the party, the take-charge guy, the one everyone looked to for advice and support. But Ronnie's death had crushed him.

I tried to approach the subject of our wedding delicately a couple of times. Postponing it seemed like the wisest thing to do given the circumstances, but I was met with a blank stare whenever I brought it up with Michael. I wondered if we might need to cancel the trip to Guatemala until a later date, too. Maybe we could go with a different group in the summer.

I had a few rare moments a couple of days after Ronnie's funeral to speak alone with Ellen. The two of us women, who had only a week earlier been so excited about a new baby, an upcoming wedding, and sharing the future together as sisters, were now barely able to talk. Christina was occupied playing with some cousins in her bedroom, and Michael was napping in his basement bedroom.

As I stood by the kitchen island and shared my decision to postpone the wedding, Ellen began to weep. She cried and cried until her shoulders shook violently, and I was afraid she might either throw up or pass out. The combination of pregnancy and grief was really taking a toll on her. I ushered Ellen to a kitchen chair and we sat together, tears streaming down our faces, wondering why it all had gone so terribly wrong.

"Ellen, you've spent more time with Michael this past year than I have, with him living at your house and all. Do you think he's capable of the trip to Guatemala? I don't know what to think; I don't know what to do. My whole life has been turned upside down and Michael will barely talk to me anymore. I'm so worried about him. And poor Christina was looking so forward to being a flower girl in our wedding. I'm supposed to graduate in a little over a week. My lease runs out at the end of the month, and my landlord has already found a new renter for my apartment. Maybe I could stay with Aunt Margaret for a little while. "

Words tumbled out of my mouth in a cascade of emotions. I didn't even know if they were making sense, but the words just had to get out of me as quickly as I could get them out. After rambling for what seemed like an eternity, I realized Ellen was looking above my head.

I turned around to find Michael standing in the doorway.

"Michael—how long have you been standing there?" I asked.

Before I could get another word in, Michael slowly knelt next to my chair. He took my hand in his and caressed it gently.

"Liv, you are the best thing that ever happened to me. Your heart is pure gold and your kindness to me is immeasurable."

He was breaking down now, crying a bit more with every word. I braced myself for the "but" that was sure to come. But...we need to wait another year to get married. But...let's call off the trip to Guatemala until the summer. But...let's start fresh in the new year after we have time to recover from Ronnie's death and plan our lives together in a totally new direction.

The "but" didn't come just then. Michael's body was racking with sobs and he couldn't get another word out. Ellen put her head down on the table and made whimpering sounds like a wounded animal.

After a few minutes, Michael composed himself. He wiped his eyes with the back of his free hand and then used his sleeve to gently brush the tears away from my eyes. He kissed the top of my head. Then he gazed deeply into my eyes with as much conviction as I'd ever seen in him.

"Liv, you're right—we have to postpone the wedding. In fact, we need to cancel it altogether."

"Oh, Michael, I understand, really I do, " I interrupted. "We can wait as long as you need. It's okay. Take all the time you need. I love you and I will always be here for you."

I was rambling again. He put his fingers against my lips to quiet me.

"Let me get this out, Liv. Don't make it harder than it already is. I love you and I will always love you. I have loved you since the day I saw you working as a checker at Charley's. I came through your line three times that evening buying things I didn't need and then waited outside the store until your shift ended just so I could see you again. We've made good plans. Great plans. If circumstances were different, they would have been wonderful."

An enormous lump crept up in my throat. I tried to swallow it away, but it was stuck.

"Liv, I can't marry you anymore. Not now and not next year. Not ever. I told my brother I'd always be here to help him. His family needs me now more than ever. Christina can't get around without help, and this pregnancy is getting so rough on Ellen. I can't leave them in the lurch. I can't. I promised Ronnie in the hospital that I'd take care of his family."

"Michael, I don't follow you, " I whispered. "We can make it all work out somehow, maybe move Ellen and Christina closer to town. Or maybe I could change my mind on not wanting to live out here so far from the city.

I could do that. I could figure out a way, Michael. We can work this out together."

Desperation and dread wrestled inside of me as I braced myself for the words that seemed inevitable at this point.

"We can't get married, Liv. I'm going to marry Ellen."

CHAPTER SEVEN

I immersed myself in studying for final exams and planning for the upcoming trip to Guatemala. I watched mindless movies late into the night—anything to get my mind off of this dismal chapter of my life. As heartbroken as I was about losing Michael in this bizarre twist of fate, I somehow loved him more now than I ever had. Who throws away his own dreams and plans in order to care for and love the family of his late brother? Surely this was a man with deep convictions and a compassionate heart.

The graduation ceremony was anticlimactic. The hyped-up anticipation of it during the past year made it all seem a bit silly once it finally arrived. But at least I had done it. I had put myself through university and gotten a degree all on my own.

After the commencement, I joined a few classmates for a Chinese lunch downtown. We shared fortune cookies one by one around the table following the meal, and mine said, "If you expect nothing, you'll never be disappointed." An awkward silence followed, and finally I excused myself to ease the tension, mumbling something about needing to catch an earlier bus. Someone tried to stop me at the door, but I forced my way out and into the cold evening air.

I was numb inside. A young couple got onto the bus and sat down across from me, giggling and holding hands. I found the girl's laughter so annoying that I got off three stops early and walked the rest of the way to my apartment. As I put the key into the lock, I panicked for a moment, suddenly unable to remember how to breathe. Then realized I had been holding my breath.

I didn't remember my mother at all and had lost my father abruptly. And now, just as I was anticipating a beautiful life with Michael and his family, I had lost all of that. I didn't know what to feel or how to feel anymore. It was as if all of my future plans were wrapped up in a picture of Michael and me together that had been dropped and shattered.

I curled up on my bed, hugging a small teddy bear that Michael had given me on our second date. Tears streamed down my cheeks as the reality sank in that I was alone. Completely alone. I had to get out of here. I had to do something totally different. I needed a do-over in an entirely new place. But what could that be? And where?

The following week, on Christmas Eve afternoon as a matter of fact, I had a meeting with Stanley. He was the main group leader for the Guatemala trip and the pastor who would have married Michael and me. A single man in his mid-30s, he led trips to various Central American destinations a couple of times every year. Stanley had gotten to know Michael and me quite well over the past few months and expressed his deep sympathy for the loss of Michael's brother. There was an awkward silence after that, as he didn't quite know how to approach the topic of Michael's taking on responsibility for Ronnie's family. No one knew how to approach it.

Finally, I broke the silence with a well-thought out statement.

"I want to go to Uganda with you instead of Guatemala. I know you are headed there on January 1, a little over a week before the team goes to Guatemala. There is no reason for me to wait here any longer. Besides that, I was supposed to be getting married this week and living somewhere else. I have to be out of my apartment by January 3. I need a new beginning. Please say yes, Stanley. Please."

Stanley cleared this throat and opened his mouth to speak. Then he closed his lips and cleared his throat again. There really was no reason to say no, and this would be a way to help me get a fresh start somewhere else. He nodded slowly and then more eagerly. I was a desperate young woman. Yes, I could go with him to Uganda. As he had been planning to go alone, he could use the extra help.

"Hmm. I guess I am actually looking forward to having you along, although this is very much unexpected," Stanley remarked. "Good thing I can be spontaneous. Does Michael know?"

I shook my head. Stanley sat there thinking for a moment, then went on.

He said he hoped that the tragic events of the previous month wouldn't dampen my enthusiasm for the actual work in Uganda, which would be similar to what we had prepared to do in Guatemala. "So much for all of your Spanish studies!" he chuckled.

I hurried back to my apartment, filled with a new desire to move ahead. I could close the door to all that was here and move forward. There was no chance of Michael going on the Guatemala trip anymore, and the only member of the Uganda team who knew him very well was Stanley.

No one would ever mention Michael to me in Africa. This would be a safe group as I went through the process of rebuilding my life.

I decided to write a letter to Christina. I loved that little girl so much, and I felt badly that I hadn't seen much of her lately. My left hand instinctively reached for the pendant that no longer hung around my neck as my right hand picked up a pen with purple ink. She and I shared the same favorite color.

Dear Christina,

I love you so much! I am so sorry about your daddy, but I am glad that Uncle Michael can step in to be your new daddy. No one can ever take the place of your real daddy, but Uncle Michael is the next best choice in the whole wide world.

My cell phone began to ring. I saw Ellen's number come up and refrained from answering. Ellen had been leaving messages for the past three days that I hadn't returned. I wanted no more crying, no more trying to repair whatever was broken or weird. None of this was Ellen's fault, anyway. It was better for that family's healing if I would just move on and get out of the way.

I turned back to the note I was writing.

Christina, please give your mommy a big hug for me. I'm sorry you didn't get to be my flower girl after all. You would have been the most beautiful one ever. I love you so much!

I drew some fancy hearts with the purple ink and signed my name. As I licked the envelope shut, I wondered when they'd tell Christina about the baby. My heart swelled with love for Michael once again. It was weird and complicated and there probably wasn't anyone else in the world who knew exactly what I was going through. But I was a survivor, and I had to go on. Somehow, some way. Yes, Michael was a good man doing the right thing. Even if it shattered my dreams and broke my heart to admit it.

CHAPTER EIGHT

I was waiting at the door when Stanley pulled up to the curb in front of my apartment at 8:00 PM on December 31. There was a light snow falling and a pleasant quietness filled the air. A dog barked rhythmically in the yard next door.

I had sold my furniture to the incoming renter and had dropped off most of the rest of my things to a second hand store. The remainder of my earthly possessions now fit into one large suitcase and one backpack. I also pulled a rolling duffel bag filled with medical supplies and donations for the children at the orphanage where we would be helping.

Jesse was accompanying us to the airport. He would drop us off and then take care of Stanley's car during the time we were in Uganda. Jesse hopped out to help me load my bags in the trunk and then insisted that I ride in the front with Stanley. We exchanged a hug and I quickly hopped into the car. I hadn't seen Jesse since Ronnie's funeral and his presence on this night surprised me. I wanted a fresh start and hoped Jesse wouldn't tell Michael what I was doing. Maybe Michael wouldn't even care, but I asked Jesse not to say a word anyway.

The roads were fairly deserted at this late hour on the last day of the year. Perhaps everyone was out welcoming the coming new one already.

We made a brief stop at my landlord's house so I could drop off an envelope with the key under his front mat. I breathed a sigh of relief as I walked back to the car. A new adventure was about to begin!

The airport was almost as deserted as the streets had been. Stanley pulled up to the departures curb. Jesse insisted we could park in the ramp and he'd help us wheel in the bags, but this was fine. One less long, emotional goodbye. I hopped out and hugged Jesse, "Please don't tell," I whispered. "Just let me go quietly..." He squeezed my hand with his thin leather gloves, and I thought I saw a tear in his eye. He wouldn't say a word.

Stanley and I got through security in record time and decided to grab a coffee and a pastry. The overnight flight to London would be just over seven hours long. There would be a nine-hour layover at Heathrow followed by ten hours in the air to our final destination of Kampala, Uganda.

I was surprised at how eager I was for all of the new things about to begin. If I had learned anything in life so far, it was how to be resilient. A welcome peacefulness engulfed me, and I was asleep before the captain had turned off the seatbelt sign.

Touchdown in London was smooth. I had never flown on such a large plane before, and turbulence was all but nonexistent on a vessel of that size. My purse was filled with small Cadbury chocolate bars of every flavor, courtesy of a kind British Airways flight attendant who had taken a liking to me and slipped another one onto my tray every time he passed my seat. Chocolate mint, dairy milk, chocolate with raisins. I kept them all, knowing what a treat they would be in a few days.

Heathrow airport was crowded with travelers of all shapes and sizes, speaking a variety of languages and dragging their heels as well as their carry-ons. Stanley and I made our way down a long jetway followed by a series of hallways to finally make it to the center of the terminal. We had slept on and off during the flight but knew that this would be a difficult day of trying to stay awake until the next flight in nine hours.

We toyed with the idea of grabbing a taxi and investigating London for a few hours, but decided against it in the end. After passing one duty-free shop after another, then holding our breath as we hustled past the indoor smoking area, we found a quiet lounge.

This was an area designed especially for international travelers with long layovers. There were no televisions on the walls, only rows of lounge chairs and a couple of small couches. There was no music piped into this room. An Indian family was curled up in one corner, attempting to find comfortable positions in which to rest. A businessman sat on a nearby couch, tie loosened and jacket unbuttoned, tapping away silently on the keys of his laptop. A young mother sat near the door, gently gliding a stroller back and forth next to her while remaining in her seat.

Stanley and I parked our things along the back wall of the room. Stanley hadn't been able to sleep much on the flight, so I insisted that he take the first shift of sleeping.

"What do you mean, first shift? Why don't you catch a few winks, too?" he asked.

"I'd be so afraid that I'd fall into a deep sleep and we'd miss the flight to Uganda," I replied matter-of-factly. "I refuse to miss this flight to the next chapter of my life. I'll wander around for a couple of hours, then we can switch."

Stanley agreed to the plan. I left him to rest and found my way back into the hallway. I passed a kiosk with internet and stood there for a long time, debating whether or not to check emails. I hadn't brought a cell phone along and had no other capabilities of communication with the rest of the world if not for connecting to the internet. I knew there would be a plea from Ellen to contact her, and that wasn't something I wanted to do. I had made peace with my decision to leave and wanted to start over with a clean slate, no past strings attached.

After wandering around for a couple of hours, I eventually made my way back to the quiet lounge. Stanley was snoring so loudly that a couple of little girls were trying without much success to stifle their giggles. Their father, on the other hand, did not look pleased.

"Stan!" I whispered as I shook his shoulder. "Stanley, wake up!"

He groaned and batted me away. This wasn't going to be easy. I sat on the floor next to him and leaned my head against the wall, fully convinced that I was too excited to fall asleep.

The next thing I knew, Stanley was waking me up. I must have drifted off after all, and we only had one hour until departure. We quickly gathered up our belongings and hustled to the right gate. It seemed silly to be hurrying through the airport after having been there all day.

As we began boarding the plane, I turned to Stanley with a grin and said, "Happy New Year!" Hopefully it would indeed be a happy new one.

CHAPTER NINE

The plane arrived at Entebbe Airport in the Ugandan capital city of Kampala mid-morning. Even though it was a decent-sized aircraft, the plane touched down and then parked far out on the pavement. They didn't have jetways to connect to the terminal here. Passengers had to walk down the stairs of the plane and then stroll across the tarmac to get to the terminal.

I looked around at the small runway. There was a Ugandan flag flying above the doors to the terminal. The air smelled different here—not bad, just different. It was somehow rich and earthy, yet dusty. A faint smell of smoke was intertwined with the smell of dirt. A fellow passenger pulled out a camera to take a photo of the sign on the terminal that said "Welcome to Entebbe" and was quickly told to put it away by a flight attendant.

On the flight, Stanley had filled me in on some of the details of the reign of Idi Amin back in the 1970s. I had intended to watch the movie *Last King of Scotland* before coming to Uganda, but never had the chance. I knew the brother of Benjamin Netanyahu, prime minister of Israel, had been killed by Amin's men right in this very area. There was undoubtedly still a lot of sadness in this country due to the great losses incurred at the hands of an evil dictator.

"Olivia! Girl, you're zoning out again! Over here!" called Stanley, eager to get through customs and head into the city. It was a bit unnerving to see security guards with rifles standing inside the terminal, but Stanley assured me this was a good thing and that I needed to be prepared to see more of the same throughout the city.

All of the luggage had arrived intact, which provided a huge sense of relief. There were so many extra medical supplies along that would have been difficult if not downright impossible to find in Uganda. We loaded up on a small bus that Stanley had arranged for weeks in advance. Three other passengers boarded with us as well. The driver, a young man named Paul, was very cordial and welcoming. His eyes sparkled with life as he spoke. He had been Stanley's driver on a previous trip and the two had gotten along so well that Stanley had requested Paul's services on this trip, too.

A 30-minute bus ride took us to the Musanyufu Guest House, a quaint two-story brick building that overlooked the city of Kampala. Paul told me that the word musanyufu means "happy." There was an armed guard at the entrance gate, and row after row of bougainvillea bushes in pink, orange, and white lined the driveway.

After checking into our rooms and unloading our things, Stanley and I went for a short walk to get a feel for the area and stretch our legs out a bit. An old Anglican church was perched on the hillside behind the guest house, and we found a hidden path through some bushes that led directly to it. The doors to the church were open on one side, so we stepped into the dark sanctuary. The stained glass windows were very modest, yet allowed for a particularly lovely and colorful beauty to bathe the room in the fading sunlight of the day. As we sat on one of the wooden pews near the back of the church, I was overcome with the simplicity of this place. Although halfway around the world from my home, I felt a strange sense of belonging rising up from deep within me on my first day in this new country.

Jet lag kept me up for a few hours in the middle of the night, and the next morning arrived a little too soon. After a breakfast of scrambled eggs and fresh pineapple on the outdoor veranda at the guest house, Paul arrived to pick us up, but in a car this time. The first stop was at Barclay's bank to exchange American money for Ugandan shillings. I was prepared for an armed guard at the door.

Stanley met with a banker in a back room because he had some business transactions to go over with a bank official. He had been gone for about twenty minutes when I finally got my turn at the counter with a bank teller. While he was counting out the money to me, I noticed out of the corner of my eye that a tall Ugandan man wearing a white dress shirt had walked into the bank and was scanning the area. I wondered why the security guard was sitting down and looking half-asleep with his loaded rifle pointed at a dangerous angle. I tucked the shillings into my purse and held it very tightly against my body as I uneasily made my way to the sitting area.

The Ugandan man's dark brown eyes followed me to my seat. I tried not to make eye contact, but it was too late because he was suddenly right next to me.

"Would you happen to be Miss Olivia Hanninger?" he asked in a voice so kind and gentle that it startled me.

I must have looked puzzled, because the man's face suddenly broke out into a big grin and the creases around his eyes crinkled with happiness. I noticed a tiny scar on his left cheekbone, and he smelled very fresh, like a mixture of citrus and peppermint. Even in my sleep-deprived state, this well-groomed man looked quite handsome.

"I am Salvador. Stanley didn't tell you I'd be meeting you here to catch a ride out to Okusuubira orphanage?"

"Uh…I think he forgot to mention that," I said a bit timidly. Stanley had told me that okusuubira means "hope," but that's all he had said about the orphanage.

"Well, my dear, I am sorry to have alarmed you, but I am so very pleased to finally meet you," Salvador stated, his grin not fading. He reached out his hand to meet mine in a warm, friendly clasp just as Stanley emerged from around the corner.

"I see you two have met!" he exclaimed. "Sal, my friend!" The two men exchanged a big hug in the lobby of Barclay's. That got the attention of the security guard, who shifted in his seat and propped his gun at a safer angle while eyeing the men.

Stanley, Salvador, and I went outside and found Paul waiting with the car. It was about an hour's drive to the orphanage, so there was plenty of time to get acquainted with both Salvador and the sights, sounds, and smells of Kampala. Stanley and I sat in the back seat and Salvador was up front with Paul. Salvador kept turning around to explain something or point out a landmark in his beloved hometown.

"See those tortoises? The huge ones in the yard? Aren't they amazing?" His enthusiasm was infectious.

As we approached the outlying areas of the city, the paved roads disappeared, replaced by rutted red dirt roads. It was stuffy in the car, but we kept the windows rolled most of the way up because plumes of dust surrounded the car as it bumped along and jostled us to and fro.

The children were already waiting for us when the car finally arrived at Okusuubira School and Orphanage. Paul parked at the bottom of the hill and the four of us prepared to walk up to the school buildings. Salvador hopped out and reached his hand back to pull me out of a cramped position in the backseat of the two-door car. I gladly accepted his help.

The children stood in lines on both sides of the steep driveway, probably close to 200 children altogether. They were clapping and singing a welcome song. "Welcome to Okusuubira, we are so happy you are here! Welcome to our wonderful school that is full of hope! We receive you with great joy!" My best guess was that the children's ages ranged from probably 4 years old to about 15. The music their voices made was magical, blending together in intricate harmonies. The dark eyes on each shaved, brown head shined brightly with curiosity as they followed their white visitors up the hill. A couple of the little ones came over to me and touched my skirt. A brave one stroked my pale arm and giggled.

Desks and chairs had been pulled out of a classroom at the top of the hill and this was where Stanley, Salvador, Paul, and I were directed to sit. The teachers and headmaster of the school came over to greet us, and then the children started up a program. Not one of the students was shy about performing. The boys took turns drumming. The girls twirled around and around in bright yellow and blue dresses. The whole area was filled with dancing and singing and beautiful smiles.

After the wonderful display, the students dispersed to their classrooms while the headmaster ushered us across the schoolyard for a tour of the newly finished clinic. Paul had organized a group of students to carry up from the car some of the medical supplies that Stanley and I had brought along from the US. These items were lined up along the far wall of the clinic which consisted of two freshly constructed rooms with cement walls painted a light yellow. There were two blue plastic chairs in each room, and a small cabinet and old desk in the back room.

Although this would be considered a meager set-up and a sorry excuse for a clinic in America, it was an amazing and wonderful addition to this rural school. The clinic would eventually benefit the members of the surrounding community as well, many of whom had never been seen by a doctor in their entire lives. For a brief moment, I thought about Michael and our mutual love for children. I remembered the day he decided he was going to become a pediatrician and we made plans to go to Guatemala. Now here I was in Uganda, halfway around the world from Michael and far away from our dreams. Yet there were children here that I could love even without Michael.

"I guess we'll start checking the children by age levels starting tomorrow," decided Stanley. "Just basic comprehensive stuff."

I turned to Salvador and asked, "So, are you a pediatrician? Internal medicine? Infectious diseases?"

Salvador let out a soft chuckle. "General practice with an emphasis in obstetrics," he said with a grin. "But I'm a doctor with medical training and that's all that matters here."

"Oh, I see," I answered. It sure was different here. Stanley had explained a few weeks earlier that I'd be expected to help with medical care because I had taken a course in basic first aid. I had thought he was kidding, but apparently not.

"Where did you get your training?" I asked Salvador.

"London," Salvador answered with a little sideways grin once again lighting up his face. "I had one semester in America, too."

"Why the emphasis on obstetrics?" I queried. "Not that it's not a good thing, but why not something else?"

"I grew up in a small village in western Uganda where doctors never visited," explained Salvador. "My mother lost three children during childbirth before I was born. My sister lost two babies pre-term, my aunt died while giving birth, and it goes on and on. Maama begged me to help, said she knew we needed to learn how to care for pregnant women and how to help them have babies safely. When I was in secondary school, a man from England came to visit. He took a liking to me and was impressed with my sharp mind. He offered to pay for me to go to medical school and let me live with his family."

"Wow, that's a sweet deal!" I exclaimed. "Do you stay in touch with him?"

"Yes! Of course I do! Dr. Rollofson and his wife are like second parents to me. They live in Uganda for a good part of every year. They run a medical clinic in the southern part of our country, near the border of Rwanda. We usually see each other two or three times per year. I owe them everything."

A couple of the older students got set up with a teacher to make an inventory list of all the items in the clinic, everything from bandages and tissues to Tylenol and antibacterial gel. Salvador and Stanley planned to arrange and organize everything the next day. It was getting late and Stanley wanted to get back to the guest house before dark. He didn't want to alarm me, but I already knew it was a safety issue. We were Americans, and because of that, it was assumed that we had access to money. Kidnappings for ransom were rare but not unheard of. It was best to do our work and traveling in the daylight.

CHAPTER TEN

Stanley had made preparations to return to the States after five days. It hardly seemed like long enough to get over jet lag, let alone make the trip worthwhile, but he had to get back and escort the group that was heading to Guatemala. He knew just bringing the medical supplies and setting up the clinic, even in a rudimentary way, was beneficial. Besides, he was confident that Salvador and I would lovingly and carefully make sure the clinic was being run well.

Salvador offered to drive Stanley to the airport early in the morning, and I decided to ride along. The change of plans in coming to Uganda instead of Guatemala had happened so fast. With Stanley about to leave, I would pretty much be on my own in a foreign land. I wasn't worried, though. It felt so right to be here now, like it was part of the grand plan for my life all along. It helped that Salvador was so kind. I trusted his judgment and felt he'd already become a good friend.

Saying goodbye to Stanley at Entebbe Airport wasn't nearly as difficult as I had anticipated. Perhaps, I later decided, it's because I had gotten so used to people leaving me—my mother, my father, Ronnie, Michael…At least Stanley would stay in touch via email. A small team from the US would be arriving within a week. It was people who had worked in Uganda with Stanley the previous year, so they were already familiar with the surroundings and general routine of being in Africa. I planned to remain with them for three months and would reassess my life after that.

Stanley's plane lifted off shortly after 10:00 AM. Salvador and I watched it take off from our vantage point in the parking lot. I looked up and waved, not sure if Stanley had a window seat or not, but it helped me to put closure on his time in Uganda. I seemed to need that—closure. I couldn't control Stanley's coming or going, but I could control my choice to wave to the plane and wish him well.

Salvador opened the door for me, but I had already walked to the wrong side of the car. Again! It was hard getting used to the steering wheel being flip-flopped from cars in America. Salvador shook his head and laughed as I grinned sheepishly.

"Olivia, dear, how would you like to see the source of the Nile River? It's not that far of a drive to Jinja."

"Oh, Salvador, I'd love to!" I exclaimed, perhaps a little too eager for adventure. I surprised even myself. Better to start exploring more of this country that was my new home than to go back to a quiet room at the guest house. Besides, if I busied myself with activities, there would be less time to think. And that might be a good thing for awhile.

"Olivia, you may call me Sal from now on. My closest friends do. And we are friends now," he said with a smile. Sal it was. My first real friend in Uganda.

After about an hour of driving, we came to a small village and traffic slowed down considerably. A bus was ahead of us on the road, and I watched intently as a group of young men swarmed and surrounded the bus. Sal seemed non-chalant about the whole thing, tapping his fingers lightly on the steering wheel and humming a soft tune.

"What are they doing?" I asked. It didn't seem to be a dangerous situation, and I could see windows on the bus being pulled down from the inside to open them.

I got my answer before Sal could open his mouth. The young men surrounding the bus were holding up skewers of meat for sale. Some skewers were being thrust directly into the windows of the bus! Other young men held up bottles of soda for sale. Money was exchanged through the windows as hungry travelers found much-desired food.

"Is it safe?" I inquired.

"Is what safe?" asked Sal. "You mean getting poked at with a skewer or eating the meat?"

"Both!" I laughed.

One of the young men from the bus had wandered back to Sal's car and held up a skewer of meat near the driver's window. Sal reached into his pocket and gave him some shillings, then handed the skewer to me.

"It's chicken. Fully cooked!" he said with a chuckle. "Better start getting your system used to our food."

Sal pulled off a chunk of meat and shoved it into his mouth. He grinned as he chewed and I couldn't resist trying some for myself. I took a smaller bit and began to chew. Not bad! Not bad at all. In fact, it was rather tasty.

Within a few minutes, traffic began to move a little faster along the Nairobi-Kampala Road. The chicken skewer was picked clean well before we arrived at the town of Jinja. It was smaller than Kampala, but still a fairly good-sized town.

"We have to go about 7 km more to get to Bujagali Falls," explained Sal.

"Oh boy, I have to convert kilometers to miles! Hang on a minute! I know a 5 km race is about 3 miles, so let's see…7 km…"

"Olivia dear, let me give you a formula! It's not perfect, but it's quick and easy to remember. Do you know Fibonacci numbers?"

"Yes!" I replied, thrilled that I had retained something of the mathematics world. "It's where you take $1 + 1 = 2$, $1 + 2 = 3$, $2 + 3 = 5$, $3 + 5 = 8$, $8 + 5 = 13$, and so on. And there's something about pinecones and snail shells, but that's all I can recall!"

Sal smiled. "That's good! Now dear, list out the Fibonacci numbers and that will help you convert kilometers to miles. 1,2,3,5,8,13,21, and so on. So 2 km is approximately 1 mile. You already know that 5 km is close to 3 miles. 13 km would be close to 8 miles. It's not a perfect system, but it's close enough for stressed-out Americans who cling to their strange ways of measuring."

"I like it! Anything to help me remember something!" And then I added softly, "and to keep my mind busy."

"What was that?" asked Sal.

"Oh, nothing," I replied, picturing Stanley on his flight back to Heathrow and then catching the next one home. In four days, he'd be on the way to Guatemala with the group Michael and I would have been in.

Out of the corner of my eye, I could tell that Sal was looking at me. I did not turn to catch his gaze for fear that the waterworks would start and I'd be unable to stop them. I didn't know what, if anything, Stanley had shared with Sal about my recent past, but I didn't care to bring that up right now. It was a lovely day and there was no need to put a damper on discovering more about this beautiful land called Uganda.

We parked the car in a lot and walked to Bujagali Falls. Dark blue water turned frothy white as it crashed down the different levels of rocks. It was really more of a series of large rapids than a true waterfall, but spectacular to behold nonetheless.

A man holding onto a yellow jerry can was wandering amongst the tourists, looking for donations. Sal explained to me that he was trying to collect enough money to make it worth his while to jump over the falls.

"Is that safe?" I asked.

"Do you mean safe as in eating chicken-off-a-stick safe?" joked Sal. "No, it's not safe. Somebody died jumping in with a jerry can about a week ago. But these guys can make pretty good money, so to them it's worth the risk."

"How much is considered good money?"

"About $10 US. But they can jump a few times per day and bring that total closer to $40 or $50."

"That hardly seems worth risking one's life!" I exclaimed. "Could you pay him not to jump?"

Sal laughed again. I decided he wasn't always laughing at me, but just had a happy countenance about him. I was grateful he wasn't yet annoyed with my incessant questions.

"The average annual salary in Uganda is equivalent to just a few hundred dollars US, dear. This is good money."

Sal bought a can of Pringles and two Cokes at a nearby shop. We sat on the grassy field, enjoying the view and watching as the young man gingerly climbed his way up the slippery rocks to the top of the falls. He waved to onlookers, then jumped in holding tightly to the jerry can which was also tied with a thin rope around one of his wrists. I held my breath waiting for him to resurface.

Suddenly the crowd cheered. I scanned the base of the falls and didn't see him anywhere. Sal pointed. The water had carried the young man to a different spot than I had been expecting him to pop out. He was sputtering, but appeared to be just fine.

"Come with me, "said Sal after a few minutes, reaching for my hand to help me up. "I want to show you something."

I followed him to a small memorial garden where a bronze bust of a man stood tall and proud. Was it a famous Ugandan? Perhaps it was John Speke, the British explorer who discovered in the early 1860s that the source of the Nile River was right here at Lake Victoria. Speke was the one who had named nearby Lake Victoria, the largest body of freshwater in all of Africa, after the queen of England.

"It's Gandhi?" I exclaimed upon further investigation. "Really? Why is there a statue of Gandhi here? I thought he was from India."

Sal filled me in on the many years Gandhi spent in Africa. It had been his wish to have some of his ashes sprinkled in the Nile River, among other major rivers in the world, and so it was done following his death.

"What other surprises does Uganda hold in store for me, Sal?" I queried. He smiled and motioned for me to follow him once again as we made our way along the edge of the Nile River. He found a spot that was not as crowded as the main grassy area and directed me to a small bench.

We sat down and looked out over the water again. The sound of waves crashing over the rocks made a soothing background noise. This was a nice place. Sal was becoming a good friend. I had a warm, peaceful feeling inside, and knew I was going to make it.

Suddenly, Sal put one hand lightly on my knee and pressed a finger from his other hand to his lips, as if to quiet me. He nodded his head over my shoulder to the right. I turned slowly and saw a pair of long-legged birds walking on the grass. They stood tall, probably one meter. I was getting the hang of this metric system! When the birds flapped their wings, the wingspan looked to be about twice as wide as their height. They had grey feathers and a small patch of white in the middle of their bodies. Their most fascinating body part was their heads, the top of which was a rich, deep black color. Above that, each bird had a tall plume of stiff golden feathers. Their faces were white with small red patches near the eyes, and they had bright red pouches near their throats.

"Those throat pouches are inflatable," explained Sal in a whisper, although he probably could have spoken in a regular voice. The birds didn't seem frightened at all by our presence.

The birds began to hop around and flap their wings. The one nearest to our bench made a noise that sounded more like a low dog's bark than a bird's call.

"Crested crane," said Sal before I could even get my question asked. "It's the national bird of Uganda." He reached into his pocket for a coin and placed it in my palm. On it was a bird that looked exactly like the ones hopping in the field next to us. "Look for it the next time you see our flag, too."

We started walking back to the car and Sal asked, "Well, my dear, have you enjoyed our visit to Jinja?"

"Oh, yes, thank you!" I exclaimed. "This is a beautiful place. Uganda is beginning to feel like home already."

As I was bending down to get into the car, some kids in the parking lot pointed at me and called out, "Mzungu!"

I knew that word from our first visit to the orphanage. "White." They weren't trying to be rude; rather, it was just an observation of my skin color. I supposed this was something I'd just have to get used to.

CHAPTER ELEVEN

The team from the US arrived a few days after the trip to Jinja. I decided to continue staying at the guest house with them. Management was giving us a good deal since most of the team members planned to stay there for the full three months. This was a safe location. Breakfast was provided on the veranda each morning, and the armed guard at the gate added a sense of security. While I wished I could have access to laundry facilities for myself, I knew the women who collected my bag of dirty clothes each week relied upon the extra income to sustain their families.

The next few months went by quickly. We stayed busy with setting up the clinic, assessing the health of each of the children at the school, and beginning medical services for the community. I got used to our daily routine, and the local rooster's crow didn't always wake me in the wee hours of the morning anymore.

I seemed to click especially well with April, a divorced nurse in her mid-50s from Ohio. For the past four years, she had spent three months out of every year doing medical work in third world countries. I admired her passion and commitment. She taught me basics of health care as we worked side by side.

Sal usually came out to the school to help us about twice per week. Sometimes I worked with him directly and sometimes I didn't. He had such a calm and caring demeanor with all of his patients, from the youngest of children to the blind 80-year-old widow from the nearby village. I felt more peaceful just being in his presence.

During one stretch of time, Sal had not been to the school for two weeks. I wondered where he was but didn't have time to ask anyone. Our days were so busy. My heart swelled with love for the children, and I had a couple of favorites who came to visit me at the clinic every day.

My heart skipped a beat when I heard Sal's voice outside the clinic walls one day.

"Olivia, dear, are you in here?" Sal called through the window. It was funny to call them windows because there wasn't any glass, just a square hole in the wall and a metal frame.

I tried not to sound too eager with my greeting. It surprised me how much I had missed him.

"I have been upcountry, dear," Sal explained. "A small group of children was found in poor condition, rescued from the LRA near the border."

I had heard about the Lord's Resistance Army from April. The children were likely rescued from slavery and sex trafficking. They had probably been beaten, raped, brain washed, and who knows what else. I was glad Sal did not provide me with a more detailed description about his activities over the past two weeks.

"I was wondering if you might accompany me to dinner this evening?" Sal inquired. "I have missed your company. And I would like to quiz you on your metric conversions!"

I laughed. "The whole group of Americans is planning to go to Munyonyo for one last tilapia dinner before returning to the States," I replied. "Why don't you come with all of us? We can't fit it in over the weekend, so this is the only date that works for everyone."

"It's time for the team to return already?" Sal asked. He sounded so surprised. Frankly, I had been pushing the return trip out of my mind and hadn't given it much thought until that morning when one of the guys discussed plans for the farewell dinner.

"Um, yeah. It's been over three months since I first came to Uganda," I said slowly. "Hard to believe it, huh?"

"Well, then," replied Sal slowly, "I guess Munyonyo it is. I better get home and clean up after my long day of travels. I shall see you this evening, dear." And with that, he turned to leave somewhat abruptly.

I felt a lump rising in my throat. What was that all about? Was it because of Sal? Or because my time in Uganda was nearly over? I fought the urge to rush out the door after Sal. I eased myself onto a bench in the now-empty examination room and rested my head in my hands. Was it time for another loss? Another painful goodbye? The feeling was familiar, but that didn't make it any easier.

"Hey, Liv, what's up?" asked April. She had walked into the room to put away a few supplies at the end of a very long day and sat down next to me on the bench.

I leaned my head on her shoulder and sighed. She knew all about Michael and Ellen from previous conversations we'd had.

"Are you dreading the return to the States?" she asked gently. "I bet it will be hard to see Michael with Ellen and the baby. Want to come to Ohio with me instead? I've got plenty of space. We'd be great as roomies."

I thought briefly about April's generous offer but knew in my heart it wasn't what I wanted to do. But I didn't want to return to Minnesota, either. I belonged to Uganda and she belonged to me. The rich red earth, the bright green trees, the beautiful brown-skinned children, the rhythmic drum beats, the never-ending line of patients at the clinic... They were all wrapped up into who I had become over the past three months. I couldn't leave now. I had to stay.

"Oh, Liv, I see it in your eyes. You've been bitten by the Africa bug," said April. "Bad."

"I know," I whispered hoarsely. "April, what do I do? I can't go home. And as kind as your offer is, I don't want to go to Ohio. I...I want to stay here."

"Then stay."

"Really? Just stay here and not go back at all?" My eyes began to well with tears. My heart knew where it belonged, but I had to find a way to make sense of it all.

"Why not stay? Stanley will come back to check on things in a few months. There's always a group of Americans coming to the guest house if you miss a familiar accent. You said the money from the trust fund your father left you will keep you going for years and years. You love the people here and they love you. Stay, Liv. "

We heard a low cough at the window.

"How long have you been standing there?" April asked, eyes wide. Sal was standing just outside the window.

"So sorry, ladies, I inadvertently set my keys on the window sill. I didn't mean to intrude on such a personal moment. Please forgive me." He backed away slowly and turned to go.

"Oh, Sal, it's okay," I said, wiping my teary eyes on my shoulder. I hadn't yet washed my hands thoroughly after seeing patients and didn't want to touch my face. "How much did you hear, anyway?"

I looked up when he didn't answer. His eyes were focused at a spot on the floor and he acted as though he hadn't even heard my question.

April broke the awkward silence by announcing that she still had about twenty minutes of work to do before she could return to the guest house to clean up for dinner. She had a ride with two of the other Americans and suggested that Sal give me a ride since I was already done and the guest house was on his way. I guessed at what April was plotting, but was too emotionally wrung out to dispute anything.

Sal and I drove in silence. This was rare indeed, because he usually had a story or a lesson about something Ugandan. Perhaps he knew I needed to be alone with my thoughts for awhile. It caused a pang in my heart as I realized that Sal's silence reminded me of the times Michael knew I needed quiet time.

About ten minutes before arriving at the guest house, Sal asked if I'd mind a quick stop at the internet cafe. He hadn't been able to get on a computer for the past two weeks and had a few important messages that needed to be sent out soon. I didn't mind. I hadn't checked emails for a couple of weeks myself. There was a business center at the guest house, but the power was so unreliable that the experience of checking emails there often turned out to be more frustrating than rewarding.

As we entered the internet cafe, Sal pointed to a computer near the door for me, and he walked toward the back of the room to another that was available.

I breathed deeply and entered my password. If I really decided to stay here in Uganda, who would need to know?

Who would even care? I had cut off all contact with Michael. Ellen sent an email every few weeks, but even those were beginning to dwindle because I didn't send replies. What was there to say?

What about Stanley? He would want to know my plans. I'd let Stanley know. As I thought about what to write him in an email, my inbox beeped with a new arrival. An email from Jesse. Good old Jesse. He faithfully wrote to me every week and I usually replied, although I averted many of his questions and instead chose to keep it light and told him about the sights and sounds of Uganda.

I clicked to open Jesse's message and the word "baby" jumped out at me. He hadn't mentioned Ellen's baby at all up until now, but she was having complications and was scheduled for a c-section the next day, so he thought I'd want to know. It was 6 weeks before her due date. Jesse also told me that Christina had broken her leg. Sweet Christina. I had given her the snowflake necklace, and we'd shared such intimate sorrow. And then I had left so abruptly.

I felt a light hand on my shoulder and heard Sal ask, "Almost ready, dear?"

"Are you done already?" I asked. "But we just got here!"

"We've been here for nearly an hour, " Sal replied. "The others will wonder what has happened if we don't get to Munyonyo soon!"

An hour? Good thing no one had been waiting to use my computer station. I tapped out a quick reply to Jesse, something lighthearted about the clinic and a funny incident with a child. I didn't even mention Ellen, the baby, or Christina. I added a P.S. *I won't be coming back with the team next week. Have decided to stay in Uganda. Please inform Stanley. Will write again soon. XO*

CHAPTER TWELVE

Our evening at Munyonyo Resort was a wonderful celebration of all we had accomplished with the clinic in the past three months. On our short walk from the parking lot to the restaurant, we passed by a number of round white buildings with brown thatched roofs. A huge swimming pool was surrounded by dozens of lounge chairs. Palm trees and tropical flowers adorned the edges of brick pathways that criss-crossed through grassy fields of freshly-mowed grass. The setting sun glistened off the waters of nearby Lake Victoria.

It seemed surreal to find this luxurious tropical paradise just moments away from the desperate poverty in the city of Kampala. We trudged upstairs to an open-air restaurant and ordered fresh tilapia straight out of Lake Victoria. When it came, the fish still had their heads! The Americans in our group shuddered and sputtered while the Ugandans laughed. Fish body parts were passed back and forth around the table all evening, and by the time dinner was over, every fish skeleton had been picked clean of meat. There weren't even any eyeballs left!

"Eyeballs! Mmm, a delicacy!" remarked our waiter as we laughed and enjoyed our final evening together as a team. I had come to love this group of people, but it was definitely sealed in my heart that I wouldn't be returning to the States with them. I hadn't mentioned it at dinner though.

As we walked back to the parking lot feeling full of fish and full of life, April came alongside me and grabbed my hand. She steered me to the edge of the path so we could have a moment of perceived privacy.

"I guess you've made your decision to stay for sure," she said. "I know you didn't want to talk about it tonight, but I got a phone call from Stanley right before we came here, asking me all about it."

Stanley? How did he know already? Jesse must have gotten my email as soon as I sent it and called Stanley immediately.

"What did Stanley have to say?" I asked hesitantly. Ultimately, I should have spoken to him before making a decision.

"Oh, Liv, you know Stanley! If I could have heard a cartwheel being done over the phone, I'd tell you he was doing one! You know how thrilled he is when someone feels a deep connection to a calling. He just wants to make sure you truly feel like you belong here and it's not just that you're staying away from Michael and Ellen."

I looked at April as intently as I could. "You know as well as I do that I belong here. I've never felt so sure of anything in my life."

She nodded. "I told Stanley that. And he also said he'd feel better if you continued to live at the guest house. Even though it's a bit more expensive than finding a place to rent, it is a much safer option. And he'll work on the details for extending your visa."

We hugged, tears filling our eyes. But unlike most of the tears in my life so far, these were beautiful, joy-filled tears.

April whispered into my ear, "Stanley also said he wants you to stay close to Salvador. He's a good guy and he'll look out for your well-being. Not everyone is completely trustworthy, but Stanley says you can count on Sal."

I swallowed hard. I already knew that to be true about Sal. I wasn't frightened to be in Uganda, but I knew there were real dangers, and I was glad to know Sal would indeed be a protective friend.

We returned to the guest house and I walked room to room, informing each member of the team of my decision to stay. Every one of them was thrilled, and a couple admitted feelings of jealousy. Life was different in Uganda, harder than life in America in many ways. But there was a peacefulness in the slower pace and simplicity of life here.

A few of the team members gave me some personal items as parting gifts—a wonderful high-powered flashlight that could be transformed into a lantern (perfect for those nights when the power would undoubtedly go out), a skirt, and a pair of socks. Melissa, a college student from Dallas, offered me the rest of her anti-malaria pills. She had about two weeks' worth left.

"Thanks but no thanks, Mel. I ran out a few weeks ago and realized they had been making me sleepy and a bit queasy. I haven't gotten more than a few mosquito bites in the past three months anyway."

I did not accompany the group on the trip to Entebbe Airport a few days later. It wasn't that I was avoiding a painful goodbye this time, but because the bus Paul had been able to secure for the drive was smaller than the previous one and I'd be taking up precious space.

We said our goodbyes in the parking lot at the guest house, and I assured April I'd return emails in a timely manner. After hugs, kisses, and waving to the bus, I walked through the gate and down the hill to the small hospital around the corner. We had dropped off some slides with blood smears from children at the school a few days prior. The hospital was going to test them for HIV and malaria, and results would be done by then.

After a thirty minute wait, brief by African standards, I received the results in an envelope and was instructed that they were to be opened by Dr. Walugembe. I wasn't used to hearing Sal referred to in that way. The children at the school always called him "Doctor" and everyone on the team called him Sal.

I walked out of the hospital and ran straight into Sal. Caught by surprise and almost by instinct, I shoved the envelope into his hands. "Dr. Walugembe! This is for you!"

"Weebale nnyo! Thank you, my dear, " he laughed. "I didn't expect to see you here."

"You have a way of sneaking up on me!" I exclaimed. "That's twice this week. I didn't expect to see you here today, either!"

"My plans changed. The woman whose baby was due next month in the village had a hemorrhage last night and died. No one could reach me by phone because there is no coverage that far away. Her brother is a traditional healer and refused to let her be taken to a hospital."

"Oh, I am so sorry," was all I could think to say. There was still a lot of conflict between those who followed traditional ways, including witchcraft, and those who preferred modern medicine.

We stood there awkwardly for a moment and then began to speak at the same time. After a moment of laughter, Sal motioned for me to go first.

"I guess I should tell you that I am not returning to America," I began. "I…well, I…I belong in Uganda now," I blurted out. It didn't sound quite right, but it was all I could think of. My thoughts were getting tangled. I winced at the sound of my childish and impetuous response.

"Olivia, my dear, if this is where you are supposed to be, then of course you will know it in your heart."

"I wanted to tell you that night at Munyonyo, but somehow there wasn't an opportunity. Did you hear me talking with April through the clinic window earlier that day?"

"That was a private conversation and it was not mine," Sal respectfully described. "But I must tell you, I am thrilled indeed that you are remaining here. Stanley sent me a message this morning and has instructed me to keep you in my care." He grinned.

I grinned back. Stanley knew I was bent on being independent, but he also knew a watchful eye might keep me from inadvertently tripping myself up in a dangerous situation. "Promise you won't hover over me and I'll be happier," I said. "But I am grateful for your friendship and your care."

Sal grinned even bigger. "Since I need to keep a close eye on you, would you like to accompany me on a trip to my home village tomorrow? I promised my parents I would visit soon."

Sal had mentioned his village to me months ago when we had visited Jinja. I had been so busy with the school and the clinic that I hadn't left the Kampala area since then. Of course I was up for another adventure!

We left early the next morning. A quick stop at the petrol station and we were on the way. Sal's parents' village was a few hours' drive east of Kampala in the Pallisa district. It had rained the night before, and when we finally turned off the pavement and onto the dirt road that led into the village, Sal's car got stuck. Within about thirty seconds, the car was surrounded by six local village men who tore branches off nearby trees. These they stuffed underneath the spinning mud-covered tires, and within minutes the car was out of the deep puddle in which it had become stuck. Sal gave a quick wave of thanks and we were on our way once again.

We parked a few kilometers down from there and got out near a small building. Sal explained that this was the local church. It was no bigger than 4 meters by 8 meters. A man walked over and greeted Sal, then came over to say hello to me. I looked to Sal for translation, but surprisingly the man addressed me in English. He introduced himself as the local pastor and walked to the doorway to show me the inside of their newly constructed building.

The floors were smooth and shiny. Sal explained that their surface was actually a mixture of mud and cow dung. That was the local concrete formula!

"How many people attend the church each week?" I asked.

"About 75 men," the pastor replied. Before I could ask if they really all sat on the cow dung floor, he went on with his explanation. "Everyone brings a chair to the service."

"Are only men allowed?"

"No, no!" he laughed. "I do my counting like Jesus did in the story of the loaves and fishes. We have 75 men, in addition to women and children."

Sal took me by the hand and helped me navigate a path that led through a tangle of branches behind the church. We stepped into a clearing upon which stood two round huts with thatched roofs and a smaller brick hut. Ten people stood in a row to greet us. I suspected that this was Sal's family, eager to welcome him home. His parents were especially pleased to greet their first born. He obviously brought them much pride and happiness. They were kind and gracious to me as Sal made introductions.

Next we entered the small brick dwelling. A lingering smokiness hung in the air. This was the kitchen building. A woven reed mat was laid on the floor for Sal, and I was directed to sit on a short stool. A parade of children entered from the doorway on the left and lined up in front of us. Sal whispered to me that these were his nieces and nephews. They sang a few songs in the Luganda language, laughing and clapping all the way through. There seems to be a universal happiness to children's songs, and it was delightful entertainment even though I had no idea what the words meant.

When the singing was over, food was carefully placed on dishes for Sal and me, and then the rest of the family left the hut. Since I was a visitor and Sal didn't get home very often, a special meal had lovingly been prepared for us. I found it odd that the tradition was for them to leave us to eat by ourselves. But I had grown accustomed to differences in Ugandan dinnertime. People didn't usually chat during a meal as we did in America. Eating was serious business here.

Pumpkin greens, supa rice, millet bread, maize bread, beef, and gravy rounded out the menu. It smelled delicious and tasted wonderful. Sal assured me it was as safe to eat as the chicken sticks near Jinja, but advised me not to drink anything. I had a water bottle in the car and could wait for a drink.

Following the meal, we went outside where a few more members of the family had come to say hello. Sal was greeted with more hugs and squeals of delight. One of Sal's young nieces, a girl of about 5 years named Daisy, clucked her tongue and shook her head whenever she looked at me. She pointed at my legs, barely visible underneath the long, pink skirt I was wearing. Before I knew what was happening, Daisy came over to me and bent down. She licked her finger and rubbed it against my calf, as though trying to brush something off. She kept mumbling under her breath.

Sal looked at her and laughed, then told me that Daisy was upset by my white skin and thought something was wrong with it. She was muttering the word for "horrible" under her breath as she tried desperately to wash off the whiteness.

A shy young woman holding a baby hugged Sal, then apprehensively came over to me to say hello. I noticed a large growth on the side of her neck.

"This is my sister, Teopista," Sal explained since she did not speak English. "Don't be alarmed at the goiter in her neck. Her body is lacking in iodine. I have told her to get some iodized salt and sprinkle it on her food at every meal. She should be back to normal soon." I wondered if it would really be as simple as that. How amazing that basic health care issues could be addressed with an educated doctor available to explain things.

Teopista whispered something to Sal, sheepishly grinned at me, then averted her eyes to the ground. "My dear, she wants to know if you would bless her by holding the baby," Sal said.

"Of course!" I carefully took the precious baby girl from Teopista. She looked up at me and cooed, the picture of perfection.

"Her name is Kirabo (CHEER-a-bo), which means 'gift.' From this day forward, she shall be known as Kirabo Olivia," said Sal solemnly.

"Just because I am holding her?" I gasped somewhat self-consciously.

"Because you are here, dear. Because you are here. Not many outsiders make it to our humble village, and you are the first white person, the first mzungu, to be here. My family is blessed by your presence. The villagers are honored."

On the drive home later that afternoon, Sal explained that his sister's husband had mistreated her, so her parents invited her to come back to the family homestead with the baby to feel joy and love once again. This was the poorest family I had ever met, materially speaking. But they were by far the richest in so many other ways. Children from around the village often came to play and eat and feel the warmth and love found in their home. Sal was part of a special family indeed.

CHAPTER THIRTEEN

I was eager to get back to the smiling children at the school after deciding to permanently stay in Uganda. They greeted me with cheers and shouts of joy when they saw me walking up the hill. No one expected anyone from the team to still be in Kampala.

"Auntie Olivia! Auntie Olivia!" they shouted. "We have a surprise for you!" The headmaster came out to the schoolyard and scolded them for the commotion, then saw me and hurried over.

I told him I had decided to stay on in Uganda, and he was thrilled. One of the female teachers ran over to me and held my hands as we jumped up and down. It was amazing how much genuine love the people of Uganda could show.

A loud giggling began as I was absorbed into a group of children that made their way up and around the building and to the back. A beautiful golden cow proudly stood behind the kitchen building, held to a post with a rope that was loosely tied around her neck.

"A cow!" I shouted. "My goodness! Where did we get a cow?" This was great news, for it meant fresh milk.

"We won it at the singing competition!" shouted 200 children in one way or another. More commotion ensued as each wanted to tell me about their wonderful prized cow. Some of the classes had been in a singing competition against a number of other Kampala schools over the weekend, and apparently we had won the grand prize.

A little girl named Winnie took me by the hand and pulled me down. I squatted to her level as she proudly proclaimed, "We call her Olivia!" Her announcement was met with more cheers and shouting by the children as I learned their surprise. Today there was a cow named Olivia. The day before, a baby had added my name to hers. My heart was full. I had definitely made the right decision to stay. I was already becoming a part of Uganda.

I stopped at the internet cafe on my way home later that afternoon. Since I didn't need an entire bus and driver anymore, I had taken a boda-boda, a motorcycle taxi. Apparently, the name originated when the cycles used to take travelers from border to border. I was scared to death of them for the longest time and hadn't attempted a ride for my first two months here. But the drivers were amazing as they darted in and out of traffic, and it was a cheap and easy way to get around. Most women rode in a side-saddle fashion, but that didn't seem worth the risk to me. One big pothole and I'd be flat in the street. I tried to remember to wear pants rather than a skirt on the days I planned to take a boda-boda.

The internet cafe was crowded, but a computer opened up within about ten minutes. As I waited to log in, I wasn't sure whether it was curiosity or dread that filled me as I anticipated the message that would be waiting. Ellen would have had the baby by now.

I had three new emails. The first was from Ellen. I passed it by and opened the second, from Stanley. He was thrilled about my decision to remain in Uganda and gave me detailed instructions about making arrangements with the government to stay longer. He had been back from Guatemala for a week and was planning to come to Uganda later that year, not sure when.

The third email was from Jesse. He was very concerned about my decision to stay in Uganda and insisted on coming to visit me. I wasn't sure if that was his own idea or if Michael had somehow put him up to it, but I decided to go ahead and let him come. It might help for someone from home to see how I was flourishing in my new world. I had nothing specific planned anytime soon, so I looked at the list of dates Jesse had already prepared as potentially working out for him getting off work and chose some. It might be fun to get a visitor after all, even though it had only been a few days since the team had left.

I was about to log off when I decided to look at Ellen's email after all. I clicked to open and nothing happened. Then I could see that a photo was slowly opening. This might take awhile with the slow connection. I watched half-heartedly at first, then rather intently as the picture gradually began to take form. It wasn't a personal email to me after all, but rather I had been included on a group announcement about the baby.

The baby's name was Veronica, to be nicknamed Ronnie after her late father. She was born six weeks early but was a healthy 5 pounds. She was bald and beautiful, and I cried as I studied the family photo. Ellen sat in the middle holding little Ronnie, looking tired but relieved. Michael had one arm around her and the other around a beaming

Christina who had been propped up carefully on the bed with a new purple cast on her arm and a bow in her hair to match. Michael looked genuinely happy. His hair was a little longer than he used to wear it, causing little blond curls to gather around the nape of his neck. He had grown a goatee and it looked as though there were already some grey flecks in it. I'm sure the stress of losing his brother, getting married, caring for Christina, having a new baby, and finishing up med school in such a short span of time were all taking a toll. I touched his face on my computer screen as a tear rolled down my cheek and splashed on the keyboard.

I tried to zoom in a bit to study the picture more closely. Oddly, I looked over my shoulder to see who might be watching, as though I were somehow doing something I shouldn't be. Michael had that same twinkle in his eye that always zapped me deep within, even through a photo. Ellen's exhausted face had an underlying peacefulness to it that hadn't been evident just a few months earlier. I am sure Michael's presence was very reassuring and helpful. Darn it, I thought I was completely over all this, but why did it hurt so much to look at all of them together? I should be in that photo. Michael's arm should be around me. I was supposed to be a part of that family. I looked more closely at Christina and saw that she was wearing the snowflake necklace my father had given to me. Why did I suddenly find that irritating? It seemed like the right thing to do at the time, giving it to her. I noticed the wedding ring on Michael's left finger. It was too much. I slammed my fist on the table and stood up.

"Eradde nyabo? Is everything alright?" asked the shopkeeper. Looking at the photo on the screen, he added, "Abeeka bali bulungi? Are the people at home okay?"

I was speechless and the man's Luganda words were suddenly confusing me. I had been getting pretty good at understanding, even when I couldn't figure out how to communicate back in Luganda, but words were escaping me now. I think I had forgotten to eat lunch. Yes, that was it. Maybe I was hungry and couldn't think clearly. Tears kept streaming down my face.

The man directed me to a chair and told me to wait there. Then he quietly logged me out of the computer I had been sitting at and turned away from me to make a phone call.

I closed my eyes and leaned back against the wall. It was dirty, but I didn't care. Suddenly, I felt very alone in a foreign land. Who could understand my feelings when I couldn't understand them myself? It was only about a fifteen minute walk to the guest house, but it was getting dark out already. I shouldn't have stayed so long at the internet cafe.

I stood up and walked toward the shopkeeper. He was behind the counter, taking someone's money. He eyed me and hurried with his customer.

I stepped forward. "Nsonyiwa," I said quietly. Oh, good. The words had come back. "I'm sorry." I handed him enough shillings to more than cover my time on the computer and turned to go away.

"Wait!" he called out after me. "Please, you must wait. I have called your friend. He will be here to pick you soon."

My friend? Pick me? What? "Wanji?" I asked.

Just then Sal walked through the door.

"What in the world?" I began. Sal nodded at the shopkeeper and thanked him, then greeted me with a thin smile.

"I was in the neighborhood," Sal replied. "Let's get you home." He took me by the arm and escorted me to his car which was about five blocks away. I walked quietly and let him lead me.

We drove to the guest house and the guard waved at the car as he opened the gate. Sal had come and gone so many times over the past few months that even though he was not a guest, he was recognized as a regular visitor who was welcome. He was also very respected for the work he did as a doctor.

Sal parked the car and walked me to my room, something he had never done before. He always dropped me off at the front door, and I walked up the stairs and through the hallway to my room alone.

I fumbled with the key to my room before Sal finally took it from me and gently turned it in the lock. He was so kind. He had no idea what was troubling me, and yet he asked for no explanation.

I sat on the bed, unsure of what to do and untrusting of my voice to even try to use it. Sal pulled the chair out from the desk and set it next to the bed. He sat down beside me and took my hands in his. He breathed in a deep breath and let it out slowly. After a moment, he did it again.

"Olivia..." he started. I did not reply. For all of his medical training, surely he must have known something was wrong with me that even I couldn't pinpoint. Was I depressed? In shock? Still in mourning? We sat there for what must have been twenty minutes.

Eventually, Sal stood up. "Come with me, dear. The kitchen must still be open," he said softly. He took me by the hand and led me down the hallway, out the front steps, and down the footpath to the dining area. There were many open tables, and he chose one nearest to a pink flowering bush whose blooms gave off a delicate scent that lingered in the nighttime air.

Shortly after ordering and receiving our food, the power went out. Our waiter brought over a small candle in a jar and set it on the table. It was barely enough light to see the food on our plates, but it was enough to be able to check for bugs crawling on our food before taking a bite.

We ate in silence as was typical in Uganda, but afterwards I knew an explanation was in order. As I began to speak, Sal interrupted me, which was totally out of character for him.

"You don't need to explain anything to me," he said, and I wondered if he already knew part of the story from Stanley. But I needed to talk, to process the feelings inside of me that needed somewhere to go. And I trusted Sal. So I began. I started way back with memories of my father and of his untimely death, of not even remembering my mother. I spoke about the preparations to go to Guatemala with Michael and our engagement. I told Sal about Christina's health, Ellen's fear for her unborn baby, and Ronnie's Thanksgiving Day accident. I talked about my sadness at losing not just Ronnie, but Michael and Ellen and Christina, too.

I babbled on and on for a very long time, and Sal just sat there patiently listening to me and nodding at appropriate times. When I finally finished my story with an explanation of how I wanted to stay in Uganda because it felt so right, like I finally belonged somewhere, he just smiled.

"It's perfect for you," he said, the first words out of his mouth in nearly an hour. "You have suffered much loss and therefore you are able to relate to Ugandans in a way that many Americans cannot. You are at a point in your life when this door to Uganda has opened up perfectly for you. It's your time, Olivia. This is part of the plan for your life. Now we must find a way to reconcile the past and move ahead to a better future."

Sal took out a small notebook from his pocket and ripped off the top sheet. He took it together with a pen and pushed them across the table to me.

"What am I supposed to write?" I asked.

"Write down the aches and pains in your heart. Write down the lost dreams. Write down your fears about the past and the future."

It took a few minutes, but I scribbled down as many things as I could think of, using both front and back sides. I also knew that I needed to truly forgive Michael, once and for all, and I wrote down his name. Then I handed the scrap of paper back to Sal. "Now what?" I asked.

"Now we give it all to God," Sal said. "You don't need to hold on to these burdens anymore. It's time for a fresh start." And with that, he crinkled the piece of paper and held it over the candle. Immediately an edge caught on fire. Within a few seconds, the whole crumpled ball of paper was engulfed in flames. It stayed contained in the jar and then burned itself out quickly. In fact, the candle itself went out.

We sat in silence for a few minutes. I could barely make out Sal's face across the table in the darkness, but I was sure I saw a tear slide down his cheek.

"Olivia, I told Stanley I'd keep an eye on you. You are a strong and independent woman. You are indeed a survivor in so many ways. But I need you to do something for me." He rested his chin in the palm of one hand and glanced my way. "Don't take a boda-boda at night. In fact, don't go anywhere alone. You are well loved, but you are also an American. To many, that implies that you have access to large amounts of money. It would not look good for my beloved country if anything were to happen to you."

I looked up, barely able to make out Sal's face, yet fully aware how serious he was being. Sal hadn't told me his whole story yet, but something must have happened to make him fear for my safety. I didn't know if he was more concerned about the impact on his country if anything were to happen to me, or more concerned for himself. "I promise," I replied with a solemn nod. It was true that I had access to large amounts of money because of my father's trust fund.

CHAPTER FOURTEEN

Time seemed to crawl at a slower pace after I decided to stay in Uganda. I went to Okusuubira nearly every day to help at the clinic, but I was careful to take a boda-boda during daylight hours only, and I always returned home well before dark. I switched to using a different internet cafe because of my embarrassment from the earlier incident.

On the days I didn't go to the school, I accompanied Sal on medical visits into the country. His skills were in high demand and his expertise was highly esteemed. He did many prenatal check-ups on women who lived too far away to receive medical help, and he taught me how to assist in that.

On one such trip, we found Bernice, a younger sister of the woman we had actually gone to check on, going into labor. She looked about 15 years old. Sal had never seen her before and didn't know any background on her pregnancy. But he moved with grace and ease as he gently gave orders and organized the women of the village to assist. This wouldn't have gone over well in the past to have a man there, but since they were able to communicate that Bernice had other medical issues besides the pregnancy, the women were happy to have a doctor on site.

I carried gloves and sterile wipes from Sal's car over to the hut. The women made way for me as though I held some special position. If only they knew I had yet to experience a live birth!

Our set-up was rudimentary at best. "What if she needs a c-section?" I whispered to Sal, knowing full well that I could speak at a normal volume and no one here would understand what had been said.

"We hope and pray that doesn't happen," Sal replied. "The nearest hospital facility is well over an hour away. We'd never make it in time."

Bernice kept slipping in and out of consciousness. The baby was putting pressure on an artery or something. I really wasn't sure what was happening. Sal was concentrating so intently that it was best to keep my mouth shut and just observe.

Suddenly the baby began to come quickly. Sal was caught off-guard and I reached forward to help catch the little one. "Olivia, no!" Sal shrieked. But it was too late. I knew exactly why he had shouted. In all the commotion, I had only pulled on one glove. I had forgotten to put on the other glove and now my hands were covered in blood. It was very possible that Bernice's underlying health concerns were complications due to HIV, but we didn't know for sure since Sal had never seen her before.

Sal grabbed the baby from me and instructed me to go wash immediately. I rushed out of the hut. No one else in the room was aware that I had even left because they were focused so intently on Bernice and the baby.

As I scrubbed my hands with antibacterial solution, I could hear shouts from inside the hut. "Muwala!" It was a girl.

Sal found me out by the car about twenty minutes later. "Bernice is going to be okay, " he said. "She's stable now and the baby appears to be quite healthy, although small. These women know what to do. They've been delivering babies forever."

Sal put him arm around my shoulders and I burst into tears. "I'm sorry, Sal. I got so caught up that I forgot. I forgot! How could I be so stupid?"

"It's okay, Liv," he said. "It'll be okay." That was the first time he had ever called me Liv. "I got a sample of Bernice's blood and we'll get it tested. Do you have any open cuts on your hand?"

I held up my left hand for his inspection, although I had already checked it myself at least a hundred times. There didn't appear to be any open wounds.

We were interrupted by a young girl calling us back to the hut. As we stooped inside, we could see the baby resting on her mother's chest. Bernice smiled weakly at us and mumbled something. The others looked at me intently.

"What did she say?" I asked Sal softly.

"They want to name her after the beautiful mzungu!" Sal said.

"Oh, no!" I said. "I've already got a cow and another baby called Olivia. How about they name her after you?"

Sal shook his head. "Awkward. Salvador's not a girl's name."

But I returned Bernice's smile and whispered softly. "Sally? What about Sally? Sally!"

The little girl who had come to find us at the car heard me and whispered something in Bernice's ear. Bernice looked up at us, and with all the effort she could muster, she proudly announced, "Sally!" And it was done. These sweet people had no idea what my name was or even what

Dr. Walugembe's first name was. But now there was a brand new Sally in the village.

The next four days were a difficult test in patience as I tried to distract myself from waiting for Bernice's blood test results. Sal had to go out of town and I was not about to pick up that report on my own. While it was unlikely that I had been exposed to anything, the risk was always real. When Sal came to visit me at school one day with a grin as wide as the Nile, I knew I was in the clear.

He picked me up and twirled me around, laughing. "My dear, we need to celebrate tonight! Let me go over a few things in the clinic. Can you leave soon?"

We had a happy dinner indeed. I wasn't in the mood for anything fancy, and frankly it was hard to eat a nice meal knowing that so many people around the city were struggling to feed themselves. We went downtown for a simple meal of chicken and chips. Before we ate, Sal prayed. "There are those who have an appetite but no food. There are those who have food but no appetite. We thank You, God, for we have both." Yes indeed. We had more than food and an appetite. We had a renewed sense of gratefulness for life.

Jesse's visit was coming up soon, so I walked down to the front desk at the guest house the next morning and reserved a room for him. He was planning to stay for two weeks. I couldn't wait to hear all about his time in Guatemala. I was even looking forward to hearing about baby Ronnie. That night on the patio when I wrote down my troubles and Sal burned them seemed to really help put closure on a lot of things for me, and I felt ready to see it all with new eyes.

Sal had a meeting near the Kenyan border the day Jesse arrived, but I was able to get ahold of Paul and secure a car for him to drive to and from the airport.

It was wonderful to see Jesse! I was glad I had agreed to his visit after all. We hugged and laughed inside the Entebbe terminal. It was like a slice of the past right in front of me. Jesse remarked on how good I looked and said Uganda must be treating me well.

"Uganda treats everyone well," remarked Paul as we carried Jesse's things to the car. "She's called the Pearl of Africa."

"You look like a pearl in Africa!" joked Jesse. "I saw your pale skin glowing before the plane even landed!

I nudged him playfully. It would be good to have an old friend here. Sal was great, but he didn't joke around much.

Sal had emailed Stanley with a list of items we were running low on at the clinic that were hard to replenish in Uganda, and Stanley had helped Jesse fill both of his large suitcases accordingly. In fact, only Jesse's carry-on was packed with his personal items.

On the drive to the guest house, we passed a construction site for a building that looked like it had recently collapsed. Paul explained that it was supposed to be a new four-story hotel. It had fallen down and killed twenty-three people just the day before. They were trying to build it too quickly and the cement had not been ready. A large flowering tree stood nearby. That's the way it often was in Uganda, a juxtaposition of beauty and death, side by side.

Jesse was eager to visit the children at Okusuubira, so we headed out the very next morning. I thought he might sleep in or feel a bit jet-lagged, but Jesse was a bundle of energy. He was awake the next day before I was, enthusiastically knocking at my door and calling my name.

"Let's go, Liv, let's go! Kids are waiting for me!" I had heard Jesse was a real hit with the children in Guatemala. No doubt the children in Uganda would love him, too.

"Aw, Jess! Can't we at least get some breakfast and a coffee first?" I whined, faking more annoyance than I really felt.

He relented and we ate on the veranda. Jesse piled his plate high with fresh chunks of pineapple. He shoved bite after bite into his mouth with glee.

"Mmmm! This is better than Hawaiian pineapple!" he exclaimed. "Why don't I ever see Ugandan pineapple in the stores back home?"

"We're landlocked," I explained. "It's too expensive to ship it through other countries."

"Too bad. Hmm. Now what else can I try?" Jesse's train of thought was already back to more food. He grabbed a dark yellow skin-covered fruit off the table, peeled it, and stuck it into his mouth as he proclaimed, "Ooo! Banana!"

"Matoke!" I corrected with a grin.

It was no surprise that the children at Okusuubira loved Jesse. Amongst the medical supplies, he had carefully packed a parachute. He organized children and showed them how to grip it around the edges. Then he taught them to wave it up and down as more children ran back and forth underneath. They had to keep taking turns because everyone wanted to play with Jesse. Then he tossed on a ball and the children cheered as they flipped it up and down, trying to keep the ball from jumping out of the parachute.

Finally Jesse collapsed in an exhausted heap on the stoop of a classroom. I came out of the clinic to check on him and bring him a bottle of water. As well as I did with the food, I knew it was best not to drink the water. My American belly would never get used to that.

"Hey, Tío!" one of the children shouted as he came past and gave Jesse a high five.

"Tío?" I remarked. "Where did that come from?"

"That's what the kids in Guatemala called me. Uncle Jesse. When the kids here asked my name this morning, I introduced myself as Tío Jesse without even thinking!"

"I love it!" I proclaimed. "Come on, Tío, looks like somebody wants to show you around some more."

"Tío is not as delicate as you are, Auntie O!" shouted one of the older boys.

"Delicate?" laughed Jesse. "You're delicate? May I never be described as delicate!"

"They mean my skin," I chuckled. "When I first arrived in Uganda, the teachers told the children to be careful of my delicate skin and to watch me closely, lest it begin to turn red. There is no word for 'sunburn' in Luganda, so 'delicate' is the best they could come up with."

A group of about ten children hovered nearby, anxiously waiting for Jesse to catch his breath before taking him on a tour of their beloved school grounds. Their blue and white uniforms were tattered in places, and their shoes had holes, but these beautiful faces exuded love and happiness. They sang songs of thanksgiving every day, helped one another willingly, and always seemed to be smiling. So many of these children, poor as they were, had richer lives than many American children who were stuck in lifestyles filled with selfishness and greed. I was reminded of the happiness I had shared on that day with Sal's family.

I hadn't walked through the dorms for a few months, and it was interesting to watch Jesse's first reaction upon entering. The girls slept on bunk beds that were three levels high, and two girls shared each single-size mattress. No wonder their heads were shaved. Lice would spread like wildfire in this place. Many illnesses did.

Mosquito nets hung near some of the beds, carefully tied and tucked out of the way for the day. The floors were remarkably clean, as the children were taught to take off their shoes before entering the dormitories.

Little hands clung to Jesse's arms and legs as the girls eagerly dragged him around the room to show off their personal spaces. One of the middle beds was adorned with fancy green netting and a pink bow. Carol and Sophie, the girls whose bed it was, explained shyly that they had won the decorations for having the neatest-made-bed that week.

As we stepped out of the building and headed behind the kitchen so the kids could show off Olivia the cow, Jesse turned to me with a look of sadness.

"Doesn't it eat you up, Liv?" he asked. "These kids are all too eager to show me their most personal possessions. They have no clue who I am, yet they come running up for a hug or to sit on my lap."

"How is that bad?" I wondered out loud. "They know you're my friend and it's obvious that you love children."

"Yes, but would you have ever run up to a complete stranger when you were a child and given them a hug? Would you have invited an adult you didn't know to come into your bedroom? It's just stuff I've been thinking about ever since I got back from Guatemala." He hesitated for a moment, then asked, "Are they all really orphans, anyway?"

"No, of course not," I answered. I knew some of the children had been living with elderly grandparents prior to coming to Okusuubira. One girl's father was the school gardener. He lived in the village with his wife and other children while his eldest daughter stayed at the school. But some of the children had been abandoned at a nearby church that was known for taking care of the needy. "What are you getting at, Jesse?"

"Well, we toss the word 'orphan' around so freely. I know it helps to bring in donation money from well-meaning people when they hear about a group of African orphans, or Central-American orphans. But do you ever wonder if this is really the most ideal place for all of these children?"

"Jesse!" I retorted, perhaps a little too harshly. "This place provides them not only with a decent education, but also meals and a safe place to sleep."

"Aw, let it go for now, Liv," replied Jesse. "I'm just thinking about the beauty of families, that's all." And even as he said it, I wondered why it had never occurred to me before now. Perhaps I didn't see it because my own family had been shattered and crumbled apart, and I had grown up shuffled between distant relatives who saw me as more of a nuisance than anything. I had no siblings, so the idea of a hundred "sisters" all living together in one room was appealing to me. Yet I could see Jesse's point. I remembered afresh the crushing blow I'd felt when the dream of having a family with Michael had been shattered. I'd have to think about it some more. Later.

We went out to Okusuubira again the next day, and Jesse pulled out his ukulele after school was over. The kids had never seen anything like it and they clapped and danced as he played and sang silly songs.

"Have you ever heard Auntie Olivia sing?" he asked, as hundreds of dark brown eyes turned to me. I had sung along with them, but had never sung for them.

"Oh, Liv, really?" he asked incredulously. He and I had sung together at every planning meeting for the Guatemala trip. "Come on, girl!" shouted Jesse enthusiastically.

My reluctance was quickly squashed. We sang duets and taught the kids a couple of new songs. Jesse even taught them one in Spanish that he had sung with the kids in Guatemala. Some of the older boys dragged out the drums and soon everyone was dancing and having a great time.

Jesse wanted to learn how to play African drums, so he handed me his ukulele and went underneath the tree where the drums were set up. He had a great sense of rhythm and learned how to beat them along with the older boys in no time.

Jesse was occupied and the kids were having a blast, so I took the ukulele and sat down in a nearby empty classroom. I hadn't strummed a ukulele in over a year, but it was, as they say, like riding a bike. As I strummed quietly, the words of the song my father had sung to me all those years ago in Switzerland came flooding back to me. And I began to softly sing.

You're unique and special, you're one of a kind
There's nobody like you! I'm glad that you're mine.
You sparkle and shimmer as you dance and twirl
My favorite snowflake in all of the world!
Reflecting the light, such delicate art
It might be cold out, but you warm my heart.
You spread joy all over, an avalanche of love
We'll stick together, no matter the weather.
I'll love you forever
My favorite snowflake.

I looked out at the beautiful children, some true orphans and some not, and wondered if they knew what snow was. I wondered if they'd ever had anyone in their lives who could have told them such sweet words. Did they ever feel special and one-of-a-kind, or were they so used to being part of a large group? Quietly and with an ache in my heart, I sang this song for each and every one of the children of Okusuubira.

CHAPTER FIFTEEN

Jesse's time in Uganda was rapidly coming to an end. He wanted to have a party with the kids at Okusuubira before he left. I started to wonder if they'd be bored with me after Jesse returned to America! Looking for more of a reason to have a party than just a farewell to Jesse, I asked a few kids if they knew who had birthdays coming up soon. My request was met with blank stares.

I turned to one of the teachers who was standing nearby. "Don't they know when their birthdays are?" I asked in disbelief.

"No," she replied. "In fact, some of us adults don't know when our birthdays are, either. We are just grateful for every day we are given. I thank God upon waking every day that He has chosen to give me another day of life."

Jesse walked up behind me in time to overhear the short yet somber conversation. "Well, we're going to have to do some-thing about that!" he exclaimed exuberantly. "Let's celebrate another day of life! Who wants a birthday party tomorrow?" His inquiry was immediately met with cheers of joy.

Jesse and I found a bakery in town that said they could have eight cakes ready for us by the next morning. That didn't seem like nearly enough, but it would have to do. I contacted Sal to see if he was available to drive us out to the school the next day so we could carry the cakes in his trunk. I hadn't seen him for a few days and was glad that he was available. He willingly agreed to come along.

We stopped at a store the next morning and picked up some cases of Coke and Fanta to go with the cake. If we were going to have a birthday party, it was going to be a fabulous celebration to be remembered forever.

And indeed it was. Jesse insisted on birthday candles. He said you can't have a birthday cake without candles, but I think part of it was that he secretly liked saying "omu-subbaawa," the Luganda word for candle. The wind kept blowing out the candles at the top of the hillside where the tables had been set up, so we carried the cakes into a class-room to sing. A class representative was chosen from each grade level to blow out the candles on each cake.

After the singing, small chunks of cake were cut and carefully distributed. Each child was thrilled with receiv-ing only a small taste. They smiled and giggled and ran around the school grounds with bottles of warm soda. There had been no way to cool it, but the sweet, fizzy drinks were a welcome treat and no one complained about the temperature.

One of the teachers came up to me during the party and clasped my hand tightly. With tears in his eyes, he thanked me for the first birthday party he'd ever had and said it was one of the best days of his life.

It was a bittersweet goodbye when we took Jesse to Entebbe Airport two days later. Sal was available to drive as long as I agreed to go on to an appointment he had near Masaka afterwards.

"Well, Liv," Jesse said with glistening eyes. "It's been a real pleasure." His voice was starting to crack. I looked at him for a moment and then grabbed him around the neck and hugged him tightly, pressing my face into his shoulder. Tears began to flow and they wouldn't stop. Sal stepped back and let us have this moment.

"Oh, Jesse!" was all I could manage to say.

We stood there locked in an embrace for a long time. We had begun to grow close in preparation for the Guatemala trip the previous year. He was a rock for me during the time of Ronnie's accident. And here he was, quite likely the only friend from home who would ever come to visit me, other than Stanley. There was something about sharing experiences in a foreign country that forged a bond like no other. This was a harder goodbye than I thought it would be.

Finally, I peeled myself away from Jesse as the line he stood in began to shuffle closer to the security area. We held onto each other's hands until my fingertips slipped out as he rounded the corner of the next section of roped lines.

"Promise me you'll reply to my emails!" he croaked. "Oh, shoot, I almost forgot!" He pulled a piece of paper out of his right back pocket. By then he was too far down the line to hand it to me, so in true Jesse-form, he fashioned it into a quick paper airplane and sent it across the head of an elderly woman and right into my hands. As I lifted it up to my face, Jesse called out, "Not now. Read it later!"

Suddenly the line began to move faster. "Thanks for everything, Sal!" Jesse shouted. "And Liv—you make a good Ugandan!" He blew a kiss as he rounded the corner, and he was gone.

We didn't wait in the parking lot to watch Jesse's plane take off as we had when Stanley left. Sal had a meeting to get to and I was wrung out from the goodbye inside the airport anyway. We traveled in silence for the first twenty minutes, then Sal reached out and touched my hand.

"You okay?" he asked with deep concern. I looked over at him and his gentle demeanor unlocked a hidden smile.

"Actually, yes," I replied. I was sad to see Jesse go, but our conversations over the past two weeks helped to confirm that I was doing the right thing by staying here. I watched the countryside go by out the window. The contrast of red earth and green trees was so beautiful. The deep blue sky held just a few punches of bright white clouds. Traffic was light today on the Kampala-Masaka road.

We drove on a bit further and then Sal pulled the car to the side of the road. There was a bus stopped ahead of us and a few other cars, too. Was it more chicken-on-a stick?

Sal hopped out and helped me around the car. We walked up to a big, white cement circle with the words "Uganda Equator" at the top. At the base was a big S and N. People were taking photos of each other standing inside the circle.

A group of Australians asked Sal to take their photo. He willingly obliged as the group laughed and shoved and squished themselves together inside the circle, then he asked if they'd reciprocate the favor. As Sal and I stood together inside the equator marker, it occurred to me that this was the first photo I had taken with Sal and me together. He put his arm around me and I felt safe and loved, right here at the center of the world.

We stopped for a quick cup of coffee and Sal explained that his meeting would take about an hour, although I knew I needed to be prepared for African time to fall into play. It was possible that the others with whom Sal was meeting might not arrive on time, and the meeting could go much longer than expected. I assured him I'd be fine wandering around the nearby stalls filled with handmade pottery, wooden carvings, and woven mats. I was comfortable enough chatting with shopkeepers and could surprise them with the few Luganda phrases I knew well. There were still many hours of daylight left, and foreign visitors abounded. It would be safe.

A small group of children hung around near the stalls, hoping to pick up a few shillings from tourists. I had some candies in my pocket and found willing takers. As I reached into my other pocket for more candies, I retrieved the piece of paper that Jesse had flown to me at Entebbe that morning. I looked for a bench in the shade and sat down to look at it. It was a letter. I was surprised by his nice handwriting. With his gregarious personality, I guess I would have expected it to be somehow loud and splashy. But it was neat and quite legible.

Dear Olivia,

These past two weeks have been magically fun! I really didn't think you'd agree to me coming to Uganda, but I'm so glad you did. I didn't know you weren't going to Guatemala with us until I picked up Stanley for the airport back on New Year's Eve and we swung by to pick you up. I didn't ask you any questions and I never told Michael. I have seen firsthand that Uganda is a good fit for you. You belong here, Liv. It suits you well. The kids and teachers all love you and there is a joy in you that I never thought you'd find again.

I know you don't see it yet because you have a way of wandering around with your head in the clouds, but Sal loves you. Don't get mad at me for saying this, but when he finally gets the guts to ask you to marry him, tell him I approve. You guys will be great together. It's only a matter of time—I see it in his eyes, even more than I ever did in Michael's.

Stop crying now because I know you are! Tell the kids at school that I'll come back and I mean it! I left my uke for you with the desk attendant at the guest house. You're welcome! :-) Sing, Liv. There are songs locked up in your heart that need to come out. Yours will be better than mine! I started one last night that I call "Loole yettisse amatooke mangi!" The lorry is filled with many bananas! Hahaha!

Stay strong. You may have originally come to Africa to run away from home, but you've run right into a beautiful new life.

I love you madly!

J.

I sat there for a long time pressing Jesse's letter close to my heart. His friendship was such a gift. We had bonded in so many unique ways. I pondered his thoughts on Sal. I'd have to get my head out of the clouds, as Jesse suggested, and be more observant. Sal was a wonderful person and had grown so dear to me in just a few short months. Jesse was right about one thing for sure—I had indeed run right into a beautiful new life.

Sal found me at the bench as I was tucking the letter back into my pocket. "Have a good afternoon?" he asked. I nodded as he sat down beside me and handed me a cold Coke. He had one, too, and we sat side by side enjoying a late afternoon breeze as he filled me in on his meeting with a local doctor. Native doctors were few and far between, and any chance they got to come together and encourage one another was most welcome. There was still a lot of skepticism of their methods by those who preferred the ways of traditional medicine.

On the drive home, I happened to mention that in all the months of being in Uganda, I had yet to see a monkey. The timing of my comment was uncanny, as the parking lot for Mpange forest was just ahead. Sal assured me that we would definitely see monkeys in this area of tropical rainforest.

He was right. Less than a five-minute walk down a trail, we were greeted by two red-tailed monkeys as well as a very friendly hornbill. A few lingering brightly colored butterflies flitted around us, even though the sun was beginning to set. It was growing dark under the forest canopy.

"Sometime we can come back at night and take the spotlight tour to look for bush babies," suggested Sal. "I know you're a good one for adventure!" I laughed in agreement.

As we continued looping around the path that would eventually take us back to the parking lot, Sal suddenly spun me around, took both of my hands in his, and looked me squarely in the eyes.

"Olivia, I would very much like to have more adventures with you. In fact, I would like to ask you to go on the greatest adventure of all. I would be so pleased if you would be my wife."

I was momentarily stunned. Jesse had just mentioned how he thought Sal was smitten with me in his letter. I had thoroughly enjoyed every moment I'd spent with Sal up til this point. But I had never pictured myself with anyone other than Michael, and once I knew that was over, I hadn't given anything else another thought.

"You think as we walk," Sal suggested, taking my hand and leading me down the path. Even during such a big moment as this, he was still thoughtful of my sometimes wild emotions.

My heart was thumping so loudly inside my chest, I thought for sure Sal would be able to hear it. Why not marry him? He was kind, gentle, and would provide well for me. He was my dearest friend in Uganda and we shared similar interests. Sal didn't have a shady past or a sister-in-law who needed rescuing. Yet these sounded more like reasons to buy a puppy, not marry a man. Did I love him? Of course I did. I knew the answer to that right away. Maybe that's why my heart was thumping so loudly, like a waterfall of love gushing over. Did I deserve the love of such a wonderful man? No. Was I afraid to love someone else and risk being hurt again? Yes. And how would it work with a Ugandan marrying a white American, anyway?

Sal stopped on the path and gently cupped my face in his hands. He caressed my cheek with the palm of his hand. "My dear, I see that look in your eyes and I know your mind is going into overdrive. You deserve this happiness, Olivia, you really do. And I want to spend the rest of my life with you. I love you very much. Nkwagala nnyo. Let me make this easier for my beautiful thinker with a direct question. Will you marry me?"

I looked up into his big brown eyes and could see my own reflected back at me from the glow of the nearby path light. I smiled and he already knew the answer, but in a moment of fun, I replied, "I'm not sure yet. I need to know one thing first."

"What's that?" Sal asked inquisitively.

"You have never kissed me. What if you're a bad kisser? I wouldn't want to get stuck with that for the rest of my life." Suddenly horrified, I realized I had put him on the spot without meaning to. Ugandans are very loving people, although public affection is frowned upon and rarely seen. This was awkward.

But Sal knew he needed to seal the deal, and so he kissed me right there in the parking lot at Mpange forest while a red monkey jumped up and down behind us, screeching approval. And I said yes.

CHAPTER SIXTEEN

Life took on a new brightness as Sal and I began to make wedding plans. Was I rushing into this marriage? I wanted so desperately to be a part of a family, but I hadn't even been in Uganda or known Sal for a full year. Yet I had a sense of peace that I had never experienced before, not even with Michael. And I trusted Jesse's intuition as much as I trusted my own. In my heart it felt so right to be marrying Sal. Why wait? As I knew from past experiences, we never know how much time we might have with each other.

Ugandans usually have an Introduction Ceremony, known as kwanjula, as a way to announce their engagement. At this ceremony, the bride introduces her future husband to her family and they agree upon a bride price, which could be anything from a cow and some goats to the more acceptable modern idea of a Bible and perhaps a book of hymns. But I was uneasy with the whole idea of kwanjula. For one thing, I had no family that needed to approve of Sal. In fact, we laughed on the drive home from Mpange forest when I showed Sal Jesse's written message of approval in the letter. That would have to be enough.

I was also unsure about kwanjula because typically the couple's friends pooled their money together at that time and divvied up who would pay for what at the wedding. But my closest friends were the teachers and kids at Okusuubira, and other than a few doctors, Sal mostly knew poor villagers. It wouldn't be fair to expect them to give anything other than love and good wishes.

It wasn't too difficult to convince Sal that we could forego a kwanjula. We'd have a more traditional American wedding, anyway, and I preferred to wait until Stanley's next visit so he could officiate the ceremony. He was supposed to return sometime later that year.

Sal offered many suggestions as to a nice location for the wedding. We could go out to Jinja, one of the first places we had visited together in Uganda. There were a couple of nicer hotels in the area that offered wedding packages and Bujagali Falls would be beautiful in the background. There was also Munyonyo Resort, with Lake Victoria glistening in the distance and where we had been served fish with the heads still on. Both of these would have been lovely choices. But in the end, I really wanted to have the wedding at Okusuubira.

The children and teachers alike were thrilled to find out about the upcoming wedding. They wanted to plant more vegetables for the wedding feast and begged for chicken and goat to be on the big day's menu. They made plans to add flowers along some of the paths on the school grounds. The teachers let the kids work on decorations whenever schoolwork was finished. We didn't know what special artwork awaited us for the big day—most likely paper chains of many colors. Whatever it would be, we knew it would be made, as they say, with big love.

Sal hadn't yet given me a ring and there was no time sensitivity to it without the necessity of planning for a kwanjula. But one day he told me it was time to go shopping for a ring. Someone had informed him of the American tradition to present the woman with a ring when he asked her to marry him, and even though I told him it didn't matter, that I'd be happy even without a ring, he insisted on getting one as soon as possible after that. He picked me up from the guest house one morning and we drove to downtown Kampala. After parking in a secure lot, we walked inside one of the few malls in town.

The mall was reminiscent of many American malls, although the food court offerings were quite different, with goat and beef liver as standard fare on many of the menus. We found a nice jewelry store and met with the owner to look at rings. I hadn't worn any jewelry since arriving in Uganda. In fact, I hadn't been near a jewelry store since my high school girlfriends and I had gazed into storefront windows and imagined what sort of engagement rings we'd have one day.

We looked at a case of beautiful diamond rings. It seemed odd to find such luxury in the midst of so much poverty. I told Sal that I preferred something simple and would rather spend the money on a fun celebration for the kids at Okusuubira or medical care for the needy than on a ring. He understood and asked the owner to show us rings with smaller stones.

I tried a few on and they were stunning. As I tried on a simple band inlaid with diamonds, a ring in a lower case caught my eye.

"Can I see that one, please?" I asked, pointing to a delicate gold band with a shiny ivory-colored pearl in the center, flanked by a miniature diamond on either side.

"That isn't a wedding ring," insisted the store owner. His hopes must have been set on a more expensive purchase, especially after a passing shopper recognized Sal and greeted him as Dr. Walugembe.

But Sal insisted that we be shown the pearl ring. I tried it on and it was already an exact fit, no sizing required.

"It's perfect," I insisted. A pearl in Uganda, the Pearl of Africa. What could be better? Sal picked out a simple gold band that matched.

The days flew by quickly as we awaited Stanley's arrival and made wedding preparations. The aunt of one of the teachers at Okusuubira was a seamstress and insisted on making the wedding dress. She and I had a grand time at the fabric district downtown, searching shop after shop for just the right white satin to make something simple yet elegant. So many of the wedding dresses I had seen in Uganda were full of lace and frills, and thankfully her feelings were not hurt as I explained that as an American, I preferred a little bit less foo-foo. My dress would be a classic A-line gown with a sweetheart neckline and short cap sleeves. But there would be no getting around a big fluffy veil, whether I wanted it or not.

Sal's mother was having a new gomesi made for the wedding celebration, a traditional Ugandan woman's dress worn for special occasions, floor-length and made of brightly colored cloth. The neckline was squarish, and the sleeves were short and puffy with a couple of buttons on the left side. A wide sash around the waist would be tied just over the hips. Sal's mother would look very dignified in her new patterned dress of bluish-green hues. She had chosen a color to match the eyes of her new American daughter.

107

Sal asked if I wanted him to wear a kanzu for the wedding. We decided against it for him, but his father wanted to wear one and I thought that would be a nice touch. This white, floor-length, traditional male garment, similar to a dress, was often worn with a sport coat over it. Sal's father would be quite handsome in a kanzu.

Sal's family was proud of him and so pleased to be coming to the big city of Kampala for the ceremony. They were very loving toward me even though I was not going along with many traditions, and I was glad for their unconditional acceptance.

Stanley was scheduled to land at Entebbe in early October, just a few days before the wedding. It was a little early for the rainy season, but the clouds hung low and heavy with moisture on the day of his arrival. Sal had a medical emergency to attend to upcountry, so I asked Paul to drive me to the airport. He was available and eager to see Stanley again. The two had become friends over Stanley's past few visits.

Stanley looked tired upon his arrival and wanted to take a nap as soon as we got back to the guest house. I asked if he had been sick and he said no, but he was definitely dragging. He nearly fell asleep on the drive back from the airport. Paul helped carry the bags inside and I told Stanley I'd wake him in a few hours. I heard him cough a few times after he closed the door.

Sal got to the guest house in late afternoon and found me out reading on the patio. Stanley was still asleep.

"We should wake him or else he'll be up all night," insisted Sal.

"He didn't look well," I explained, "so I left him to sleep most of the afternoon. Could you check on him please?"

I told Sal the room number, but before he reached the room, he ran into Stanley coming down the path. The two men came back to join me on the patio.

"Oh, good, you look so much better!" I told Stanley. "You had me worried."

"So sorry, Olivia. It was a rougher flight than usual. I felt terrible when we landed," acknowledged Stanley. "Nothing that a nap and time with good friends can't cure!" He gave me a much better hug than the one I had received that morning. "And maybe some food!"

We ate at the restaurant on site. It was a night with a traditional Ugandan buffet on the menu, and we filled our plates with local foods. I still couldn't bring myself to eat the grayish-purple paste made of ground nuts. I was told it tasted a little bit like peanut butter, but I could do without finding out. The rest of the meal was delicious. We had luwombo, which consisted of chicken and beef steamed inside of banana leaves, as well as yams, cassava, and piles of fresh fruits. There was also posho, something resembling grits both in looks and taste.

Stanley expressed his happiness at our upcoming marriage over and over. When Sal excused himself to take a call from the hospital, Stanley mentioned to me that it had not been an easy year for Michael. He and Ellen were getting along well enough, Christina was currently without any broken bones, and the baby was healthy. But the loss of Ronnie still hung over Michael like a dark cloud.

I didn't know what to say. I felt sorry for him, but I had moved on. I harbored no bitter feelings and my life was here with Sal now. Part of me wondered if Stanley had told me about Michael just to see if I was really over him before he married me to Sal. I was. There was such freedom in having forgiven Michael months ago.

The next morning, I awoke to discover that Stanley was not in his room. I remembered how he had shown me the church behind the guest house and up the hill when we had come here together in January. He must have gone up there.

I walked to the outdoor seating area for breakfast and overheard an elderly couple talking over coffee at the table behind me. They had thick British accents. The guest house received many international visitors, but I was on the look-out for the Rollofsons, the couple who had taken Sal in and helped him through medical school. They would be arriving sometime this week. Sal wasn't exactly sure when, as they were coming from the southern part of Uganda where they had been for the past two months, and phone service was scarce. He only knew they planned to make it in time for the wedding that weekend.

"Excuse me," I said, turning around in my seat. "By any chance would you happen to be Dr. and Mrs. Rollofson?" I inquired with a smile.

"Why, yes, we are," said Dr. Rollofson, as he stuck out his hand in greeting. His wife did the same.

"Sal has told me so much about you! It is truly my pleasure!" I exclaimed, so happy to finally meet this couple who were doing so much to improve lives, both directly in their own medical work with the people of Uganda and indirectly through all they had done for Sal.

"We are grateful this wedding worked into our plans so well," remarked Mrs. Rollofson. "Sal sounded so happy when we last spoke and he told us all about the lovely woman he'll be marrying. He said she's the sweetest thing ever to come into his life, and that as lovely as she is, her outer beauty is no match for her inner grace. How delightful!"

I felt myself begin to blush as Dr. Rollofson patted his wife's hand, "My goodness, dear, this poor girl will be frightened away hearing you go on so." Then turning to me he said, "Now, love, how do you know Sal? Are you here for the wedding, too?"

I was momentarily stunned as I realized this couple had no idea I was the one Sal had described as his future wife! Just then Sal pulled into a parking space below us, waved, and bounded up the steps happily, two at a time. He came over and put a hand lovingly on my shoulder as he said to the Rollofsons, "Oh, I'm so glad you've already had a chance to meet my Olivia!"

Mrs. Rollofson's eyes suddenly grew wide and her husband's looked as though they might pop right out of his head.

"What's the matter?" Sal asked, wondering why they looked so puzzled.

"Ah, darling," began Mrs. Rollofson. "You failed to mention that Olivia was a white American!"

I wondered if that was going to be a problem, if they had been expecting Sal to marry a Ugandan woman as tradition would have it. But it only took a moment for them to begin laughing. The tension in the air immediately dissipated.

Mrs. Rollofson jumped up from the table, practically crawling over the chairs in her way, and gathered me in a loving embrace. "Oh, darling," was all she could manage to say at first. "Oh, my darling love."

As awkward as that misunderstanding had been, I could feel the genuine warmth and care emanating from this couple. I knew I would be welcomed with open arms just as they had done for Sal.

CHAPTER SEVENTEEN

I awoke on my wedding day to the sound of rain dripping off the roof for the third day in a row. I guess that was to be expected during rainy season, but I couldn't hide my disappointment from Stanley when he quietly knocked at my door around 7:00 AM. We made our way to breakfast with the help of an umbrella.

The wedding was supposed to begin at noon and the festivities would continue throughout the day. I could just picture how muddy the hillside at Okusuubira must be, and I felt worse for the disappointed kids than I did for myself. I knew they had singing and dancing planned for entertainment.

The Rollofsons were well-known at the guest house due to their many stays over the years. Mrs. Rollofson had a special bond with one of the hotel workers, Clarice, who had already enlisted the help of her sister to do my hair. They were going to make little braids all over my head but would need to get started soon. I hadn't so much as gotten a trim since arriving in Uganda, and there was a lot of hair to be braided.

With two of them working, they finished in about two hours. I did a double take when they finally let me peek in the mirror. I didn't think it was nearly as lovely on me as it was on Ugandan women, but they insisted mine was the most beautiful hair in the world. They were thrilled with the auburn coloring and said bits of red hair "danced" on my head when I turned in the light.

I was grateful for Mrs. Rollofson's help getting dressed. I hadn't thought far enough ahead to realize that Stanley would have been my other option! I was missing Jesse on this special day, but he had emailed the day before with good wishes. He didn't have the funds to come back to Uganda so soon, and besides, he was busy caring for a friend who had taken ill.

Dr. Rollofson was used to driving on the bumpy, red dirt roads and had a jeep they kept in Uganda for getting around, so he eagerly consented to be my ride when Sal asked. Mrs. Rollofson got an extra blanket from the guest house staff and tucked it around the front seat so my dress wouldn't get too dirty. It seemed almost foolish to think of wearing a white dress here! Mrs. Rollofson and Stanley hopped into the back and we started on the 40-minute drive out to Okusuubira, arriving by 11:50.

The rain had stopped about an hour earlier and the sun was shining through the remains of a few clouds. The school grounds didn't look nearly as muddy as I had expected they might. The children had decorated with paper chains in bright colors streaming from door to door along the front row of classrooms. They had moved the desks out of the first three classrooms and stored them in a room at the end of the building in case the ceremony had to be moved indoors.

We went into the clinic to wait. There were currently no sick children, a small miracle, and the others knew not to enter that building without permission. Soon I saw Sal drive up, and I watched out the window as he helped his parents out of the car and into the front row of white plastic seats that had been set up outside. Paul had driven some of the other relatives from the village in a rented van. They must have left home at 5:00 in the morning.

Children and teachers began to gather into position and it was nearly time for the wedding to begin.

"We're kind of winging this, eh?" chuckled Stanley. It was going to be a mixture of Ugandan culture and American tradition. We had totally forgotten to do a rehearsal before Sal left for his home village two days earlier. But it would be fine and perfect. Mrs. Rollofson fluffed up my veil, kissed my cheek, and then went outside with her husband to take their seats.

Stanley took both of my hands in his and looked intently into my eyes. "This is good, Olivia. This is really good. I've known Sal longer than I've known you, and I can't think of two people I'd rather see together. Truly." He gave me a hug, took my hand, and then almost as an afterthought, turned to me as we stepped out the clinic door and into full sunshine and said, "Who's walking you down the aisle?"

"You are!" I said brightly, as I took his arm and we made our way to the back of the last row of chairs. I felt a twinge of sadness that my own father wasn't there to walk me down the aisle. But this was all so different from any wedding I had ever imagined as a child, and the sorrow lifted quickly as I anticipated joining my life with Sal's forever. My Sal.

The wedding was more than beautiful, more than I could have hoped for or imagined. April had generously wired money a few days earlier for a bouquet, and one of the teachers had picked it up that morning. It was a gorgeous lively mixture of reds and purples and yellows.

Stanley walked me down the aisle to the sound of children's voices singing a sweet Ugandan song about love. He took my hand and placed it in the palm of Sal, who was standing attentively, waiting for me, looking more handsome than I'd ever seen him. He wore a black suit with a crisp white shirt and a turquoise tie that closely matched the color of his mother's gomesi.

Stanley's words were perfect and he spoke in Luganda for as much of the service as he could out of kindness to Sal's parents. It was a sweet gesture and they probably ended up understanding more of the service than I did!

When it was finally time for Stanley to say, "You may now kiss the bride," some of the older children had made their way to where the drums were set up underneath a big tree. At the moment Sal pulled the veil back from my face, shouts and whoops of joy erupted. The drums banged out a loud and happy beat, and soon everyone was on their feet dancing and celebrating.

The kids were allowed to wear their special singing competition clothes on this day, and they were careful not to spill on themselves. My dress, however, ended up covered in dusty red fingerprints, but I wouldn't have wanted it any other way.

The children had their wish, and a delicious meal including chicken and goat, in addition to a vast spread of vegetables, rice, and beans was served. Smiling, happy faces danced around us all day. Sal's mother kept giving me hugs, and his sister kept wanting me to hold her baby, little Kirabo Olivia. She was getting bigger now and had already developed quite a spunky personality.

Before leaving with Sal for our honeymoon later that afternoon, I said goodbye to Stanley. Sal and I were going on a safari near the northwestern border of Uganda and planned to be back in about five days. Stanley said he'd be around for at least ten more days, but travel plans often change quickly in Africa.

As Sal and I drove away from Okusuubira in the setting sun, children and adults alike ran after the car, smiling and waving and shouting their good wishes. It had been a joyous day indeed.

The drive to the safari was going to be much longer than we could safely do before dark, so Sal had booked a room in Jinja for the night. The hotel sat on a partial cliff, and the room opened up to a beautiful view that overlooked Bujagali Falls. We kept the window wide open in order to enjoy the sound of rushing waves as the water splashed over the rocks in the near distance.

I shook my head in disbelief. What had begun as one of the worst years of my life was ending up as the very best. As I snuggled up next to Sal, I felt blessed to overflowing. My heart was so full of love for this man who had literally saved my life. Sal smiled at me, stroked my cheek with one hand, and with the other reached up to pull the mosquito netting all the way around the bed.

CHAPTER EIGHTEEN

The drive to the safari was beautiful, and I understood how Winston Churchill had come to nickname Uganda the Pearl of Africa many years earlier. We passed by fields of sugarcane and coffee, and one plantation after another of tea and cocoa. We saw banana trees laden with fruit. It rained for a little while but then cleared up and left a fresh open sky.

Our destination was Murchison Falls, and it was one of the few places in Uganda that Sal had only heard about but had not yet visited. I loved all the points of interest he showed me and all the knowledge he had about his homeland, but I was secretly glad that this would be a new adventure for both of us.

Sal and I spent the first morning on a boat tour. Hundreds of hippos bathed on the muddy shores of the Nile, a sight to behold. Sal whispered to me that he was glad our boat driver knew to stay back. Hippos and elephants were the cause of more deaths in Africa than lions, a fact that would surprise many.

We caught glimpses of Nile crocodiles slithering through the muddy water on either side of our boat. Some of them were as long as the boat itself, and I shuddered as each one popped up its eyes just high enough to peek downstream, then sank back down into the murkiness.

The next morning was supposed to be our land safari and Sal had booked a jeep tour. But the light sprinkles were getting heavier, and the driver found us to ask if we'd mind waiting a bit longer to see if the weather cleared up. Not a problem.

We sat on a large covered patio that overlooked a huge expanse of land, enjoying the view even through raindrops. The passion fruit juice was refreshing, and I grabbed a roll to go with it. Sal set his glass of juice next to mine on the low table and went back inside to look for matoke. No sooner had he stepped away than a baboon came sneaking up beside me, stealing the roll from my plate. I screamed and jumped onto a chair as the restaurant staff rushed to my aid, shooing the baboon away. They called her Dorothy! Apparently this was not the first time she had wandered up here, and it was not likely to be the last.

The weather cleared by noon. We set out for another day of great adventure, feasting our eyes on giraffes, buffaloes, and even a few elephants. We rounded a corner and came upon a lion that was picking at the remains of a fresh antelope carcass about twenty feet in front of us. I was surprised at how close the driver got.

"Should we be so near while he's eating?" I asked hoarsely. I grabbed Sal's arm a little too tightly, and he gently pried my fingers away while continuing to hold my hand. But I could sense his body tensing up a bit, too.

"It's alright, nyabo," replied the driver. "Mr. Lion sees the jeep as a bigger animal than he is, so we're not a threat. As long as you stay inside the vehicle, you'll be fine. "

After a few more minutes, we carefully backed up and proceeded down another road. I felt a sharp stinging pain on my arm and smacked at my elbow. "Ouch!" I exclaimed.

A fly wiggled away but continued to buzz. Sal took off his shoe and slapped the fly after it came to rest on the seat next to him. "Tsetse," he said. "They give a nasty bite. You okay?"

I nodded. My arm was sore, but not so much that I couldn't enjoy the rest of our tour.

Our guide pointed out a leopard, and we saw a few more giraffes as we made our way back to the lodge. Some antelopes ran past the side of the jeep, and their springy, playful jumps reminded me somehow of Jesse. If Jesse was an animal, I was sure he'd have been an antelope.

It was hard to get up the next day. I didn't know if it was because I was feeling so relaxed and peaceful, or if it was because of yet another grey and rainy day. The bed sure was warm and comfy.

I awoke to find Sal sitting next to me on the bed, looking puzzled. "Sal, what is it?" I asked, suddenly propping myself up on one elbow.

"How are you feeling, dear?" he asked with a look of concern.

"I'm fine, why?" I asked. "Is everything okay?" I swung my feet around and sat up quickly.

"Oh, nothing, dear," he said, his face relaxing considerably. "It's just that I couldn't wake you earlier and now it's 11:30 in the morning."

"What?" I asked in disbelief. I had never slept past 9:30 AM in my entire life, save for a few bad bouts of jet lag. "Oh, I'm so sorry," I gasped. "We've missed today's excursion."

I knew Sal had been looking forward to our last day on the safari. He had a big medical convention coming up in

Kenya the following week and wanted to spend every minute possible with his new wife while he had the chance. And here I was, sleeping away half the day.

"It's alright, dear, really," he reassured me. "I've been watching you sleep, thinking how I must be the luckiest man in all of Uganda. Probably in all of the world."

Sal grinned at me and I felt relieved. He didn't appear to be too upset after all. He picked up my arm and looked at the spot where the tsetse fly had bitten me the day before. There was a small red bump. He rubbed it gently.

"Still hurt?" he asked.

"Not too bad," I replied. "Let me get dressed and we'll see what we can salvage out of the rest of this day. I'm surprised I could sleep at all with these cornrows in my hair."

"What do you mean?" asked Sal. "I think they look beautiful on you. Like a true African."

"Oh, but it's so hard to get comfortable on a pillow with bumpy braids all over," I said matter-of-factly, rubbing my head.

"Well, come here then, my dear," said Sal as he curled up on the bed next to me and put a pillow on his lap. I laid my head down and closed my eyes as he gently loosened each braid from its elastic band. He ran his fingers carefully through the hair to smooth out each section before starting in on the next one.

As luck would have it, our driver from the previous day recognized us when we finally got down to the lobby and motioned for us to join the small group he was preparing to take out right then. "We've got elephants today!" he said with a grin. "And maybe some rhinos."

After a fifteen-minute drive, we came upon a watering hole. It was later in the day and a few small mammals were at the water's edge. I saw a zebra making its way as well, but it was suddenly frightened off by a loud noise. An elephant was crashing through the trees on the opposite side of the water hole from us, making its way to the edge of the water, followed by another elephant. They took turns bathing each other. First one would suck water up its trunk and shoot it all over the other one. They repeated this back and forth a few times. It was amazing to watch, but Sal reminded me how good it was that we were not any closer to the elephants. He knew of someone who had driven too close to an elephant the previous year, trying to get a photo, and had gotten his car tipped over by an angry pachyderm.

On the way back to the lodge, we had to stop for a group of white rhinos to cross the road. Our driver informed us the proper name was a crash of rhinos. Although we were quite near to them, they didn't seem to mind. They looked dangerous up close with their sharp horns and strong legs, but they meandered slowly as though they didn't have a care in the world. Thirty minutes later, the rhinos finally decided to pick up the pace enough so that we could continue on our way.

We drove back to Kampala the next day and I finished packing up my meager belongings from the guest house in preparation for moving into Sal's house. Stanley was still there and informed us that he had decided to go to the convention with Sal in Kenya after all. It was for more people than just doctors, and Stanley figured if he was already this far around the world, he might as well take advantage of the great opportunity and extend his trip by a few more days.

Stanley helped Sal put my belongings into the car and we promised to come back and eat a late supper with him. If the men were leaving in the morning for Kenya, I wouldn't get much more time to spend with Stanley before he returned to America.

Sal lived in an area of Kampala that was situated about halfway between the guest house and Okusuubira. It was a modest 2-bedroom house, but practically a mansion by typical Ugandan standards. It had been painted a light yellow with white trim and was very neat inside. Sal employed Gloria, a young woman from the neighborhood, to help weekly with the cleaning and laundry. A young teenager named Daniel unlocked the metal gate for us as we pulled up. He swung it open and held it there while Sal drove into the yard, then closed and locked it behind us. Daniel's job was guarding and protecting the house. It seemed like an easy job and almost pointless, as a six-foot cement wall with spikes at the top surrounded the entire yard save for the gate. But I knew better than to argue with Sal about it. Daniel had worked for Sal ever since he moved into the house two years earlier. Besides offering steady employment for the young man, it also gave Sal a sense of safety to have Daniel there, especially since I'd be living in the house now, too.

Daniel was anxious to help bring my things in from the car. When I asked if he could take the small box off my lap so I could get out of the car, he answered with a quick, "Kale, nyabo!" and flew to my side.

"Oh, please, call me Olivia," I insisted. Daniel looked to Sal for an approving nod before answering with a spunky, "Okay, Olivia!" If I had to have a security guard at my house, at least we could be on a friendly first-name basis.

It didn't take long to get my things organized in the house. Gloria had already moved Sal's things over to leave space for my few clothes in the wardrobe that stood along one wall of the bedroom.

"Does it feel like home, dear?" Sal asked me eagerly. It didn't really, but I couldn't tell him that. I'd add my own touches to it soon enough.

"It's very comfortable, darling," was the best I could do. I didn't understand why the pictures were hung so high up on the wall, all in a row around the living room. It was hard to make out the faces of people in photos when they were so far away. And the white doilies on the back of the burgundy-colored couch and chair in the living room reminded me more of elderly Aunt Margaret's place than they did of the home of a young doctor and his wife. But this was my first home with Sal, and that fact alone made it the best place in the world right then.

I hastily put my toothbrush and hair bands in the bathroom. I was glad for indoor plumbing but knew I'd be brushing my teeth with bottled water for years to come.

We had a very subdued dinner with Stanley later that evening. I could tell something was on his mind and finally asked him about it.

"Oh, I was at the internet cafe this morning and got some disturbing news," was all he offered. Sal was content not to know more and to leave it at that, but I pushed Stanley for more information. Finally, he consented to tell me.

"Adam, one of the guys from our Guatemala group, has tested positive for HIV. It's just hitting me a little hard."

"Oh no," was all I could muster. I knew who Adam was from our group meetings the previous year and that he was going to help coffee farmers set up small businesses.

"He doesn't have any idea when he got infected, but my trip to Guatemala for next year has been cancelled until we figure this out." Stanley looked dejected.

"Are there many cases of HIV in Guatemala?" asked Sal.

"Gosh, I didn't think so," said Stanley, "but we hadn't prepared for it and discussed health risks like we do with groups coming here. I remember one young man who was very sick in one of the mountain villages. Adam was very kind to him and insisted on visiting him nearly every day. I never knew what he was sick with, but he died the day before our return to the States. Too late to test him and find out for sure."

"Surely medical care for HIV is more affordable in America than anywhere else," Sal replied after a few minutes of silence. "We have trouble getting the antiretroviral tabs to people here in Uganda mostly because of the cost. Not many here can afford the treatment."

"Yes, I'm sure Adam will get the best medical care available," replied Stanley. "It's still so hard. Apparently, his roommates have kicked him out. And his parents won't let him move home out of fear. They are so ashamed, burdened by the social stigma associated with HIV."

"What's Adam going to do?" I asked. "Where will he go?"

"Jesse offered to take him in."

CHAPTER NINETEEN

After Sal and Stanley left for Kenya, I busied myself for a few days trying to make the house look a little more like a home. They say a woman's touch can do anything, but there was only so much to work with. Fresh flowers in a vase would help.

There was a patch of dirt outside the front door that could at least sustain the growth of a few flowers if not a few vegetables, too. But I wasn't much of a green thumb. I called out the door to Daniel and asked if he had any experience with gardening. He said that his younger brother was good with plants and promised to bring him by sometime later that week.

My thoughts kept going back to Adam staying with Jesse, and when I couldn't stand it anymore, I pulled some shillings out of my money bag and asked Daniel where I could find a nearby phone. My mobile was having problems and I wanted a good, unbroken connection. Daniel directed me to a pool hall a few blocks away. I hiked up my skirt and scurried over a muddy field to get there. Hopefully, the owner would let me pay him to use the landline. He was a young man no more than 20 years old who eagerly agreed when he saw the shillings in my hand.

I called Jesse and surprisingly he answered on the third ring.

"Hello?" he said sleepily.

"Jesse, it's me, Olivia." I said. "What's going on?"

"Whoa, slow down, girlfriend!" he said in typical Jesse fashion. "Why are you asking me what's going on? You're the one calling at this most unfriendly hour."

It took a minute for me to convince him that I already knew Adam was at his apartment before he relented and gave me more details.

"I guess good news travels quickly," he replied sarcastically. "Yes, I offered for Adam to stay with me. He's got nowhere else to go. His parents won't even let him move back home. I've got a spare room since Rico left me in the lurch for that French girl, and I could use a little extra rent money. It's a no-brainer."

"Is he very sick?" I asked.

"Not too bad yet," answered Jesse, "although sometimes he coughs like a chain smoker."

"Oh, Jess, be careful," I moaned, grateful for my friend's compassionate nature but afraid for his health.

"That coming from the girl who moved to the heart of Africa!" teased Jesse. "You're in the middle of AIDS land, baby." He was waking up and becoming his feisty self again, even without coffee. "No worries, sister. I've done my homework. Stack of gloves, face masks, AIDS hotline on my speed dial. I'm good, kiddo." He chuckled.

"I just worry about you, that's all," I confessed. "You're like family to me, Jess. You and Sal are all I've got. Please be careful."

"Hey, I've got an idea," suggested Jesse. "Why don't you find yourself an HIV friend over there to take care of and then we can compare notes. You're a doctor's wife now. He'll know how to keep you safe. Might even be able to give me some tips."

I remembered my scare with Bernice's delivery earlier that year and how careless I had been. I was much more cautious now, even around sick kids at the school.

"Jesse, that's a ridiculous idea and I'm not going to do it. But I will check in with you about Adam and how you're getting along with your new roommate."

We chatted for a few more minutes when I realized my conversation was being listened to. The pool hall owner stood across the room from me holding a receiver to his ear. He returned the phone quickly to its cradle when he caught my gaze. I wasn't sure what he hoped to gain by listening in.

Before hanging up, Jesse pronounced his undying love and affection for me in what could only be a display of bad acting for anyone within earshot of him. I laughed, made the sound of blowing him a kiss, and hung up. Even in the midst of troubling circumstances, Jesse could be counted on to perk things up. I felt better for having called.

I thanked the pool hall owner for the use of the phone, paid him way more shillings than the call was worth, and started down the steps. He called to me before I hit the bottom one and I spun around.

"I heard what your friend said," he told me, looking me squarely in the eyes.

"What's that?" I asked, playing dumb. What was he getting at?

"About finding someone with HIV to take care of." My heart sank. Did this man have HIV and want me to take care of him? Was he going to follow me home and insist I pay for his medical treatments?

127

"My sister's not doing so well these days. Would you come take a look? You are the doctor's new wife, right?" Apparently, my reputation had preceded me into the neighborhood. "Doc used to come check on Robinah, but he hasn't been here in over a week. I figured since you're his wife now and all, that you'd do the same."

He had put me on the spot and now there was a small crowd gathered around, listening intently to our exchange of words. I could hear a couple of children murmuring "mzungu" to each other as they pointed in my direction.

Why did I venture out on my own and not just stay home until Sal's return in a few days? How come I hadn't taken Paul up on his offer to drive me to Okusuubira today? I could have been happily working at the clinic and playing with my young friends out there. Would I ruin Sal's good name in this community if I did not follow this man to see his sister?

I cleared my throat, swallowed hard, and said, "Where is Robinah? Why don't you take me to see her now?"

The man introduced himself as Richard and led me down a path next to the pool hall. We went through a rickety metal gate and came to a small doorway, covered only with a tattered beige sheet. Richard pulled it aside and motioned for me to step into the poorly lit room.

A small female body lay on a woven mat in the corner, facing the wall. She was nothing but skin and bones, and she shivered underneath a threadbare blanket even though it was a warm day. Richard kicked at her curled-up feet with his toe and mumbled something in rapid Luganda, so quickly that I couldn't understand any of it. She replied in a faint voice.

"She said you're welcome to visit her today. I'm going back to the shop." Richard looked at me for a moment, then turned and left. I was alone with his sister.

The girl slowly turned to face me, using all of her energy in the effort. She couldn't have been more than 11 or 12 years old. She forced a weak smile and mumbled something, then motioned to a glass near her on the floor.

"Do you want a drink?" I asked. She nodded. "Mpa ku mazzi."

I picked up the glass and searched the room for some water. A small dirty jug half filled with brown water sat near the door. "Is this what you want?" I asked, sick to my stomach that she would actually drink something so dirty. She nodded again.

I filled the cup part way and held it up. It took a moment for her to open her mouth, and swallowing seemed to be difficult. Maybe just wetting the girl's lips would be good enough for now. Her cheek bones were sticking out and I could see open sores inside her mouth. I carefully put the cup down when she stopped sipping.

"What's your name?" I asked quietly, as though a louder voice might somehow cause her more pain. "Ndi Olivia. I'm Olivia."

"Ndi Robinah," murmured the girl. "Mpulira obunyogovu." She was cold. I scanned the room for another blanket and found a small shawl on a chair. I carefully laid it over her shoulders and she closed her eyes. I backed out of the room, silently promising to return soon.

As I passed by the pool hall on my way home, Richard poked his head out the door.

"You'll come back tomorrow?" he asked. I nodded slowly. How could I not? I could feel his eyes watching me as I crossed the field and waited at the gate for Daniel to let me into the yard.

Sal called to check on me later that night. The phone connection crackled, but I made sure to sound upbeat enough not to cause him any worry. I wasn't going to tell him about my conversation with Richard or my visit to Robinah while he was still in Kenya.

I woke up the next day with a plan. I'd go to visit Robinah after breakfast, maybe even take her a few bites of something soft like a boiled egg. I'd be careful to wear gloves every time I went there. And then Paul could drive me to Okusuubira. That sounded like a good day. Sal and Stanley would be coming back the day after that.

I stood up to go into the bathroom and fell back onto the bed with a thud. It surprised me. I felt a little dizzy, so I stayed on my back with one hand against the wall behind me for a few minutes, trying to ground myself somehow. The room was spinning. Waves of nausea coursed through my body and I thought I was going to throw up right there, all over the bed. In a burst of effort, I managed to run to the bathroom just in time. I knelt down, clinging to the edge of the toilet as everything in my stomach emptied out. I wiped my mouth on the sleeve of my pajamas, too exhausted to reach for a towel.

I sat on the cold tiles of the bathroom floor for a long time, slumped against the wall and desperate for a friend who could sit there with me. I thought of Jesse taking care of Adam and wished he could be here taking care of me instead. Sal and Stanley were still a day or two from returning. Other than Daniel out in the yard, there was no one I knew nearby and I suddenly felt very alone in this strange new house. I got dry heaves a few more times and then the nausea seemed to ease up. I crawled back to the bedroom and somehow got dressed, then fell back onto the bed. It was going to be a long day.

Daniel knocked at the front door around noon and shouted that he was going to run home for his lunch and he'd be back in half an hour. I felt alone after he left, even though he'd been outside all morning. But at least the queasiness was beginning to subside.

I walked outside to take a look at where the garden could go. Daniel had set a metal folding chair next to the front door and I pulled it across the front porch to get a better view of the side yard. My energy was returning just from being outside.

I heard a car horn and thought nothing of it until the beeping persisted. When I realized it was a car at our gate, I stood up to go open it since Daniel had not yet returned.

I peeked through the cutout door within the larger metal gate to see who it was, then swung the gate wide open. It was Sal! What a welcome surprise!

He pulled into the yard by the front door and turned off the car, then hopped out as I eagerly greeted him with a welcome home hug.

"I missed you so much!" I exclaimed a little too truthfully.

"Oh, I missed you, too!" Sal proclaimed. "Stanley's a nice guy and all, but I have really missed you!" He told me that Stanley insisted on staying at the guest house that night even though he had been invited to come to our house. They made plans for us to get together the next day before Stanley headed back to America.

After entering the house again, I got another wave of queasiness. I hid it from Sal, for fear I'd have to tell him about Robinah before I was ready. He'd worry and probably want me to get another blood test, even though I had only been there one day earlier and I had been very careful. Sal was already worried enough about that tsetse fly bite, although the wound had just about disappeared by then. No sense causing unnecessary alarm.

I followed Sal down the hallway and lost my balance while entering the room. I crashed against the door jamb and hit my head. I eased myself onto the bed and sat down to rub my temple.

"Silly me," I said, trying in vain to cover. "Tipsy and I haven't even been drinking!"

Sal sat down next to me on the bed and I knew he was about to go into his concerned doctor voice. "Look at me, dear," he gently commanded, and I did. He took my hands in his and suddenly I couldn't focus on his face. I rushed to the bathroom just in time to throw up the small bit of food I had managed to keep down since that morning. Oh no, I thought. He's probably going to haul me off to the hospital and all I really want is to lie down and take a nap.

I wiped my face and stood up. Sal was standing in the doorway.

"How long has this been going on?" he asked, staring at me intently.

"Just since this morning," I replied. "Oh, Sal, please don't take me to the hospital. I could pick up something worse there. I will be fine, really I will. It's nothing that a nap won't fix. Just help me to the bed and all will be well soon."

Sal reached down to give me a hand up. As I stood to look at him, suddenly he couldn't hold it in any longer and his face broke into a wide grin.

"What are you laughing at?" I asked.

"Oh, my darling, this is nothing that nine months won't cure. Do you think I can't guess exactly what's going on?"

My eyes opened wide in disbelief. Pregnant? Already? As overwhelming as the prospect of becoming a mother sounded, it was a much better alternative than having a terrible illness. A honeymoon baby was on the way.

CHAPTER TWENTY

Stanley was thrilled with the baby news when we met him for a breakfast of scrambled eggs and fresh pineapple at the guest house the next day.

"Please don't say anything to anyone back home just yet," I begged. "I would like to tell Jesse myself, and I'd prefer that Michael and Ellen don't know anything."

"Michael and Ellen don't even know you've gotten married!" teased Stanley. "I only told a handful of people that I was coming back to Uganda a few weeks ago. Don't worry, Olivia, your secret is safe with me."

About a week after Stanley left, Sal told me he needed to check on a container of medical supplies and asked if I wanted to get out of the house for awhile. I had been keeping a low profile, in part due to not feeling well, but also because I hadn't yet mentioned to Sal my meeting with Robinah and was hoping Richard wouldn't come snooping around to look for me. So far that day I was feeling okay, but I didn't want to ride in the car any longer than necessary. Sal assured me it wasn't too far from home.

"I met a man named Dr. Alexander at the meetings in Kenya," Sal explained. "He's a doctor from Colorado with a big heart for Africa. His church filled a container with all sorts of wonderful medical supplies and sent it to Uganda months ago, but they have somehow lost track of it. He doesn't know if it was inadvertently shipped to the wrong location or if it is being detained somewhere."

"How will you locate it?" I asked.

"Dr. Alexander gave me an address and I know that general vicinity of Kampala. He had to go back to America straight from Kenya for his daughter's wedding, but will be returning here within a few months. He is willing to share some of the supplies with me to use at Okusuubira clinic if I can help locate the container."

Sal was beaming. He loved to meet new people and help others, and the prospect of gaining some top-notch medical supplies, even if they were older, was very appealing.

We drove around for awhile as Sal scanned various streets. They were not labeled very well in this section of the city and he couldn't find the right sign post. Short buildings intermingled with makeshift huts that had been fashioned together from scraps of wood. It was a rather desolate area.

Sal spotted a man walking along the road with a child and pulled the car over near them. He spoke to the man in Luganda, asking for directions to the container storage facility. After exchanging a few words I couldn't quite make out, the young boy hopped into the backseat of our car. He knew where we needed to go and would escort us there in exchange for a few coins. Sal handed the boy some coins over the seat and shifted the car into reverse. The boy's father suddenly knocked on the front of the car and shouted something that sounded a bit frantic. Sal waved out the window and shouted back.

"What was that all about?" I asked.

"He wanted me to know that his boy has been circumcised and there has already been spilled blood, so he wouldn't make an acceptable sacrifice. I assured him we are born-agains and will bring no harm to his son."

Sal said this so matter-of-factly that all I could do was stare at him in amazement. "You're joking, right?"

"Oh, no, dear. Children often disappear from this area to be used a sacrifices in witchcraft rituals. But they won't take a child whose skin has been pierced. Why do you think so many baby girls are given holes in their ears immediately after birth? Many parents believe that will protect their girls from the risk of abduction."

I thought back to the girls at Okusuubira. Not all of them had pierced ears, but many did. They didn't wear earrings, however; it looked more like a thick piece of straw or a sliver of wood sticking out through each of their earlobes.

The boy directed us to a building on a nearby street, then hopped out of the car and skipped down the road, happily jingling the coins Sal had given to him.

"Shouldn't we drive him back to his father?" I asked, somewhat alarmed.

Sal put his arm around my shoulder. "Olivia, you cannot live every minute in fear. Yes, there are bad people. But there are also many good people. He'll make it home. He knows his way around here." I shuddered and thought of our unborn child's future.

A man who introduced himself as Leonard came out to help us. He assured us that Dr. Alexander's container was indeed at that location, but that insufficient funds had been received and therefore he did not have permission to release the contents.

Sal asked if we could see inside the container. Reluctantly, Leonard grabbed a large ring of keys from inside his office and we followed him along a narrow path. He walked so quickly that branches brushed off of him and slapped me in the face. Sal ducked ahead of me and held back the branches so I could proceed unscathed.

Leonard stopped in front of a large grey container, checked the number on the outside of it against the slip of paper in his hand, and then slid a key into the padlock. He tugged down to unfasten it and swung the door wide open.

It was hot inside and the contents smelled musty, but Sal gasped with excitement as he spied an examination table. He brushed dust off the lid of a nearby box, then carefully lifted it and nodded his head excitedly. He turned to me with a look of delight that one might find on a child's face Christmas morning.

"How much is the extra fee?" Sal asked Leonard.

Leonard gruffly mumbled something, then motioned for us to follow him back to his office after he secured the padlock. He pointed to two hard, blue plastic chairs and we sat down. Leonard shuffled through a few papers in a folder, then scribbled something down and handed it to Sal.

"That's the price if you pick it up by next Wednesday," Leonard muttered. "After that, it will go up."

Sal studied at the slip of paper intently, then looked up at Leonard.

"Are you serious?" he asked. "This is almost the price it would cost to ship the container here from America in the first place."

Leonard shrugged and didn't say a word.

"We'll be in touch," Sal murmured, then stood up. He turned to go without even shaking Leonard's hand.

Sal opened the car door for me, then shuffled around to the driver's side somewhat dejectedly. "I just don't get it," he said. "Obviously this guy is a rip-off artist and is looking for a bribe. As much as I want to get Dr. Alexander's container released, I won't do it. I won't."

"Shall we call the police?" I asked innocently.

Sal shook his head slowly and chuckled. "Are you hungry?" he asked, changing the subject. We got to the end of the dirt road and pulled onto pavement once again.

We stopped at a deli that was next to a pizza place. Crackers and cheese sounded better to me than a deluxe pizza, but Sal had been such a trooper waiting on me for the past week that I insisted he get something he really wanted. We chose a table outside in order to enjoy the sun. We were having a brief respite from rain over the past few days.

"Sal, I need to tell you about something that happened while you were in Kenya," I blurted out before he had even opened the lid on his box of pizza. "I should have told you sooner but I didn't know where to begin."

Sal kept quiet and lifted a slice of pizza to his lips. He bit off a piece and I continued.

"I went to use the phone at the pool hall to call Jesse because I was worried about him taking care of Adam with HIV and all, and I wanted a good connection, but my phone was giving me trouble. Daniel told me the owner would let me use his phone if I paid him. And then the owner, Richard, wanted me to go see his sister."

I stopped to catch my breath, aware that I was rambling and that Sal was watching me with a puzzled look on his face.

"This is about Robinah?" he asked.

"Umm, yes," I said slowly, surprised that he didn't seem more upset, and that he mentioned her name when I hadn't yet gotten to it.

"So did you go?" he asked.

"Yes. I went, " I replied. "Are you upset?"

"I figured you'd find her soon enough."

"So...do you mind if I go back?" I asked. "I promise to be careful."

Sal consented. "I've gone to see her a few times myself. Richard was hoping I could work miracles since he found out I'm a doctor, but Robinah is way too far along with AIDS to be able to do much for her other than keep her comfortable. I'm surprised she's still hanging in there."

"She looks miserable just lying on the ground on that mat," I said. "Could we get her a new mattress? Maybe some fresh sheets and a thicker blanket? And what about some medicine?"

Sal shook his head. "You can visit her and take some food, but that's it."

"Why, Sal, I thought you'd care more than that! She's suffering right under our noses and we can't do more?" When he didn't respond, I thought for a moment. "Maybe I could get Paul to come out with a car and help me bring a new mattress. I have money from my father's fund just sitting in the bank."

"No, Olivia," Sal said rather sternly. Then softening, he said, "We can't. It wouldn't be fair. You don't understand, dear."

Not fair? I wondered. He was right. I didn't understand. Had this tenderhearted man suddenly been drained of all compassion?

"Liv, you'd be surprised to find out how many people are dying all around us. It happens all the time. Everyone

139

needs a new bed. Everyone needs just a little more medicine. If we help one and word gets out, there will be a never-ending flood of requests at our door."

"So? Why can't we help them all?" My eyes began to fill with tears and I wanted to pound on Sal's chest and beat some sense into him. There were people who needed help and we could help them, couldn't we? Was I being a naive American who actually thought I could save the whole country?

"Olivia, it doesn't work that way. It would be too much and there's no other way to explain it. We just can't." He put his head down sadly.

"Don't you care?" I blurted out. But even as I said the words, I knew Sal did care. I knew he cared so much that sometimes it caused him to lie awake at night and stare at the ceiling when he thought I was asleep. I knew he cared so much that he hadn't told me about his secret visits to Robinah because he knew I would have worried. Sal was right—we couldn't help everyone in the way that I wanted to. I had to toughen up if I was going to make it in this country, so far away and foreign from the one in which I had grown up. Life was a beautiful thing, but sometimes it could be so cruel.

As we drove home, we passed by a casket maker's shop. We had been down this road many times before, but we were usually going the opposite direction and I hadn't paid much attention. Today, however, I took notice. Five smaller wooden caskets had been propped up along a bench by the side of the road, tiny enough to hold infants. They were as much a part of the shop's regular inventory as the larger adult-sized ones. Death and life were closely intertwined here in Africa.

I was suddenly desperate to get home and see Robinah. After Daniel opened the gate for us, I rushed into the house to grab a water bottle and a container of broth that was in the fridge. Good, it was cold. Amazingly, the power must have stayed on all day. As an afterthought, I pulled a straw out of a box that was in the cupboard and stuck it in my pocket.

Sal came out of the bathroom and knew immediately what I was up to. He asked if he could join me and pulled some gloves out of a box on the top shelf. I would have forgotten...again. Together my new husband and I made our way across the rutted field to the pool hall. Richard was sitting on the stoop, smoking. I wondered how much food he could have gotten for his sister for the price of a pack of cigarettes, then batted those thoughts out of my head. His actions were not mine to judge. Richard looked right through me and nodded at Sal.

Sal and I made our way down the path and through the rusty gate to the sheet-covered entrance of Robinah and Richard's place. I pulled the sheet aside, being careful not to rip the hole in the sheet any wider where it hung on a nail at the top of the doorway, and whispered Robinah's name.

"Robinah?" I called softly into the dark room. There was no answer. "Robinah?" I called again, a little louder this time. She stirred. What a relief.

I stooped down next to her and Sal crouched beside me. He slipped on a pair of gloves and picked up her wrist. I was sure he was checking her pulse, but he covered up well and an onlooker would have suspected he was only holding her hand. As much as I wanted her to be able to feel the warmth of a human touch, I knew it was too dangerous to hold her without the gloves. A fresh sore on the back of her elbow was oozing.

I pulled on a pair of gloves that Sal handed to me and gently caressed Robinah's face. She moaned as though the pressure of my hand was too much, and I withdrew.

"Oyagala eky'okunywa?" I asked. Sal looked up at me, seemingly impressed that I knew how to ask if she wanted a drink.

Robinah didn't respond, but motherly instincts must have already been kicking into high gear due to the hormone levels raging through my pregnant body. This child needed some nourishment. I peeled the plastic cover off the container of broth and set it on the floor next to me. Then I took the straw out of my pocket, dipped it into the soup, and stuck my index finger over the top of it. I placed the straw inside Robinah's partially opened mouth and released my finger as the broth dribbled onto her tongue.

Most of the broth came running back out of her mouth, and I used a corner of the blanket to wipe her chin. I tried the straw method again and this time Robinah was able to swallow a little bit. I thought to myself how strange that this was one of the biggest successes in my life so far and almost let out a giggle. Why did laughter sometimes creep up at such inopportune moments?

Robinah stopped swallowing after that and writhed a few times as though her hands and feet hurt. Sal directed me to put the lid back on the soup. I wasn't sure why it mattered to him if I did it right then or in a few minutes, but as I bent to snap the green lid in place, out of the corner of my eye I saw Sal take something out of his pocket and push it gently behind Robinah's back. Oh my goodness, was he giving her a shot of morphine to ease the pain in her final hours?

I heard the rusty gate creak outside and knew Richard would be inside the room in moments. "Hand me the soup, Olivia," Sal suddenly ordered.

"What?" I asked. "But I don't have the lid on tight yet."

"Just hand it to me," he ordered with pleading in his voice. There was no sense arguing. I handed him the soup just as Richard peeked through the doorway.

"How is she doing, Doc?" Richard asked, as Sal handed me back the container of broth with the lid snapped in place. What was this? Musical soup bowls?

"She won't be with us much longer," Sal replied sadly. "She's put up a good fight."

Richard nodded and Sal stood up to go. I brushed my hand lightly against Robinah's forehead, then stood to follow Sal out.

"Thanks," mumbled Richard as we passed him in the doorway. He stood there unmoving as we made our way down the path.

We walked in silence past the pool hall and out into the field.

"What was all that with that soup?" I asked Sal when we were out of earshot of anyone.

"Oh, my dear, let's just say it's better if you don't know everything. Trust me on that."

I didn't ask any more questions, but soon after we got home, Sal set the soup container into a doubled-up trash bag, the type I had seen him use for medical disposal. Before he could pull the bag over the sides of the bowl and tie it up, I saw something glisten from inside the bowl. It was most definitely a needle. He must have forgotten to think of how he'd dispose of it in my haste to get to Robinah. What if I hadn't brought the soup along? Well, it didn't matter. Dr. Walugembe's secret act of kindness was very safe with me. I prayed Robinah was resting peacefully in her final moments on earth and that her suffering would soon be over.

CHAPTER TWENTY-ONE

Morning sickness got the better of me for the next two months, and I only made it out to Okusuubira a handful of times. Sal had found a young man named Ezekiel who was very well suited for running the clinic, and he was doing a wonderful job. My visits these days mostly consisted of playing with the children and encouraging the teachers. It was a strange transition as my role changed, but I knew I'd be a mother soon enough and my role would change yet again.

Christmas came and went with few complaints. We spent two days with Sal's family at their homestead. It was my first overnight inside a hut and I did surprisingly well. How could I complain when this was all these people knew? Sal tucked an extra blanket underneath me to add a bit of cushion.

I steered clear of using the phone at the pool hall. I couldn't bear to look at Richard after Robinah died. I tried calling Jesse from my mobile a couple of times but got no answer, and I wondered how things were going for him with Adam.

I avoided riding on a boda-boda anymore because my bladder couldn't handle it, but Sal was so good to take me to the internet cafe at least once per week. He knew I needed those connections with the few people I dearly loved back in America. I wrote to let Jesse know about the baby via email about a week earlier and had yet to get a reply.

Sal and I headed to the internet cafe on a Saturday afternoon in the first part of January. I sat down by an open computer, anxious for some news. I was a little stir-crazy and couldn't wait to hear when April's group would be returning. I had decided not to tell her about the baby yet and to save it for a surprise.

I opened up my email account and had two emails waiting, one from Jesse and one from April. I clicked on the one from Jesse first. He said Adam was doing remarkably well. The ARV medication had really slowed the disease's progress and to someone who didn't know, Adam appeared to be quite healthy. What a stark contrast to Robinah's experience.

Jesse said he did both a cartwheel and a backflip upon learning I was pregnant and insisted that the baby be named after him if it was a boy...or a girl! We'd see about that! He had a difficult semester coming up with school and couldn't get away anytime soon. He hoped to be able to come for a visit before the end of the year, as long as Adam was still doing well. Then he mentioned that Ellen was pregnant. I skimmed that part over, then went back and re-read it again. Ellen was pregnant? She and Michael were going to have a baby? Little Ronnie wasn't even one year old yet. Jesse thought Ellen was due sometime in mid-July. That was near my due date, too.

Next I clicked on April's email. She and most of her usual team would be arriving in two weeks. Yay! I was so excited for female companionship! The women of Uganda were truly wonderful, but I sometimes got a funny feeling that they were not too keen on a white American having married one of the most eligible Ugandan men around.

April's church was getting very involved with Okusuubira, and in fact many members were now sponsoring individual children. April was bringing along gifts to distribute to the children. Her group also wanted to bring some special movies along to show the kids at Okusuubira. They had a movie projector, but she asked if I'd be able to get ahold of a movie screen.

After I replied to Jesse and April, I found Sal at another computer. He was just finishing up. He smiled at me and took my hand as he logged out with the other one.

"You are positively glowing, my dear," he told me. "Radiant is the best word I can come up with to describe you!" He grinned at me and I felt beautiful.

"My goodness, Doctor, you are making me blush!" I replied. "It's not fair that I can never make you blush!" He laughed.

"Say, April wants to know if we have access to a movie screen to use at Okusuubira." Sal looked at me and laughed again.

"Sure, " he replied. "I'll take you on another adventure and you can see how we find movie screens in Uganda."

We were close to the downtown area and it was easier to leave the car parked where it was, so we hopped into a taxi and Sal gave directions for the fabric district.

I never tired of watching the bustle of activity in downtown. We passed by the taxi park where dozens of old cars and vans waited to be put into use. We snaked our way through traffic that had trouble deciding which lanes to stay in as it wound through the streets of Kampala. I saw a man with ten mattresses balanced of top of his head, running down the street as though late to make a delivery. I nudged Sal and motioned for him to look out my window. He looked beyond that man and nudged me back. There was a different man with fifteen mattresses on his head!

We got out near the fabric district. Areas of downtown Kampala were divided into very distinct sections. The stationery district sold paper, copy machines, writing utensils, and all sorts of office and school supplies. The electronics section had televisions and radios for sale. Some of the smaller electronics were housed behind glass cases. It seemed strange to find all of the shops in an area selling the same thing and I wondered why they didn't spread them out across the city. Perhaps this made haggling on the price easier when you could simply walk to the shop next door if you weren't satisfied with customer service.

The fabric district consisted of row after row of sewing machines and sewing supplies, such as thread and needles. Piles upon piles of fabric in assorted colors and textures were stacked on top of tables and counters. I followed Sal into a shop where he seemed to know the owner. Either that or the man thought we looked ready to make a big purchase. He was right.

Sal turned to me and explained what we were doing there. "We'll need to buy three large sheets of white fabric and have them sewn together. Then we can hang it up on a rope. That's how we'll get a big enough movie screen." How clever! The resourcefulness of Africans never ceased to amaze me.

Sal paid the man after they scribbled down measurements on a piece of paper and made arrangements to pick up the finished product a few days later. The man was so excited by the purchase that he didn't mind when Sal offered a price outright and didn't leave room for haggling. Sal knew I was getting tired.

We stopped at a place for supper before finding a taxi to take us back to the car. My appetite was returning with a vengeance. Chicken and chips for me while Sal enjoyed some beef liver. He knew I wouldn't be cooking that for him at home.

I felt a small bite near my ankle as we walked down a street filled with shops carrying mosquito netting. It was the first mosquito bite I had gotten in the past six months. We usually avoided being outdoors after dark when the mosquitoes were more likely to be out. I was surprised at how many people got malaria each year because there just didn't seem to be that many mosquitoes around. Sal always insisted on sleeping with the mosquito net pulled over our bed. I loved how he called it a mos-KWEE-toe net, just like the kids at Okusuubira did.

The next two weeks crawled along, but finally the day came when April's team was set to arrive. I planned to go out to Okusuubira the next day and greet them there. Sal had to go upcountry for a week, so Paul picked me up and drove me to the school.

April saw me getting out of the car and came running over. "What in the world?! I hear you're going to be a mama! Why didn't you tell me sooner?" she exclaimed, catching me up in a big hug.

"Sorry, April, I wanted to surprise you. I forgot the children would be so excited and would tell you the good news! I had to tell them about the baby early on. I was so sick, they all thought I was dying!"

"Well, you look great! Are you feeling well enough to help me distribute some things?" she asked. I nodded, eager to do something meaningful.

Four suitcases were hauled into the headmaster's office. They contained gifts from members of April's church in Ohio for their sponsored children. Since I hadn't been around much in the past few months, I wasn't sure which children were sponsored or even how many, but April had been given a list. I wasn't even sure who had compiled the list.

April and I sat in a back room behind the main office as the headmaster called in children one by one, according to our list. The gifts in the suitcase had been arranged in the same order.

The first child's name was called. He entered the room, and after receiving his gift, he bowed to the headmaster, and then dropped to his knees in front of April and me in a gesture of gratitude. We looked at each other quizzically as we handed him the letter and a shiny rubber ball from his sponsor.

The next child to enter the room was a girl. She also bowed to the headmaster and then dropped to her knees on the ground in front of us. I started to get choked up. She looked sad when there was only a letter from her sponsor, no gift. I quickly reached into a nearby bag and pulled out a sparkly pencil for her.

"April," I whispered as the next child entered the room. "Was there no set monetary value for each of the sponsored kids?" I asked. "Aren't they all getting the same thing?"

April looked at me with teary eyes and shook her head. "I have no clue," she whispered back. "But this is painful."

The boy standing in front of us next was named David. We were supposed to measure his feet for shoes because his sponsor had sent enough money to buy him a new pair. After tracing around David's foot with a pencil on a piece of paper, the headmaster looked up. "Oh, sorry," he remarked. "Wrong David." And he sent the boy away.

That was almost more than I could take. "This seems so unfair!" I exclaimed. "There are only about 50 sponsored kids out of the whole bunch. What about the other 150? They won't be getting anything today."

"It's okay," the headmaster assured me. "They know that this is not their day for a big blessing. Maybe their day will come soon." April and I exchanged a look with each other.

The next child to enter was a small boy. He received a backpack filled with paper, markers, a ball, and a jump rope. There was also a small stuffed bunny in the side pouch. He bowed to the headmaster and dropped to his knees in front of us.

We finished distributing the gifts and went outside in the late afternoon sunshine. A few children straggled around the building and watched us get ready to leave for the day.

"April, do you see that?" I asked.

"See what?"

"In their eyes."

"You mean that sadness in the ones who didn't get anything? The ones who weren't fortunate enough to have been 'chosen' by a sponsor? Yeah, it's about killing me," remarked April sadly.

"There's definitely sadness," I agreed. "But there's something else I've never seen in the eyes of these children before today."

"Oh, yeah? What's that?"

"Jealousy and greed."

CHAPTER TWENTY-TWO

I asked April to come to the house and spend the night with me. Sal was out of town, anyway, and she and I needed to process the happenings of the day together. Something needed to change about the way children were being sponsored and fast.

Paul stopped off at the guest house so April could get a few things and then took us to the house. Daniel was faithfully waiting to open the gate, and he had already turned on the porch light. I thanked him as he carried April's small bag into the house.

After a light dinner of some vegetables from my garden, we got ready for bed and then propped ourselves up on the couch to talk awhile. But I was so exhausted from the big day and April's eyes were heavy with jet lag, so the conversation didn't last long. I set up April in the guest room and made my way to bed.

I woke up in the middle of the night feeling hot. In fact, I was drenched in sweat. I had to think for a minute—no, it wasn't a really hot time of year. Then I started to feel sick to my stomach. Don't tell me morning sickness was making a comeback.

I called out to April, but she was in such a deep sleep that she didn't hear me. I sat up on the edge of the bed and slipped on some flip-flops. As I made my way to the bathroom, my head started to throb with such intensity that I thought it might explode. I must have eaten something that I shouldn't have. Maybe I had rinsed off the vegetables with the wrong water. Had I remembered to use the bottled water to cook them? I made my way back to the bedroom and fell into a fitful sleep for the rest of the night.

I awoke the next day and shuffled into the kitchen, where April took one look at me and declared, "You look terrible."

"Gee, thanks," I said weakly. I didn't feel hot now. In fact, I was rather chilly and grabbed a blanket to pull around my shoulders.

"Olivia, what is the matter?" April asked. "Are you getting sick?"

"I don't know," I mumbled. "It must be something I ate."

I declined going to Okusuubira that day but assured April a nap would do wonders for me. And it did. Paul brought her out to the house later that evening and I was much better.

But I woke up in the night with horrible back pain and a high fever. I called for April and she rushed into my room.

"Something is very wrong," I mumbled as she pulled back the mosquito netting to take a look at me. "I thought I was better, but it's all come back."

April checked my pulse and then asked for my phone. I pointed to the bedside table. I could hear her punch in a number and eventually figured out that she had called Sal.

She hung up after a minute and sat back down by me. I was so weak, I could barely hear her voice. "Sal is on his way home," she told me. "He can be here in two hours." Then squeezing my hand, she said, "When I told him what was going on, your man actually swore! Olivia, I didn't think he had it in him!"

Sal's car pulled up exactly two hours later, or so April told me later. By then I was so weak, I couldn't even get out of bed. I kept holding my head. Oh, it hurt so much. My stomach felt like it was cramping and I feared for the baby. And I was so hot. April had been sponging me off with a wet washcloth. She tried to get me to drink some water but I just couldn't do it.

I remember Sal running right in to the bedroom the minute he arrived home and checking me over like a good doctor, but I think he was sort of crying as he did it. He and April kept whispering back and forth, and I heard them mention something about the baby.

I kept hearing "malaria" in the conversation. Was Sal talking to April or was he on the phone? Words like mefloquine, doxycycline, atovaquone, and quinine rang in my ears like a strange melodic poem. Sal asked me if I knew exactly how far along the pregnancy was. I remember telling him 9 or maybe 10 weeks and then he swore. April was right—I didn't think he had it in him, either.

More loud voices and then the next thing I knew, April was taking blood from my arm. She and Sal were arguing about a hospital. I just remember their voices becoming loud and then soft. There was anger and then strangely, laughter. Oh, but my head still hurt. And my legs ached so much.

The next thing I remember was waking up in the bedroom with an IV in my arm. I don't know how long I had been lying there. Sal was slumped in the chair next to me, asleep. He must have heard me stir because he suddenly sat upright and turned to face me.

"Oh, my dear, dear, Olivia," he said, gently kissing my hand. "How are you feeling?"

I tried to form words but no sound would come out. He told me to just be quiet and rest. I must have looked confused because he went on to explain, "Malaria, darling. You have malaria."

"The baby?" I was able to gasp. "What…about…the baby?"

Sal shook his head. "I don't know. There aren't many medications safe for the baby during the first trimester. But we have to get you well so I chose the one with the least risk. We can only hope and pray our little one is okay."

April popped her head into the room when she heard us talking. "Hey, beautiful! Welcome to the land of the living! It's been a few days."

I gave her a wan smile. I wasn't feeling a whole lot better. "You can thank me later for keeping you out of an African hospital," she said. She knew as well as I did that the possibility of picking up something far worse was a real danger of being in a hospital here.

"I had forgotten April was a nurse skilled with poking in needles," commented Sal. "When I wanted to take you in for an IV for dehydration, she insisted we could keep you home. What a miracle that she was here! I've been able to put medication from the hospital in your bag as well."

Sal went on to explain how he had consulted with Dr. Rollofson and a few others as to the best medication for malaria in a pregnant woman. It was complicated because I was still in the first trimester.

"Just tell me the risks to the baby," I insisted in a weak voice. Sal and April exchange a look with each other.

"You rest now, dear," Sal said to me softly. April began to tiptoe backwards out of the room.

"Tell me!" I croaked.

Sal couldn't keep the truth from me. He explained that malaria is often passed from mother to unborn child. There is risk of miscarriage, low birthweight, premature birth, abnormalities, and possibly stillbirth.

"April and I have been praying over you and the baby, my dear," Sal choked out. "We can't worry. We just need to concentrate on getting you better."

There was a knock at the door and April went to get it. Within a few moments, Dr. Rollofson appeared in the doorway. He nodded at Sal, then sat down on the bed next to me and patted my arm. He took a strange looking stethoscope out of his bag and put it on my abdomen. It had a small box attached to the cord. I looked from him to Sal and wondered what this instrument would do. Sal had mentioned the possibility of liver damage from malaria.

Both men grew quiet as Dr. Rollofson moved the device back and forth. Suddenly, he stopped it and a muffled sound like horses galloping through water could be heard. Sal shouted and jumped up from his chair.

"That's our baby's heartbeat, Olivia!"

I was stunned. The heartbeat? The baby was okay?

Sal grabbed me in an embrace, then stepped back quickly when I cried out in pain from being squeezed. Oh, did my muscles ache. Dr. Rollofson explained how he had been given a fetal doppler stethoscope a few months earlier. It had been a source of joy and wonder to pregnant women in the communities he visited. It definitely brought joy to our household as well.

"We usually can't find a heartbeat until at least 12 weeks along," Dr. Rollofson commented. "You've got a strong fighter here!"

"Strong like her mother," Sal stated confidently.

"Her?" I mumbled.

"Or his!" laughed Sal.

Happiness filled the air for the moment. I knew the baby's health was not yet in the clear, and neither was mine. But for now, we had hope.

I gradually began to feel better over the course of the next two weeks. It was a long, slow journey through recovery, and I couldn't imagine how difficult it must be to be a pregnant mother with malaria out in the villages. Or to be anyone with malaria for that matter, with no access to medical attention. I was never more grateful to have a bed, indoor plumbing, and a husband who was a doctor.

April only had a few weeks left of her visit to Uganda. She had been such a good friend to help Sal care for me on and off over the previous weeks, but she really needed to spend more time with her team at Okusuubira before they left. I was feeling well enough by then to remember to ask her about the sponsored children and if anything had been done to alleviate the unfairness of the gift fiasco.

"We're only going to allow gifts from now on if all children at the school receive the same thing," April explained. "We had a big meeting that lasted into the night. It was so crazy—we had students begging people on our team to be their special friend and sponsor. It's like a panic was going on because no one wanted to be left out. Even some of the teachers were pulling us aside and wondering if we could sponsor them!"

"How's the progress coming with electricity?" I asked. April's church had raised funds to bring electricity to Oku-suubira. Work had started but it was progressing slowly.

"I don't think we'll see the lights go on before we leave," April replied. "As you know, this is Africa!" She laughed. "Let's just hope there's electricity out there before we come back next year!"

One day soon after that, I decided that I needed to get out of the house. The shaking chills had subsided a week earlier, and my appetite had been back for a few days. I begged Sal to assist me in getting outside. He helped me out the front door and as I walked down the steps, I noticed my garden in full bloom.

"Oh, Daniel!" I exclaimed. "You must have been taking care of the flowers and vegetables while I was recovering! They look wonderful! Thank you!" Daniel beamed from where he was standing.

"I had some help from my cousin, Isaac," Daniel said. "He's good at making things grow."

Sal looked up from where he was standing. "Where's Isaac now?" he asked.

"He went back to his homestead for a few days," Daniel replied cautiously. Sal nodded.

After sitting outside for about ten minutes, I was ready to go back in. It wasn't very long, but the fresh air felt so good. I took a few deep breaths and then asked Sal to help me back inside. He really only needed to stand near my side because I was doing quite well on my own, and that feisty, independent streak wanted me to do everything for myself that I could, especially after being waited on for so long.

After we got inside, Sal helped me to a chair at the kitchen table and said he'd get some food together. He brought me a bowl of vegetable soup and a few crackers. He got a bowl for himself, the sat down with a thud. He had a puzzled look on his face.

"What is it?" I asked.

I couldn't imagine what would have him stressed right now. I was feeling better, and Dr. Rollofson had brought out the special stethoscope again a week earlier before leaving town. The baby's heartbeat was stronger than ever. Dr. Rollofson insisted it was a boy based on the number of beats per minutes, but Sal thought it was a girl. Well, either way, I'd be happy with a healthy baby. It would be a surprise, anyway, since I wouldn't be getting an ultrasound unless something went really wrong.

Sal let out a long, slow breath and then asked what I knew about Daniel's cousin, Isaac.

"I don't know the boy," I insisted. "Why do you ask?"

"I found him snooping around in the kitchen last week when you were asleep in the bedroom. He must have thought I was in there with you because the door was closed. I came out of the bathroom and he was going through the pantry."

"What do you think he wanted?" I asked.

"I'm not sure," Sal answered. "But Daniel knows better than to come inside without being invited. We need to keep an eye on this Isaac. I might forbid him from coming around."

"Oh, Sal," I sighed. "He was probably hungry and wanted a snack. Can you blame the boy for being hungry?"

Sal looked at me intently. "Just be careful."

Our serious conversation was interrupted by the sound of my mobile phone ringing. I'd know that ringtone any-where—Jesse! I looked for my purse and then remembered I had hung it on a peg in the pantry before getting malaria a few weeks earlier. Hmmmm. My purse was in the pantry.

"Jesse!" I cried in delight.

We caught up on the past few weeks of life. He had heard about my malaria from Stanley, who had found out from Sal, and expressed his concern. "Bad news travels around the world quickly," I said sarcastically.

After chatting a few minutes about how his classes were going, I asked, "How's Adam?"

"Oh, he's not here anymore."

"Oh, Jesse, I'm so sorry."

"What?" he asked. "Oh, no, not like that. Adam is fine. He was feeling good and his symptoms are totally under control, so his parents actually let him come home for a visit. As long as he eats healthy and keeps up with meds, he could continue as he is, virtually symptom-free for easily another ten to twenty years."

What a stark contrast to Robinah's relatively brief battle with the same horrifying disease.

CHAPTER TWENTY-THREE

My pregnancy continued without complications, and I seemed to have made a full recovery from malaria. Sal kept a close watch on me in case symptoms returned. He said some malaria parasite strains were getting resistant to the medication and a relapse could occur. But so far, so good.

The baby was beginning to kick strong enough for me to feel it now. And Sal finally felt his first kick.

"I can't believe you are so excited!" I declared. "You've probably felt hundreds of babies kick."

"Oh, but this one is special!" His eyes danced. "This one is mine!" Then he played a little game where he'd poke on my belly twice and then the baby would kick twice. He poked three times and sure enough, the baby kicked back three times.

"Looks like we're going to have our hands full!" he laughed. It was so good to finally have things going well in our lives. I was well, the baby seemed to be well, and Sal's trips away weren't as frequent. I wasn't sure if that's just the way it happened to be or if he was trying to stick around home more often. Either way, I was grateful for his presence.

The week following April's team's departure, Sal announced to me that he had to go upcountry.

"It's only for a few days," he explained. "You'll be fine. You can call me in a pinch, although mobile service won't be very good out there. But Daniel can help you get ahold of someone should you need help."

I assured Sal I'd be fine. I didn't go out to Okusuubira as often anymore because Sal didn't want me to be around kids who could potentially expose me to illness. With my immune system finally getting stronger, I reluctantly agreed to stay closer to home.

To keep myself busy, I had befriended Justine, a young neighborhood woman. She came to the house a couple of mornings per week to use the sewing machine Sal had recently purchased for me. I was glad Justine could use it and make things to sell to help support her family. I was also grateful for some company, as it offered me a good chance to keep up with speaking in Luganda. Sal's English was so good that we rarely spoke anything but that.

Sal left on a Wednesday afternoon in mid-April. The following day, Justine was supposed to come over and sew. She had a six-month-old daughter who accompanied her, and it was fun for me to entertain the baby while her mama sewed men's shirts for a clothing booth downtown.

I heard Daniel open the gate and went to the front door to greet Justine. She had baby Leah securely strapped to her back with a cloth as I had seen many Ugandan mothers do with their babies. It was very convenient and kept the mother's hands free. I'd have to get lessons how to tie on my baby like that. These women were real pros with breastfeeding, too. There would be no trouble finding help should a need arise.

I rocked baby Leah in a chair on the front porch while we listened to the hum of the sewing machine just inside the door. Leah started to fall asleep and nuzzled her nose into my neck. I was glad that I had remembered to put a thick cloth pad underneath her. She didn't usually come with a diaper on, and I had gotten wet on more than one occasion. I kept a stash of cloth diapers on hand for her to use but had forgotten to put one on her before we sat down that day.

I started to fall asleep, too, but was awakened when Justine came to the door to tell me my mobile phone had been ringing. I sighed and rocked for a few more minutes. Not many people called me, and whoever it was would surely call back if it was important. I had a snuggly baby on my lap.

The phone rang again about a minute later and Justine brought it to me before it stopped ringing.

"You better answer it. It's Doctor Sal," she said, handing me the phone.

"Hello," I answered. "This better be important, darling—I am having a delicious moment with a precious little love!"

Sal wasted no time with what he wanted to say to me. He had just received a call from Robinah's brother, Richard, the young man who worked at the pool hall a few blocks away. Richard had gotten wind of some news while overhearing a conversation between a few customers and thought Sal would want to know. Apparently, Daniel's cousin, Isaac, really had been snooping around in my purse when I was down with malaria. He had found information about my bank account. Although unable to access the account directly, he had somehow managed to find out that I had accounts both here and in America. He was convinced I had access to a lot of money, and he was correct.

I was speechless as I listened to Sal unfold a plot to kidnap me and hold me for ransom. I could hear the hum of Justine on the sewing machine once again, and Leah was still asleep on my shoulder. I hoped my now-shaking hands wouldn't wake the baby.

"Don't act obvious," instructed Sal. "I don't think Daniel would willingly be in on it, too, but one never knows."

I glanced over and spied Daniel weeding in the garden.

"Has Isaac been around lately?" Sal asked. I didn't think so. "Richard said it sounded like the plan was to take you away before I get home tomorrow night."

"Are you sure Richard isn't in on something?" I whispered. "He could be wanting reward money for alerting you to danger." Suddenly, I didn't trust anyone.

Sal didn't think Richard was a problem, but he left me with careful instructions so as not to make it appear that I was behaving differently than the norm. He told me to pack some clothes and make sure to tell Justine that we were going to spend a few days with Sal's family after he got home the next day. He said to tell her that as she was leaving so that Daniel would be within earshot. Poor kid. We had trusted him, but he was probably being threatened by his older cousin and forced to divulge information on us.

"I'll come home tonight when no one expects me," Sal explained. "Be ready when you hear me pull in. We'll load up quickly and then spend a few days out of town. We'll see if the police can dig anything up while we're away."

"Are you sure this could really happen?" I asked quietly. This sounded like the plot of a bad movie. Just when things were finally settling down.

"I'm sorry, dear," Sal said sadly. "But I need to keep you and the baby safe. Now say something loud for Daniel to hear about me coming back tomorrow. I love you and I'll see you in a few hours." And he hung up.

"Well, little Leah, it looks like I need to lay you down inside so I can start to pack my bag," I said to the sleeping baby, hoping it was loud enough for Daniel to overhear. His head tilted in my direction. "We're going to visit my in-laws tomorrow after Sal gets home in the afternoon."

I stayed as calm as I could so as not to alarm Justine. I didn't want her to know any details in case someone threatened her after we were gone.

Sal got home just before sunset. Daniel was there to open the gate for him, but it was obvious he had been startled by the car's arrival.

Sal rushed into the house and found me sitting at the kitchen table. "Are you ready?" he asked with wide eyes.

"Yes, I've packed a couple of dresses and a few snacks. How long do you think it will be before this blows over?" I couldn't hide the fear in my voice. "Two days? A week?"

Sal ignored my question. "Do you have your passport?"

Was he serious? "Passport? Do you really think that's necessary? Are you overreacting?" I couldn't believe this was happening.

Sal looked up from the table and saw small lights coming across the field toward our house. It might be nothing, perhaps just kids who had the good fortune of finding a flashlight. But he wasn't taking any chances with his wife and unborn child. "Get the passport now," he instructed.

I squatted down in front of the wardrobe in our bedroom and retrieved my passport. It was in the safe box that was sitting on the bottom shelf behind a box of shoes. I didn't see Sal's passport in the box, but he often carried it with him due to his frequent travel. Quietly, I closed the wardrobe door and looked around the room, wondering if it might be for the last time. I took Sal's hand as he picked up my bag and we walked out to the car.

Sal turned the car around in the yard in preparation to pull forward out the gate. Daniel walked over to open the gate, then stopped and ran behind the car. What was he doing?

Momentarily, there was a knock at my window. Daniel was standing there with a few flowers in his hand that he had just picked from the garden.

"Ebimuli," he said softly, holding up a fresh bouquet. "Flowers for your journey."

"Weebale nnyo, Daniel," I replied, taking the flowers from him. "Thank you. They are beautiful."

"Will you be returning soon?" he asked.

Sal was growing impatient and before I could think of how to carefully respond, he said gruffly, "Open the gate, Daniel."

I wondered if Daniel was interested in our sudden change of plans out of sheer curiosity, or if he was fishing for details as an accomplice to the bigger scheme. I didn't know whether to feel sorry for him or to be angry with him. But it didn't matter. Sal pulled out as soon as the gate was wide enough for the car to clear it and sped down the road.

CHAPTER TWENTY-FOUR

We drove without speaking for thirty minutes before Sal pulled the car into a parking area along the side of the road. He stopped the car. And then he began to weep silently, his body racking with violent sobs as he rested his head on the steering wheel.

"Oh, my dear, sweet Olivia," he moaned. "What would I ever do if something happened to you?" He was visibly agitated. I had never seen so much emotion coming from Sal, and it frightened me.

"Oh, Sal, " I began, a lump forming in my throat. "I'm right here. You spoiled their evil plans and rescued me off to safety."

He looked at me with dark eyes. This was no time for humor, even if it was true. He really had rescued me in more ways than just this one. Sal had helped me recover from the losses that weighed so heavily on me when I first arrived in Uganda. He opened my eyes to be able to see the beauty and wonder of this magnificent country. He showed me how to find joy amidst the pain that so often accompanied life here.

Sal finally composed himself, but by then I was crying.

He took a handkerchief out of his pocket and carefully wiped away my tears with his strong yet gentle hands.

"Olivia, you outshine anything that has ever happened to me in my life. You have brought me more happiness than I ever dreamed possible. I will do anything to protect your life, to keep you safe. Anything." Then he added softly, "And our baby, too."

We sat for a few minutes just holding hands and staring out the front window. I wanted to get out and stretch my legs for a few minutes, but I was paranoid of being followed even though we both knew that hadn't happened.

"What can we do, Sal?" I asked weakly. I had visions of him returning to the house with a weapon and hunting down the boys who had plotted to kidnap me. I shuddered at the possibility. It seemed very out of character for Sal, but then again, he did say he'd do anything.

"We have to get you out of here. You need to go away for awhile until things are sorted out," he replied. I didn't know how long that would be, but it sounded like a much better plan than where my mind had been going.

"Where can I go?" I asked. "Who would take in a pregnant woman indefinitely?"

We turned to each other without having to think for very long and said at the same time, "Jesse!"

Sal started up the car and we drove to a restaurant located inside a hotel on the outskirts of Kampala. We decided to stay there for the night and make sure things made sense in our minds. And also we needed to get ahold of Jesse to see if this plan might even work. Sal didn't put anything past Isaac and his buddies, and he forbade me from using my mobile phone anymore.

"Do you think they are sophisticated enough to track my whereabouts?" I asked somewhat incredulously. "And what about your phone?"

"My phone never leaves me," Sal replied. "I don't know if they could track your location or not, but I don't want to risk anyone finding out about your travel plans. It will be easier to catch them if we leave them guessing as to where you are. As far as they know, you're staying local, or at least within Uganda, with the baby due in a couple of months."

"Not for three months," I moaned. "How long do I need to stay away? A few weeks?"

"We'll see how it goes," replied Sal. "Now look up Jesse's number for me so I can plug him into my phone." And then with a small grin, he added, "Please." As serious as the situation was, Sal and I both loved adventure. This definitely qualified.

Jesse answered on the second ring. He recognized it as a Ugandan number and worried that it was news about a relapse of malaria. I was sitting next to Sal and could hear Jesse talking. He was actually speechless for a full ten seconds after Sal explained what was happening and asked if he'd welcome me into his home.

"Well, my friend? What do you say?" asked Sal, suddenly worried that this idea might not be sounding as good to Jesse as it was to us.

"Oh, sorry," Jesse replied. "I was already rearranging furniture in my mind, planning where to put Olivia and how I can fit a crib into this apartment."

I grabbed the phone from Sal, "Jesse!" I shouted. "So is that a yes or no?"

"Yes, of course!" he laughed. "You are welcome here anytime! My home is your home."

"I don't know about the crib and all that," I said. "Hopefully, it's only for a couple of weeks."

"Okay, well I'll be prepared for anything. When are you coming?"

"I don't know." I looked at Sal and he was mouthing the words to me, "as soon as possible." "Umm, I guess as soon as possible?"

"Do I need to meet you at Heathrow dressed as an undercover agent and whisk you off to safety?" Jesse asked. "Because I could do that, you know!"

"I'm sure you could, Jesse!" I replied with a chuckle. "But there's no need. Really." I told him I'd be getting a new phone and that he'd have to stay in contact with Sal as to my whereabouts until I landed at the Minneapolis International terminal sometime in the near future.

Sal was able to make travel arrangements for me using the hotel's business center computer. It was an old computer that had seen a better day, but at least it worked and the electricity stayed on. I was scheduled to depart from Entebbe at 1:10 the following afternoon.

"When is my return flight?" I queried. Sal looked at me with a face set like stone.

"Oh, Sal, you got me a one-way ticket?" I complained. I was concerned that there was no foreseeable end to this scenario.

"Olivia, dear, it's for the best right now. We can fly you home at a moment's notice," Sal explained. "When it's safe."

"Yes, but if I'm there for more than a few weeks, it will be too close to my due date for such a long flight."

"When thrown into the sea, the stone said, 'After all, this is also a home.' "

"What in the world does that mean?" I asked.

169

Sal laughed. "I'm not sure. It's an old Ugandan proverb that I used to hear in my village as a boy. I guess it means that you can make a home wherever you are."

"I guess that's sort of like 'bloom where you are planted,'" I replied. "But Sal, when will we be together again?"

"If it takes too long to sort things out here and the time for the baby has arrived, I will come to where you are," promised Sal. He took my face in his hands and lifted it up. "You have my word."

The drive to Entebbe the next morning was somber. I was usually excited for big trips, but the circumstances surrounding this one were so bizarre. And I had such little luggage along that I didn't need to check any bags. Just my purse and a small tote bag.

After a very sad goodbye, I proceeded through security and then walked outdoors and onto the tarmac. As I lifted up my carry-on bag and prepared to ascend the steps of the plane, thoughts raced in my mind. How soon would I be coming back? Would I be returning with a baby in tow? Would I ever return to my beloved Uganda again? And what about Sal? Did I need to fear for his safety? We hadn't discussed that.

A man standing beside me must have seen the distressed look on my face. "Here, let me help you with that," he offered, taking the tote bag from my hand. "Looks like you're already carrying quite a load," he observed, looking down at my rapidly growing belly.

"Oh, thanks for the help," I replied. An American. He was holding a small white box in his other hand and looked a bit distressed himself.

"Have a hard goodbye?" he asked. This guy was in a chatty mood. He seemed nervous.

I nodded. "You?" I asked, trying to be polite but wanting to just find my seat. This line was moving very slowly.

"Yes, I just got married," he answered. "This is a piece of our wedding cake that I'm taking home to show my parents."

"Where's your wife?" I asked, scanning the area for someone who looked like she might belong with him.

"She's had some trouble obtaining her visa," the man replied sadly. "She's Ugandan. I have to go ahead to the States and work on things from that end."

"Oh, I'm sorry," I replied. He was apart from the love of his life indefinitely, too.

"Say, my name's Kenneth," he said. "Kenneth Frymont. I'd shake your hand, but mine are a little preoccupied."

"No problem, " I said. "I'm Olivia. Walugembe."

"So are you going to the States, too?" Kenneth asked a little too eagerly. I nodded. "'Cause I was thinking, since we're both traveling on our own and there's an overnight stay in London til the next flights out tomorrow, I sure don't want to spend the night on the floor at Heathrow. Want to split a room with me somewhere?"

I must have looked surprised because Kenneth's eyes suddenly got wide. "Oh, no, not like that!" he exclaimed, turning bright red. I had to laugh. Innocent blunder. I told him that might be a good idea and we'd have to see once we landed. The line started to move again and I stepped into the huge British Airways vessel.

I dozed on and off fitfully during the flight. I hadn't slept much the night before in the hotel with Sal, but it was hard to get comfortable sitting upright with a bigger belly than I was used to, and the seatbelt dug into my bladder. Kenneth found my seat and wandered past half a dozen times to say hello. He seemed like a nice enough guy. Perhaps it wouldn't be such a bad idea to share a room somewhere. Just to catch a few hours of sleep. That would be much safer than venturing off on my own in London.

We landed at Heathrow around 8:00 PM local time. I told Kenneth I'd share a hotel with him after all and he seemed relieved. As he waited at the carousel for his bags, I found an internet kiosk. At least that's what I called it. I put in a pound coin and had five minutes to get connected to the internet. It was difficult typing on the little keypad. The silver keys were shiny and slippery, probably from the sweat of a thousand other hands that had used it that day. I sent Sal a quick email, said the package had arrived in London in fair condition and was awaiting final shipment the next morning. Hopefully, he'd appreciate my humor.

Kenneth insisted he knew of a great place to stay that was just a few stops away on the Piccadilly line of the tube. He'd been there two years earlier and said it was located near a few good restaurants, too. I followed him to the tube, being careful to "mind the gap" as I stepped inside the subway car.

We passed by two stops and Kenneth looked a bit confused. The train came above ground at this point and we could see the outlines of buildings glowing amidst the misty light of street lamps. I could tell Kenneth was trying to recognize the area. Finally, he said we should get off at the next stop.

We walked for two blocks through a lightly falling rain. The skinny sidewalks were uneven, with some parts cobblestones and other parts cement block. Finally, we came upon some sort of bed and breakfast. I wasn't sure if this was the place Kenneth had in mind, or if he was lost and trying to cover. But I didn't care. I was exhausted.

The desk clerk looked bemused when Kenneth insisted on a room with two beds. We walked up an old staircase with threadbare green carpet to the second floor. As Kenneth opened the door to the room, a musty smell greeted us. This was definitely an old building. There were two double beds and two twin beds inside the massive room. A large floral patterned bedspread covered each of the beds and the curtains had a pattern that matched. I claimed the bed nearest the windows, pulled back the covers, flopped inside fully clothed, and was asleep within seconds.

Kenneth sheepishly woke me up at 5:00 AM. "Sorry, we forgot to talk about departure times last night. I need to get to Heathrow soon. When is your flight?"

I groaned and checked my boarding pass. My flight didn't leave for two hours after his, but I decided to go back to Heathrow with him then so I didn't have to travel alone later.

Kenneth and I said goodbye soon after entering the airport, and I laughed out loud wondering if he'd ever tell his new wife that he spent the night with a strange pregnant woman in a London hotel room.

My first leg out of Heathrow was a flight to Chicago. A direct flight to Minneapolis would have been nice, but at least I could get customs out of the way at O'Hare and head straight off the plane in the Twin Cities.

I hadn't been back to America since leaving for Uganda just a little over a year ago. So much had transpired in such a short span of time. I hadn't felt homesick one bit, but after the plane touched down in Minneapolis, I felt apprehensive. The clean facilities, the familiar food, the recognizable landmarks, the cordial flow of traffic on the highways… It would soon be all too apparent that I was no longer in a third world country. What if I didn't want to go back to Uganda after being here?

Jesse was waiting for me with a bouquet and balloons.

"I knew not to make a WELCOME HOME sign for you because you're such a Ugandan now!" he said happily as he scooped me into a big hug.

"Whoa, hello there, little fellow," he exclaimed after inadvertently bonking bellies with me. He reached out a hand to pat my abdomen. "Nice belly, Liv!"

We drove the short distance to Jesse's place and he chattered the whole way, asking questions about the children at Okusuubira and wondering what it felt like to have malaria. After he parked in the lot at his apartment, he turned to me with a serious look on his face.

"Was it really as dangerous as Doc said it was? Was someone really planning to kidnap you for ransom?"

I nodded, still in disbelief at the events of the past few days.

"Well, not to worry here, Liv," Jesse said confidently. "I'll keep you safe."

CHAPTER TWENTY-FIVE

Jesse's bachelor pad apartment was surprisingly neater than I expected. Since Adam had moved out, the spare room was available. It was small but comfortable. After a call to Sal to let him know I had arrived safely, I crashed out for the next twelve hours straight.

I woke up the next day to find a note on the kitchen table. Jesse was at class and would be gone most of the day, but he had left a spare key in case I wanted to go for a walk. I looked around the room and sighed. This was my new home for the next who-knew-how-long. I wanted to see if Sal had sent me an email, but Jesse had his laptop with him. I didn't think there were internet cafes around here anymore. Then I remembered—the library had computers. And I still had a library card.

I changed into my last clean outfit and made some toast with honey. Then I ventured out into the beautiful spring day on the half-mile walk to the nearby library branch. I spotted a robin in the yard and saw flowers peeking up along a nearby driveway. The air smelled so fresh.

My library card was still good, so I wandered in and found an open computer. I got a few funny stares and decided it was because I was wearing a Ugandan dress. Might need to go shopping soon.

I logged on and found only one email waiting for me. It was from Sal, dated just a few hours earlier. He explained that things were much more complicated than we had first suspected. The authorities wanted him to pretend that I was out of town for a few days and would be returning the following week. They were arranging for a woman to disguise herself like me as part of a sting operation to catch the guys. Easier said than done, trying to make a Ugandan woman look like a pregnant white American! Isaac and his cohorts were possibly part of a larger group that had kidnapped a Canadian couple for ransom a year earlier.

Sal shared how exhausting it was to keep up a charade with Daniel and hide what was going on. The police wanted Sal to act like nothing out of the ordinary had happened. But Daniel kept asking about me. Maybe he thought I had already been kidnapped and he hadn't been let in on it? The poor kid was tangled up in a mess that he didn't ask for. But it's all about choices.

Sal was confident Jesse would be treating me well and wondered if he might even fatten me up with some rich American food! He told me how much he missed me and asked how I was feeling. I could sense the sadness in his message. As I typed out a reply, I kept things upbeat and happy. I was anxious about Sal's safety, but didn't want to let on. He'd only say it wasn't good for the baby if I was upset.

I made my way back to the apartment after checking out a couple of novels at the library. I flopped down on the couch and promptly fell asleep.

I woke up to the sound of a key in the door and was startled for a second, trying to remember where I was. A young man in his early 20s entered the room. He had short dark hair trimmed very neatly and wore black glasses. After an awkward greeting, I realized this was Adam with a new haircut and glasses, and he recognized me as Olivia. We had been at a few planning meetings with the Guatemala group nearly two years earlier. He apologized for barging in on me and was quite surprised that I was in the States. Jesse really had kept my journey under wraps!

"I thought you had moved in with your parents," I said, a bit puzzled. "Have I invaded your room?"

Adam told me that he had indeed moved home, but that there hadn't been enough room to take his piano keyboard when he had left a week earlier. He was just here to pick it up.

I asked Adam if he wanted to sit down for a few minutes and talk. I was in the mood for some company and Jesse was at least three hours yet from returning. I wanted to hear Adam's thoughts about orphanages in Central America and compare them with orphanages in Africa. Jesse and I had never talked about it after that initial brief conversation, but I had done a lot of thinking since then.

What followed was an amazing discussion that lasted for nearly two hours. Adam was very passionate about the Guatemalan children and wanting to help them in the best way possible. He explained that the whole orphan system had become corrupt and international adoptions had been halted a few years earlier. Orphanages were filling up with children who still had family members with whom they could live.

Child trafficking became a concern when it was discovered that nearly 1 out of every 100 children were being adopted. Poor families were coerced into believing that a new life for their child with an adopted family in another country was better than staying with their poor family in

Guatemala. So they were in essence "selling" their children to orphanages.

"So what do you think about that, Adam?" I asked. I didn't want him to just spit out facts at me. I wanted to know his heart.

"It's hard," he began. "We want to help these children. A good education and enough food is so important. And adoption is a wonderful way to provide for those needs and more. But should we do it at the expense of forcing children to leave their families? Convincing parents that the best way is to give up their children?" He stopped for a minute, then went on. "My childhood neighbors were all set to adopt a beautiful baby boy about ten years ago. They flew to Guatemala and met him, took photos with him, and even picked out a name. They returned to the States to finish paperwork and were supposed to go back a few months later and bring him home. But in the meantime, an auntie was found. She decided she wanted to keep the baby, and the whole adoption was cancelled."

"That must have been devastating," I said sadly.

"It sure was. Had my neighbor known the baby might have relatives who would want to keep him, they never would have proceeded and allowed themselves to fall in love with this little boy. There are two sides to the story and both are sad." He was quiet for a moment, then went on. "Did you know that a couple of celebrities have adopted children whose parents are very much alive and well? They offered a bunch of money and convinced the families that it was in the children's best interest to be raised in America, the land of a million and one opportunities."

Adam shook his head sadly and teared up. I was getting choked up myself.

"Human trafficking, that's what it is. A couple of countries have shut down adoptions for this very reason. Poor families, desperate for another meal, have allowed themselves to be convinced that they need to give up their children in order for all of them to have a better life. We're ripping apart families and making up our own definitions of what makes the best family."

I thought about the kids at Okusuubira. At least a third of them had relatives living within the surrounding area. But the children received an education and good meals at the school. They had a safe place to stay and a bed to sleep on. Granted, we knew they weren't all orphans. But surely this was better than begging on the streets. And their situation seemed so much different than what Adam was describing.

"I bet you think it's different with the kids you were with in Uganda," said Adam. It's like he had been reading my mind! "Jesse told me they are not available to be adopted. But do you think anything is done to tug at heartstrings of well-meaning Americans to convince them to donate even more money, which may or may not directly help the kids at the school? Maybe a little emotional manipulation?"

I thought for a minute, then remembered Jesse's comments from when we had walked through the dormitories.

"They freely allow visitors to tour Okusuubira, including the children's personal spaces," I offered. "The first time I found out that those kids sleep two to a single mattress on bunk beds three levels high, my heart nearly broke. Are you saying it's a bad thing to have compassion? To care about someone and want to help? I'm not buying that argument, Adam. We're supposed to love. We're supposed to help. If we don't help, who will?" I was getting a little irritated with this discussion and it was obvious.

179

LISA J. JISA

"Hey, Olivia, it's okay," Adam said in a gentler tone. "Let's take a break for awhile and sit out on the patio."

That sounded like a good idea, although this topic was far from over. "As long as we continue later," I said.

"To be continued," said Adam with a chuckle. "You guys got anything good to drink around here?"

I poured us each a glass of lemonade as Adam pulled the sliding door and held it open for me to step through. There were two wicker chairs covered with green and orange paisley cushions on the patio.

"I do just want to say one more thing," Adam said after getting settled. "So we can end on a good note." He looked at me to see if I was okay with another comment. I smiled, so he proceeded.

"I never got to see it, but when we were in Guatemala, someone told me about a bed and breakfast place deep in the jungle for the truly adventurous. Apparently, it is attached to an orphanage and the kids do most of the work. They clean the rooms, they make the food, they help the visitors with their luggage. You get the picture. So the kids are directly involved with helping to do the work. It doesn't feel like a hand-out because it isn't. No manipulation, no coercion."

"Sounds interesting," I replied. "And the kids are getting valuable experience with managing a business."

"Exactly," replied Adam. "I'm not sure that exactly fits with what we were talking about, but at least it's a hopeful image." I nodded in agreement.

"So on to a new topic," I said. "Tell me about school. What are you studying? What's your major?"

"Oh boy, we haven't left the land of difficult topics," sighed Adam. I was about to ask what he meant by that when we heard the inside door to the apartment open. Jesse was home.

"Hey!" he exclaimed. "How's it going?" And then before either Adam or I could say a word, he went on. "I am starving. Let's order pizza! You want to eat with us, Adam?"

Pizza! Mmmm. I hadn't had a decent slice of pizza in well over a year. There was a place in Kampala that served pizza, but they often substituted items that were unrecognizable. Once I had ordered a slice of chicken mushroom pizza. The meat sort of resembled ham, but I didn't want to ask. And there had been no mushrooms.

We consumed two pizzas that night, pepperoni with extra cheese. One for the guys and one for me. I'd probably be up in the night with little junior protesting my dinner choice. Adam and I never did resume our conversation that night, but I hoped we would someday soon.

CHAPTER TWENTY-SIX

After two weeks in Minneapolis, Jesse and Adam were still the only ones who knew I was there. Not even Stanley knew yet. I'd have to let him know soon. I just hoped he wouldn't accidentally tell Michael. I really didn't want to run into him. Stanley had been good about not leaking any details of my wedding, so I was sure I could trust him. Come to think of it, he had never told me about Michael and Ellen's wedding. Maybe he was keeping secrets for both of us.

Since I didn't have a phone yet, I asked Jesse to call Stanley and fill him in on the details of my situation and ask if he wanted to come and visit me. I knew he'd understand the anxiety and stress of a possible kidnapping plot. But I wasn't sure how he'd feel about me staying with Jesse. We were the dearest of friends and even Sal had no problem with me being there, but I wondered about Stanley. He got uptight if things didn't "look" right. Perhaps that's part of the reason he was so upset when Adam got infected with HIV.

Stanley and I got together a few days later. We planned to meet at a nearby coffee shop. I walked over in the mid-morning sunshine and chose a table outside to wait for him.

Since I didn't have a phone, there was no way for me to contact Stanley. We had planned to meet at 10:00, and by 10:30, he still wasn't there. I decided to wait another ten minutes. Just as I was getting up to walk back to Jesse's apartment, Stanley arrived.

"Olivia!" he exclaimed as he caught sight of me and headed to my table. "You look lovely! So good to see you! I stood up and he gave my shoulder a squeeze, carefully avoiding my ever-growing belly.

"So sorry for the delay. Did you order anything yet?"

Stanley ordered a cup of coffee for himself and an orange juice for me. The baby got so hyper when I drank coffee anymore that I reluctantly had given it up.

We settled back into our chairs and Stanley told me the reason for his lateness. The woman I had fondly referred to as Aunt Margaret, Michael and Ellen's neighbor, was quite ill with pneumonia and had been admitted to the hospital the previous night. Stanley had gone with Michael to visit Margaret that morning. Her health was rapidly failing.

"Oh, no, that's so sad," I lamented. Aunt Margaret was such a dear, sweet woman. I often thought of her and missed her friendship. I tried to think up some way to get myself to the hospital to visit her. But I knew it was unwise for me to visit a pneumonia-filled room. And I thought my presence might only serve to confuse Margaret.

"You do know that Ellen is pregnant now, too?" Stanley asked. I nodded. I wanted to ask how she was doing. I really did care, but I just couldn't bring myself to ask.

"How's Christina?" I blurted out.

"She's doing quite well," Stanley informed me. She must have been getting close to six years old by now. Stanley told me she was enrolled in kindergarten at the local school and was having a good year. She loved her little sister, Ronnie, who was nearly one now. And she couldn't wait for her new sister to be born.

"Oh, another girl?" I asked. Stanley nodded.

"Yep, Michael sure is gonna have his hands full with all those little blonde girls!" Then he looked at me with wide eyes and gasped. "Oh, I'm really sorry, Olivia. That was so thoughtless of me. I'm so sorry."

I placed my hand over his on the table. Really, it was okay. I patted my belly and smiled. "I may not have a blondie, but I'm gonna have my hands full, too!" I wanted to say that my heart was already full, but that seemed corny and cliché.

Stanley left soon afterwards and promised to keep me filled in about Margaret.

I walked home to find Jesse was already back from classes. He told me Sal had just tried to call and handed me his phone so I could call him back. "When you're done talking, let's take you to get a few American outfits."

Sal answered right away. He was getting ready for bed and wanted to tell me about the progress on the kidnapping ring. They were so close. And then he got very quiet and said there was something else I needed to know.

"My sister, Teopista, has given Kirabo Olivia to an American couple."

"What?" I exclaimed. How could that be?

"They are a lovely couple who came to do work near our home village. Teopista became convinced that the baby would grow up with a better life if she could live in America. So many more opportunities. And so they agreed to take her home and love her as their own. They'll be leaving here in a few days."

Tears filled my eyes. "Was it because of money?" I asked, not really wanting to know. Sal didn't think so.

"I wonder, my dear…" he started. Then he grew quiet. "I wonder…" He cleared his throat. "Olivia, will you decide to stay there with our baby? Will you see that America does indeed offer more opportunities for our little one than Uganda ever could?" His voice was barely a whisper now. "Will you come back to me?"

By then I was crying. "Oh, darling, of course I will come back to you! As soon as this child is born and I can get clearance, I will come back!" Clearance. That reminded me that I really needed to find a doctor and soon.

"Do you happen to know of a city called Edina there in Minnesota?" Sal asked. "Is it far?" I told him I knew where Edina was. It was about a fifteen-minute drive from where Jesse lived.

"Oh my goodness, that's where the family lives!" Sal exclaimed. "Do you think you could go to see them? Maybe check in on little Kirabo?" I promised that I would after giving them some time to settle in. Goodness, they hadn't even left Uganda yet!

Before hanging up, Sal remembered one more thing he wanted to ask me. "Is the name of April's church in Ohio called Brookwild Baptist?" he asked. No, that wasn't it.

"Why do you ask? Did something happen there?" I realized I hadn't informed April yet of my visit to America.

"Oh no, nothing is wrong there," Sal explained. "It's just that I was out at Okusuubira yesterday and there was a big sign they were hanging up that said BROOKWILD BAPTIST, THANK YOU FOR THE ELECTRICITY."

"That's strange," I replied. I knew April's church had raised $25,000 specifically to bring electricity to the school.

I asked Sal to find out from the headmaster what that sign was all about.

After saying goodbye to Sal, Jesse insisted on taking me to the Mall of America for some new clothes. I had been there many times before, but it was a strange feeling to enter the building with Africa so fresh in my mind. Store after store was filled with clothing and shoes and jewelry and perfumes. It was odd how it used to be no big deal, but now it seemed so excessive. Then we walked through the amusement park in the middle of the mall and I observed children running and laughing as they waited in line for a ride. It was definitely a different life here. But was it really better?

"Stick it in a box, Liv," said Jesse as he looked at me. "You can't keep comparing life here vs. life there or you'll go nuts."

We purchased a few outfits that would get me through the summer and headed back toward the car. I had to step around a young child who was throwing a fit about which flavor ice cream he wanted. His mother looked frazzled. Did too many choices make one cry? I didn't think African children threw tantrums like that, but suddenly I couldn't be sure.

On the drive home, Jesse's phone lit up with a text. He handed it to me to read. It was from Stanley. Margaret had just passed away. That was sure fast. She was a few weeks from her 90th birthday.

"Will you want to go to the funeral?" Jesse asked me.

I shook my head. While I had loved the woman like she had been my own aunt, it would be too much to see Michael and Ellen. And Christina. I hadn't seen that sweet little girl since her father's funeral. I wondered, would they take her to Margaret's funeral?

Jesse felt he needed to attend the funeral a few days later, so he planned for Adam to come and keep me company.

"Now don't upset her like you did the last time," Jesse insisted. "Keep it light, Adam!"

Adam laughed and held up a movie in his hands. "Just a little fun viewing," he stated.

"What is it?" Jesse asked, grabbing the DVD out of Adam's hand. "*Slumdog Millionaire*? You've got to be kidding. No way, man."

"It's okay," I said. "I've already seen it. If you're wanting me to see the part where they burn the boy's eyes to conjure up more sympathy for bigger donations, I already know about it."

Adam looked dejected as though he had wanted to surprise me with that scene somehow.

"We can still talk about it," I said. "We do need to finish our conversation."

Jesse raised his eyebrows on his way out the door as if to ask if I'd be okay, and I smiled. I was actually looking forward to getting back into it with Adam.

As soon as the door clicked, I started right in.

"You never told me your major," I said. "You said it was a sad story. What in the world could be so sad about a degree?"

Adam flopped on the couch beside me. "It's only sad because I see the inevitable. I was majoring in elementary education. I really love kids!"

"I can see that you do!" I exclaimed. "So why the change of heart?"

"Who wants their kids to have a teacher with HIV?" he asked.

I had almost forgotten that Adam was infected with HIV.

187

He appeared to be so healthy on the outside. And I knew he could pretty much live symptom-free for years.

"I know I wouldn't have to say anything. But someday someone at the school would run into someone else who knew, and then the kids in my class would find out, and their parents would get in an uproar. Then the principal would call me down to the office and reprimand me for not disclosing something so huge. It would turn into a disaster that I'd rather avoid altogether."

"Adam, I'm surprised at you," I said. "You're such a fighter for the rights of orphans around the world, yet you seem to have given up on what you want to do for yourself based on what may or may not happen someday."

"Oh, it's okay," he replied. "I told you I had changed my major. It'll take me longer to finish school now, but I'm going for social work instead. My mom is happier, anyway, if I stay out of the public schools." He had an odd look on his face, sort of a forced resignation.

"What is it?" I asked. It seemed like he was hiding something.

"Oh, it's nothing. I was looking forward to having summers off from teaching for travel, but if I can get on with an international group as some sort of advocate for children, perhaps they'll want me traveling for them, anyway. At least I can still dream big!"

"What else?" I asked. "I know there's more." I stared at him intently.

After a few minutes, Adam told me a little more of his story. He shared how upset his parents had been when they first found out about his HIV diagnosis. People who had been their friends suddenly shunned them, believing that Adam was somehow bringing a punishment upon himself.

His parents turned against him for awhile and that's when he moved in with Jesse.

"They thought HIV was only contracted through drug use or promiscuous behavior or a tainted blood transfusion. They didn't believe that I picked it up from helping a sick boy I had been visiting in Guatemala. They said you can't get HIV from vomit. And that's true, but this boy had been coughing up blood. I had a blister on my finger. And it had popped, but I didn't know. I didn't know. I only wanted to help him and he had no one else to help him."

Adam broke down in a flood of tears. His words came out in choking sputters now. "I was holding him when he died. I cradled him on the dirt floor of his little hut and rocked him in my arms. No one else from his village would go near him. No one else from my group would come in, either. But I couldn't leave him to die alone."

Adam rested his face in his palms and his whole body shook with sobs. I scooted closer and put my arm around him and we sobbed together. We cried for that little Guatemalan boy, for Robinah, and for the countless others who would die rejected and abandoned. I shed a few tears for Aunt Margaret, too.

What did we consider a life well-lived? Was it simply a large number of days on earth? Was it having worthy accomplishments? And who decides what is considered worthy? A Ugandan friend once told me that the first thing she does every day is to thank God for waking her up with another day of life. Maybe that's the best attitude. To simply view every day of life as a precious gift and leave it at that.

CHAPTER TWENTY-SEVEN

The next month and a half dragged on. Jesse and Adam were both taking summer school classes, so I didn't have them around to entertain me very often. Stanley wasn't very happy about my friendship with Adam, but there was little he could do about it. Apparently, Stanley had forbidden Adam from going to visit that boy in Guatemala, but Adam had gone against Stanley's wishes and he went anyway. Stanley saw the whole thing as a big black mark against him somehow. He still came to visit me, but we kept things light and he always made sure Adam wasn't there before coming over.

Jesse was usually gone with his laptop, but the walk to the library was getting difficult. My belly was huge and I could barely see my feet. I was afraid of tripping on the uneven sidewalks. And the humidity was increasing.

I watched some tv for a few days, but most programs left me feeling discouraged. Especially the decorating shows. I used to love watching rooms transform before my eyes as an expert decorator worked magic, but now I saw it as a waste because I knew people who didn't even have beds. And the shows about home purchases almost made me physically ill. Granite countertops and a lovely fireplace with a big backyard may have mattered to me at one point in my life, but they sure didn't anymore. As long as I felt safe and had my loved ones with me, that was enough.

Sal and I talked on the phone a couple of times per week. The sting operation had gone wrong and Isaac had skipped town. Someone must have informed him. It was most likely Daniel, and Sal had finally let him go a week earlier. Sal assured me that those boys wouldn't come around our house ever again, but I begged him to let us move to a new neighborhood after the baby and I returned.

It was too complicated for Sal to get a visa last minute and come after all. As an American, I'd had no problem returning to my home country. I'd be having the baby without him. I tried not to let on how heartbroken I was about that because I knew he was just as devastated.

Sal had asked the headmaster at Okusuubira about the thank you sign and was told that absolutely it was April's church that had funded the electricity. But there were other groups from other churches who visited them, too. And nobody would want to see their name on a thank you sign for a new pit latrine or a roof on the kitchen. So they made everybody think theirs was the money that went for the "good" stuff like electricity, water, and new dormitories.

April was busy at work in a new position working the night shift, so it was hard to find a good time to call each other. But we tried to catch up at least once a week.

Mosquitoes were coming out in droves every evening. The first time I got bitten, I absolutely panicked until Jesse reminded me that we didn't have malaria in the US. And I wondered why not. I discovered that there had been malaria-carrying mosquitoes in the southern states in the 1940s, but the liberal spraying of DDT had eliminated them.

I found an OB doctor that I liked. She was very kind and understanding of my situation. Although I didn't have American insurance, I was able to pay cash for my visits and was given a discount. I was down to one visit per week. So far, all had looked good and so an ultrasound hadn't been necessary. That was an extra expense we didn't need. It would be a complete surprise on the day of delivery to find out if we were having a son or a daughter.

About the third week of July, I woke up in the night with a start. I couldn't figure out what was wrong until I realized that I was sleeping in a puddle. My water had broken.

I woke up Jesse and he panicked. He had been preparing for this day for the past two months, but it was as though he had suddenly lost all common sense. He hopped around looking for his clothes, shouting commands at me.

"Jesse! Settle down!" I said firmly. "I'm not even having contractions yet. We still have plenty of time."

"Yeah, but I heard once about a woman who gave birth in a taxi on the freeway. I love you, Liv, but I'm not delivering your baby in my car."

I laughed. "It's a twenty-minute ride to the hospital. What could possibly go wrong? We have time to call Sal and let him know the big day has arrived!"

We arrived at the hospital without any issues. There was hardly any traffic at 3:00 AM. Jesse pulled me up to the ER door and a nurse wheeled me in with a wheelchair. I could have walked if Jesse had parked in the lot, but he insisted on doing this in the way he had envisioned.

I was checked into a beautiful birthing suite and positioned in a bed. The room was larger than Jesse's living room. It was also larger than many of the homes I had been inside in Uganda.

Jesse plunked himself down in the chair next to me, rested his chin in his hands on the side of the bed, and gazed up at me with a look of expectation.

"Well, let's get this show on the road!" he exclaimed.

"Um, Jess, some women don't go into labor right away after their water breaks. This could be awhile. Do you want to go to class today and I'll call you when contractions start to get close?"

He shook his head. "I am not missing this day for anything. I told Sal I'd be here for you. I'm not leaving. You can count on me, Liv. I'd do anything for you." His voice cracked.

"Jesse, are you getting choked up?" I asked. His joking mood had turned to seriousness.

Suddenly the old Jesse bounced back. " Oh my gosh! You're going to have a baby in this very room today! I am freaking out!"

I insisted that he walk down to the cafeteria and get a cup of coffee or some food. I didn't know how I'd handle this bundle of energy today. Maybe Adam could come down later and distract him.

By the time Jesse got back to the room, I had already experienced two contractions. That was fast. Sal told me about all the different scenarios he had seen with pregnant women, so I at least thought I was well-prepared for anything.

Two hours later, I was beginning to feel some serious pain. Contractions were about ten minutes apart. A nurse came and asked if I wanted an epidural. I'd have to decide soon. If I waited too long, it would be too late to get one. I hadn't originally wanted one. I had seen women give birth in Africa without the aid of drugs, and I was certainly as tough as they were. But three contractions later, I asked Jesse to call the nurse in. I wanted the pain meds.

"But Liv, you told me you wanted to do this the natural way. You insisted that I hold you to that."

I turned to Jesse and grabbed his collar so fast, it even scared me. "You get that nurse in here now!"

Twenty minutes later, she finally wandered in. I was pretty upset by then.

"Sorry, sweetheart," she said. "Full moons and babies. Go figure. Happens like this nearly every month. This floor is packed solid with moms in labor today."

The epidural was a magnificent thing. I felt a twinge of guilt thinking of my African friends, but only for a brief moment. Jesse called Adam, but he couldn't miss his lab class that day. He said he'd be down later. His sister took three days to finally give birth to her first baby, so he didn't feel any sense of urgency.

Two hours later, my doctor came on call. She said I was dilated to 6 cm. I told her the doctor who had been in an hour earlier had told me 7cm. My doctor said that woman had smaller hands and her measurements couldn't be trusted. That about made Jesse livid and I had to send him to the cafeteria again.

He came running into the room five minutes later. "You'll never guess who's here!" he said breathlessly. "Michael! He didn't see me in the cafeteria, but I overheard him telling a doctor that his wife is in labor!"

It hadn't even occurred to me that Michael would be at this hospital. It wasn't the one he was at for his residency, but things change. Or maybe this was just where Ellen was going to have the baby. Oh well. It didn't matter.

About an hour later, my doctor came back and checked

again. I was close to 10 cm. It wouldn't be long now, she told me. I asked how I'd know to push since I was numb from the epidural and she said they'd back it off. Jesse panicked and asked if there was any other way. The doctor told him that blowing up balloons uses the same muscles as pushing, so I was welcome to blow up balloons. Of course Jesse loved that idea! The nurse brought in some balloons and Jesse blew up two right away.

"Save some of those for me," I teased.

Within thirty minutes, the doctor came back and told me it was time to push. I knew from Sal's stories that this could go quickly or it could take a few hours. Sometimes African women squatted and allowed gravity to assist them, but I couldn't do that with the epidural.

Jesse looked a little green at one point and asked if I really wanted him to stay in the room. Of course I did. But did he really want to be there?

"Umm, I want to be here for you, but do you mind if I turn around?" he asked. So Jesse turned his chair around and faced the wall at the head of my bed. He could still see my face and hold my hand, but he said that was all he wanted to see of me.

About two hours into pushing, it was finally time. The moment for my baby to arrive in this world had come. With one final push, the baby popped out. I waited for a cry and it came almost immediately. Strong, healthy lungs! "It's a boy!"

A nurse placed the baby on my chest. "Congratulations!" she said. "Your son."

Jesse turned his chair back around to look at my son. My precious baby boy.

"Obviously you're not the father," the nurse said as she looked from Jesse to the black baby resting on my chest and then back again. The doctor gave her a dirty look.

"Oh, no!" exclaimed Jesse. "I'm the…uncle! And this here is my little namesake! Welcome to the world, little Jess!"

"Uh, Jesse, we never said anything about naming the baby after you." I didn't know if he was kidding or serious. He looked serious.

"Well, then what will you name him?" Jesse asked. "Let me get your husband on the phone and we'll get his input!"

Jesse dialed up Sal's number and congratulated him with the happy news about the birth of his son. Sal wanted to talk to the doctor before he even talked to me, and I could tell he was asking all sorts of questions about the baby's health. We still didn't know if the baby might have contracted malaria from me, so the doctor was planning to run a blood test. Otherwise he seemed healthy and fine. Then Sal got on the phone with me and we cried tears of joy.

"I keep counting his fingers and toes," I told him. "I keep getting five fingers on each hand and five toes on each foot. But then I count them again to make sure. Oh Sal, he's absolutely perfect!"

Then we talked about a name. We had discussed a few names, but the ones we had in mind just didn't seem to fit this little guy. Sal mentioned another possible name to me that sounded perfect. Emmanuel. God with us. God had surely been with us and seen us through so many things. I looked at the baby.

"Emmanuel," I said. "That's it! It suits him well." I said Jesse would send some photos. I promised to call Sal again later and we hung up.

A nurse took little Emmanuel from me to clean him up a bit more and Jesse got a big grin on his face.

"You and Sal didn't choose a middle name yet. We could give him my name for a middle name! What about Emmanuel Jesse?"

"Umm. It doesn't really flow off the tongue," I said, trying not to hurt his feelings. Jesse had been such a great help and I'd love to give his name to my baby in some way. So I decided to ask what his middle name was. I asked a bit hesitantly, hoping it was something I could live with.

"James!" he replied. "Emmanuel James! I love it!"

"No way! Your name is not really Jesse James, is it?" I asked.

"Yes ma'am, it is!" he replied. "Long story for another time. So how about it, Liv? Emmanuel James Walugembe?"

"Walugembe Emmanuel James," I corrected with a smile. Last name first in Uganda. I didn't have the heart to tell him that James had also been my father's name and so it was a logical choice. I wanted Jesse to have his moment. He grinned from ear to ear.

And so on July 23, at 4:55 PM, weighing in at 6 lbs. 1 oz. and 18 inches long, Emmanuel James entered this world. Healthy. Loved. American.

CHAPTER TWENTY-EIGHT

About an hour after Emmanuel was born, Adam showed up at the hospital. He couldn't believe I'd already had the baby but was thrilled to finally meet him. Jesse went on and on about how the baby had his middle name. So Adam decided to top that.

"Fine, then I'll give the baby a nickname," he said.

I groaned. "Guys, please. I am exhausted and I don't care to hear you two get into a big argument. This is really stupid. You do know that, right?"

But Adam was relentless. He came over and stood by the bed. Emmanuel was wrapped up in a blanket in my arms.

"May I?" he asked, reaching for the baby. I handed him over. As silly as this competition was, I enjoyed the attention my child was getting from his "uncles."

Adam paced around the room with Emmanuel, mumbling things to himself. Finally he stood still and announced, "I've got it! Drumroll please! Ready? It's Manny!"

"Brilliant!" declared Jesse. "Manny it is! Manny the little man! Now let me hold him for awhile. I want to take him for a walk down the hallway, introduce him to more of the world."

I said it was okay. Adam handed the baby to Jesse as I declared my desperate need for a nap. Adam said he'd sit by me for awhile working on his laptop and wait around to make sure Jesse actually brought the baby back.

Jesse stepped out into the hallway with Manny and I heard a voice say, "Hey, Jesse! Surprised to see you here!" I'd know that voice anywhere. It was Michael.

"Uh, yeah, hey Michael," Jesse said, surprised. "What are you doing here?" They were just outside my door.

"What am I doing here? Look at the beautiful baby in my arms! I am holding the newest addition to our family! This is Margaret Rose. Isn't she the sweetest thing you've ever seen?"

I panicked for a moment, still woozy from the medication and unsure as to what was happening in the hallway. Michael must have looked at Manny because he said, "Oh wow, this can't be your sister's kid. Walugembe?" Oh dear. He must have seen my name on the door. Would he recognize it? I didn't think he knew my married name. "One of your international friends?"

"Sure is," mumbled Jesse. "Hey, let's pose for a photo with us and the babies together. They're like twins, born on the same day and all. Hang on a sec."

Jesse popped back into the room for his phone.

"What in the world are you doing?" I asked him.

Jesse grinned. "Just a little photo op. Because I can. And because I know you're curious. And I'll have you know, that baby will be nicknamed Maggie before we get to the end of the hallway. Just wait and see!" He gave Adam a thumbs up.

I was dismissed from the hospital the following evening. Jesse drove us home and we avoided running into anyone from Michael's family, although I saw his mother stepping off the elevator as we were getting on. But she never would have recognized me standing next to Jesse and holding a brown-skinned baby.

Manny's blood work came back as abnormal, but that wasn't completely unexpected. I figured it was probably because there could be something residual from my bout with malaria in his blood. I'd keep a close watch on him and get a re-test before heading back to Uganda. The only thing preventing us from returning to Uganda now was waiting on Manny's passport and my energy level. Shouldn't take more than a couple of weeks. Manny was born in America and therefore would be a dual American/Ugandan citizen. I was so anxious to get back to Sal and introduce him to his son. And as much as I loved being in America, I was missing Uganda.

Jesse was wonderful at sending photos to Sal. He sent so many, in fact, that Sal's computer froze up and he had to call and ask Jesse to stop sending photos for now. Jesse did not send Sal the one of him and Manny with Michael and Maggie. Yes, Jesse had succeeded in convincing Michael that his daughter needed a nickname before they got to the end of the hallway.

When Manny was two weeks old, I called the family that had adopted Kirabo Olivia and explained who I was. I asked if we could meet them and they invited us over.

Jesse had a big group project he was working on for school, so Adam volunteered to take me. I could have borrowed Jesse's car, but I had gotten so used to driving on the other side of the road in Uganda and then being chauffeured everywhere here. I was glad for Adam's help. And I liked spending time with him. He was a deep thinker like me in many ways.

We pulled up to a two-story white house with rust-colored shutters in a lovely neighborhood in Edina the following afternoon. There were enormous oak and maple trees in the yard and a basketball hoop in the driveway. Two kids chased each other down the sidewalk on their bikes. It looked like a wonderful place to grow up.

A cute brunette with short hair and long eyelashes opened the door and introduced herself as Jill. Her husband, Derek, came down the stairs as we were entering the front door. He was holding Kirabo Olivia. She had grown a lot since I had last seen her. When Derek set her down, she began to run around the room in that awkward way babies have when their legs are still getting used to standing.

"So the babies are cousins?" Jill asked. Why yes, they were. Jill and Derek agreed to taking some photos that I could take back and share with Teopista. They had promised to stay in touch with her through Sal.

"We're calling her Cora now, after Derek's grandma," explained Jill. I nodded in understanding.

I could see Adam looking around the house, eyeing everything. He took notice as Cora walked over to Derek's outstretched arms and was scooped into a big hug. Jill took us upstairs to see Cora's room and it was a little girl's fairytale. She had a beautiful pink and green patchwork quilt hanging over the edge of the crib, a shelf full of books, a bin filled with toys, and a large stuffed giraffe standing guard near the closet. A little white table with two chairs sat near the window, ready to host a tea party at a moment's notice.

On our way back home, Adam asked me what I was thinking.

"I don't even know what to think," I said. "Obviously, they love Cora dearly. They have the means to take very good care of her. It's a beautiful home and she'll lack for nothing. You already know that the worst school in this city is better than the best school she'd ever be able to attend in Uganda. She'll get great health care and great dental care. She can probably be on a soccer team or take ballet lessons. I know Teopista believes this was the best decision for her little girl to have a bright future. And I'm sure she'll have a wonderful life here. There will be opportunities galore. It's all just a little confusing." Adam nodded.

We drove in silence for a few minutes. Sometimes it's hard to see the world through someone else's eyes. This sweet family had brought a baby from Africa to America to give her a better life, and her mama had been the one to push for it. I just had a baby in America and was anxious to take him to Africa so our family could all be together. Were they doing the right thing? Was I?

"I think we'll just chalk today up to a nice outing with some lovely people and leave it at that for now," I decided. "My brain can't do anything else with it right now. And neither can my heart." Adam nodded again. I thought of the deep heartache I felt when Michael chose to break off our engagement so he could marry Ellen. There are two sides to every story.

The day soon came when Manny's passport arrived in the mail. The moment I had it in my hands, I made arrangements for us to fly back to Uganda.

"I'm really going to miss you and Manny the little man," said Jesse sadly. "It's been great having you here."

His phone rang right then and I was glad for the diversion. I was dreading the goodbyes and I didn't want to start crying already. We wouldn't be leaving for two days. But Adam wanted to come over and say goodbye already.

I shook my head and mouthed the words, "No, not now," to Jesse, but he told Adam sure, I was looking forward to seeing him.

When Adam arrived, I suggested we take a walk. I had to finish nursing Manny, so Adam and Jesse chatted in the kitchen for a few minutes before Jesse left for the grocery store.

Adam's oldest sister had lent me her stroller. Adam carried it down the stairs and I held Manny in my arms until we were on the sidewalk. Then I laid him down and started to push. There was a lovely park nearby and we headed in that direction.

"Adam, I've been thinking," I said.

"You do that a lot, " he said.

"Do what?"

"Think."

He was right, but I ignored that comment. "Adam, I know you love children. And you're sensitive to people with HIV and AIDS because you know their dilemma."

I could see the wheels spinning in Adam's mind as I continued. "What if you came to help people with AIDS in Uganda? Especially the really sick ones who have no one else to care for them. They'd feel loved and cared for right up until their dying day. Sort of like Mother Teresa's Home for the Dying and Destitute in Calcutta. Give people food and love. And if we could drum up donations to pay for the medication that slows down the disease's progress, all the better."

Adam's face lit up. "I'll think about it."

"Look who's doing the thinking now," I said, nudging him with my elbow. We could get Sal to help with medical things and perhaps I could help, too. I was even willing to use some of my father's money to buy land and get the building process started. No exploitation of children necessary to stir up emotions and open up pocketbooks. The reality of these stories would be sad enough.

We walked past the park and stopped on a bench to watch some kids playing. A few danced in a splash pad, happy and carefree. There were no parks like this in Uganda. My boy would grow up without any of this. Should I regret going back? Because I didn't. Not one bit. I was ready for Uganda if she'd have me back. And my baby.

After arriving at the airport two days later, Jesse and I became so choked up that we couldn't even make eye contact. Finally, we dissolved into tears as Manny and I were about to enter the security line. I had already said goodbye to Stanley the day before, so this was it. The final person to whom I had to say goodbye. For now. Although they were still hard, I didn't mind so much the goodbyes that were just "for now."

Jesse kept kissing Manny's toes while talking a mile a minute. "I'll come to Africa and see you, buddy; you can count on your ol' Uncle Jess to follow through! Just let me graduate first."

We hugged through tears, and I couldn't find enough words to thank him for all that he had done over the past few months.

The flight to Heathrow was uneventful. Manny was a good baby and slept most of the way. It was difficult keeping him calm during the 8-hour layover until the flight to Uganda from there, but at least I managed to stay awake. I wandered around and found the quiet room where Stanley and I had spent time. But it was too quiet in there and I felt my eyelids getting heavy, so we kept moving. Sleep could meet me on the plane. I was not going to miss this flight.

We touched down at Entebbe on an overcast day. As I stepped off the plane and walked across the tarmac, I remembered my first time experiencing this nearly two years earlier. The smell of warm, rich earth combined with a faint smokiness greeted my nostrils, and this time I had a name for that smell. Home.

Sal was waiting inside the terminal. After giving me a great big hug and a kiss, he took Manny from me and hugged him tight. I have never seen a father who was more proud to hold his child. We stood together in a big embrace for a long time, tears of joy streaming down our faces. My sweet little family was finally together.

I was relieved to find out that Sal had secured a car seat for Manny to use. The Kampala traffic frightened me more than ever with a little one in the car.

I thought Sal had missed the turn to our house. But maybe I had forgotten from being gone for a few months. Then he took another turn that I definitely didn't recognize.

"Where are you going?" I asked.

"You'll see. It's a surprise," he answered. A few minutes later, we turned on to yet another road. Sal stopped in front of a gate and honked the horn. The door slowly opened.

"A new house?" I gasped. "Did you move us to a new house?"

"I knew you had bad memories of the other one," Sal replied. "This one is in a neighborhood with quite a few expatriates. They've all pooled together and hired a security guard who patrols the street day and night. No harm can befall you here, my dear."

"Oh, Sal!" was all I could manage to say.

I had been dreading the fear that I was sure would come upon returning to the old house, especially with a new baby. But this place felt so safe. Sal had taken great pains to decorate the rooms as closely as he could to how I had them in the other house.

"There's a spot for you to have a garden again," Sal explained, waving his hand by the side of the house. He was so excited as he showed me around our new home.

It was perfect. I was back in the country I loved and with my husband whom I adored. We had a beautiful, healthy baby boy. Life was good at that very moment, and I chose to view it as a precious gift.

CHAPTER TWENTY-NINE

Manny adjusted well to life in Uganda. It was such a joy to watch his inquisitive, big brown eyes taking everything in, and his first smile came on a morning when Sal and I were both with him. There could not have been a more beautiful child.

I had to get used to cloth diapers. The day Sal had a washing machine installed at the house was one of the best days ever. I used disposable in America, and they would have been so convenient here...but cloth was a better choice now, and I was grateful for them. I knew many women who didn't even have that luxury for their babies.

Sal wasn't taking as many trips as he had in the past because he wanted to stay close to Manny and me. But I knew Sal thrived on helping people who weren't easily reached by a doctor. When Manny was about five months old, I suggested that he and I accompany Sal on a short trip. We hadn't ventured far from home at all since coming to Uganda, and I was up for a little adventure.

"Are you sure, Olivia dear?" he asked. "It would only be for a few days. They really need me for just a few days."

I laughed. Of course I was sure. It would be fun to see

Sal light up doing what he loved and what he was made to do. He brought such hope to people who felt hopeless. He had such a gentle way of explaining basic health care. And I especially loved listening to him speak in his heart language, then say something to me on the side in English, then slip right back into Luganda.

We took a three-day trip to a small village near Pallisa a few days later. The timing coincided with the week of Christmas. We were close enough to stay with his family at the homestead, which was good because we hadn't taken Manny to meet the family yet. Deep inside, I knew that Sal was worried about Manny's health in case there were complications from my bout with malaria during pregnancy. And it occurred to me that I had forgotten to get a follow-up blood test with Manny while in America. But he seemed to be healthy and he was definitely happy. We'd be fine away from the big city.

Sal's family was thrilled to meet the newest member of the Walugembes. Manny was greeted with kisses and laughter. He took it all in stride and was joyfully passed back and forth between family members. And Teopista was delighted to see photos of Kirabo Olivia thriving in her new home. Sal explained the name change to Cora, but I knew she'd still be fondly referred to as Kirabo Olivia around here.

The goiter in Teopista's neck was almost completely gone, and I marveled at the usefulness of the basic information Sal had given her about using iodized salt. He looked at an uncle's foot and checked his mother's blood pressure. The family loved having Sal around, and he humbly accepted their confidence in his medical expertise. He knew how privileged he was to have gotten a good education.

The next morning, one of Sal's distant cousins brought her toddler to the home for a check-up. I wondered if we'd make it to Sal's appointment at the nearby village on time. But this was Africa, and African time ruled. We'd get to our destination eventually. Sal loved to help his family, and he showed no stress about the interruption.

The toddler's name was Ebenezer, and that's what he was called. I laughed to myself, thinking of the nicknames that Jesse and Adam could come up with for this darling child.

Ebenezer was nearly two years old, but he was small for his age. His mother explained to Sal that he coughed a lot and had bouts of severe pain that would sometimes last for a few hours, but other times they would last for a few days. Sometimes his hands and feet would swell.

I appreciated Sal's willingness to translate their conversation to me throughout the check-up. I stood near his side and appeared to know what was going on, but the reality was that unless Sal told me, I was as clueless as the people coming to see him.

Sal's best guess was sickle cell anemia, a disease that mostly affects Africans. Healthy red blood cells are doughnut-shaped and flow easily through the bloodstream. But sickle cell disease causes red blood cells to be shaped like crescent moons. This causes them to get stuck in the tiny blood vessels of the body and can cause extreme pain. Sal suggested that his cousin take Ebenezer to a hospital in Kampala for a blood test to confirm. He didn't want to misdiagnose anything.

"Is it serious?" I asked Sal when we were in the car an hour later.

"It can be," he replied. "Based on Ebenezer's symptoms, I would highly suspect he has sickle cell disease. It does unfortunately run in our family."

I must have gotten an odd look on my face, because suddenly Sal asked me, "Manny's blood was tested at the hospital when he was born, right?"

"Yes..." I replied. "His results were abnormal, but I forgot to get him retested. I thought it was probably an odd reading because of the malaria. Oh Sal, I'm so sorry that I forgot."

Sal explained to me that the odds of Manny getting sickle cell were not high because I was not of African or South American descent and both parents needed to carry the gene. There were a few Mediterranean countries whose citizens also carried the trait. I quietly tried to review genealogy in my mind. My father died when I was ten and I didn't remember my mother at all. I couldn't remember if my father ever told me about my mother's ethnic background. I knew she was European, but our trip to visit locations from her heritage was cut short when my father died.

"I'll get myself tested when we get back to Kampala," I declared matter-of-factly. "I don't want Manny to have to go through any unnecessary pain."

"It's just a little prick," chuckled Sal. "But why would you do that, dear? Is there something you aren't telling me?"

I didn't really have anything specific. When Sal's cousin explained that Ebenezer's hands and feet sometimes swelled, that had concerned me. I thought Manny's feet appeared to be a little swollen a couple of times and that they had felt cold to the touch, but I never bothered to mention it to Sal. Whenever he came home in the evenings, Manny always seemed to be fine. I didn't want to cause unnecessary alarm, and besides, we were more concerned about malaria side effects. But suddenly I felt uneasy.

Sal brushed it off and said we'd enjoy the rest of Christmas week without any worries, and we did. After two days of routine check-ups and assisting with one baby delivery at a nearby village, we made our way back to Kampala.

Manny continued to be a good baby, eating and sleeping well, although Sal insisted on taking him for a blood test. To my horror and dismay, he did indeed test positive for sickle cell. I knew Sal was well educated on the disease, but I also knew he'd try to hide things from me so I wouldn't worry. Babies don't often display signs of the disease until at least four months of age, and other than a couple of times when Manny's hands and feet had seemed a bit swollen, he had shown no symptoms.

Sal took a few two-day trips, but was never gone for more than one night at a time. I felt very safe in our new home and had gotten to know a few of the other neighbors. A Canadian family across the street had three children, including a little girl a few months older than Manny. Perhaps they'd be playmates one day.

Justine had started coming over again a couple of times per week. It was a greater distance for her to travel to our new home and added another twenty minutes to the trip by boda-boda. But Justine was eager to sew and provide extra income for her family. I enjoyed the female company and knew that by offering the use of my sewing machine to her, it was a small way I could help contribute to the well-being of another family. I hoped to one day be able to provide even more machines for others, but right now I needed to make sure my baby would be healthy.

One afternoon when Justine was over and Manny was napping, I was able to get away to a nearby internet cafe. I wrote to April and begged her to research sickle cell disease and bring me all the information she could find when she arrived in Kampala the following week.

I had emails waiting from Jesse and Adam. Jesse was fine, enjoying the last few days of winter break and eager to finish up his last semester at school. He was missing Manny the little man. He added that, of course, he missed me, too. It had been such an odd and interesting bonding time we shared for a few months earlier that year. But it was a bond that ran deep.

Adam was also fine, and that amazed me. His medication was working. Every few days I learned of someone nearby in Africa who had either been diagnosed with HIV or had died due to complications from AIDS. There were still a lot of superstitions surrounding the disease. Education was so key. People needed to know how it spread and how to lessen the fear.

April's arrival a week later was a joyous reunion. Sal insisted on driving Manny and me out to the airport to surprise April in person. I knew she'd be exhausted from jet lag, but there's nothing like that welcoming hug from a familiar face at the airport after 24 hours of travel. April and Manny took to each other immediately. It was as though he could sense her love for children. He laid his head on her shoulder and melted into her arms. And she was in love.

April soon boarded the bus with the rest of her team, but we made plans to meet for breakfast at the guest house the following morning. Sal could drop Manny and me off while he did some things in town.

I was finding it a lot more difficult to be spontaneous with a baby. There was no way I felt safe enough to strap him to my back and get on a boda-boda, so I had to wait for Sal to give us rides. His busy schedule made that difficult, but he willingly helped out whenever he could. I was hopeful for a ride to Okusuubira sometime soon. It had been so many months since I had been there, and the teachers and children hadn't yet met Manny. I used to go out there nearly every day. How life changes.

It was drizzling the next morning when we arrived at the guest house, but April had found a table that was covered. Sal promised to be back in about two hours. Give or take a few hours.

As soon as I sat down, April whipped out a thin, green folder from her bag and set it on the table. Then she took a sleepy Manny from my arms and cooed gently to him.

"I looked up everything I could get my hands on," she explained. "Has he gotten fevers yet? Bouts with severe pain? What about jaundice?"

"Now how would I know if a dark-skinned baby has jaundice?" I asked.

"His eyes," April explained. "They'd start to look yellow."

Immediately I pried open a sleeping eye to look at it. The white part still looked white.

"What about his spleen?" April asked. "It helps filter the blood. Because its job is to pull out unhealthy cells, the sickle-shaped cells can get stuck there and cause severe pain." She gently rubbed the left side of Manny's belly just under the ribs. I had seen Sal do that to Manny a few times but never questioned him on it.

"Tell me long term, April. What's going to happen to him?" I begged for answers.

"Since the spleen is so involved with protecting and cleaning the blood, Manny could be more susceptible to infections if his spleen becomes damaged. Also since red blood cells carry oxygen throughout the body and some of his are misshapen and therefore not properly functioning, the lack of oxygen could potentially damage major organs."

By then tears were streaming down my face and I didn't want to believe any of what I was hearing. My baby looked so healthy on the outside.

"Sal is a good doctor," insisted April. "He'll know what to do when a need arises. Antibiotics are a necessity to have on hand since the spleen's compromised function will set Manny up for various infections. His body won't be able to fight off things that you and I easily could. And his lungs will have a harder time trying to get enough oxygen. They may even hurt sometimes."

Suddenly, I was grateful that I hadn't taken Manny to Okusuubira yet. The children and teachers would all want to hold him. They'd breathe on him. Who knows what sickness he could be exposed to out there?

April knew what I was thinking. "You can't hide him in a bubble, but you do need to be careful."

Just then Manny started to cough in his sleep. April gently rubbed his back and he relaxed.

"If the need for a blood transfusion arises, would you do it here?" she asked me.

I looked at the intensity in April's eyes and felt bewildered. "Blood transfusion?"

"Yes, it could become necessary if his body needs a boost of healthy cells," said April as she started to cry softly. "Oh, Liv, please tell me you'd take Manny back to the States for a transfusion. Or at least to England. Don't do it here."

I nodded my head slowly. April and I both knew that safety standards for blood collection were getting so much better in Uganda than they had been in the past, and it was very unlikely that Manny would receive tainted blood. But once again, I was aware how privileged I was to have access to perks that so many here could never imagine. If the day ever came when my baby needed blood, we'd be going elsewhere.

CHAPTER THIRTY

After my father's death, people told me that God doesn't give us more than we can handle. As if that would somehow ease the pain or make me feel more courageous than I was. I tried to believe it, really I did, but there were some days I thought it would be easier if I died, too. I definitely had a lot more than I could handle...on my own.

But there were always people who came along and helped me just when hopelessness was creeping in and beginning to take over. My grandmother welcomed me into her home after my dad died, even though I barely knew her. She took care of me in the best way she knew how and we grew to be friends in the years that we had together. Then there was my seventh grade science teacher who used to ask me to babysit her children every Friday night. That was a few years after my father had died. Yes, I think it was so she could go out with her husband. But more than that, I think she asked for my help to give me a purpose beyond my own daily existence.

Stanley had helped me get settled and find a purpose in Uganda after my future plans suddenly changed. Sal rescued me in more ways that I can count when grief at the loss of Michael, Ellen, and Christina threatened to over-whelm me. Jesse gave me a place to live and spend those precious first weeks with Manny. Adam became a dear friend and challenged me to think deeply. April was a voice of reason and also a shoulder on which to cry as we navigated the waters of life. Yes, life often gave me more than I could handle, but I was never meant to do it alone.

Manny continued to grow over the next few months, but Sal and I both noticed as Manny began to crawl that he would bump into things. We placed a thick rug on the living room floor, but sometimes Manny's hands and feet got so swollen that he would sit and cry instead of trying to crawl across the floor to me. It was too painful to put pressure on his extremities. So I held him and we cuddled a lot, gently.

Manny had a few weeks of intense coughing in late March, and Sal put him on an antibiotic right away. Those poor little lungs were trying so hard. I was grateful that Sal caught it before it turned into pneumonia.

April told me about her adventures at Okusuubira every week, but I never took Manny out there. I didn't want him to be exposed to anything, not even a misdirected sneeze. I felt guilty about it for a little while, but when April told me that one of the kids had contracted tuberculosis and they had to quarantine a whole wing of the dormitories, I knew I had made the right decision.

The day after April went back to America with her team, Manny had his first bout with acute chest syndrome. He got a high fever and the deep coughing returned. We took Manny to a hospital where Sal knew he could get access to oxygen. As Sal explained it, the infection from a few weeks earlier had most likely weakened Manny's lungs.

Once admitted to the hospital, Manny was given pain medication and put on an antibiotic. I hated to see him suffer so much to get a deep breath. He struggled and gasped for air, which caused him to get agitated and cry. Sal and I took turns walking around the room while holding Manny, trying to distract him and calm him down. The lack of oxygen was making him sleepy. I didn't want to walk him in the hallway for fear of being exposed to something else. I opened his window for some fresh air and tried to imagine a breeze sweeping all of the bad germs out.

Sal had to push his weight around to get oxygen for Manny. He didn't like to do that, especially since he knew some of the other patients at the hospital who were also in need of oxygen, and the supply was far from plentiful. But for his own child, he would do anything.

The next morning, Sal told me the hospital staff was recommending a blood transfusion. I came unglued.

"There is no way my child is getting a blood transfusion in Africa. Take my blood and give it to him. I know we have the same type." I rolled up my sleeve and sat in the chair.

Sal shook his head sadly as he rocked back and forth while balancing Manny on his hip. Sal explained something about how my blood was too similar to Manny's because I was his mother, and therefore I would not be a good donor for him. It sounded so backwards to me, but I let it go.

"Let's take him to America," I insisted. "Or at least England. Surely Dr. Rollofson would help."

"Oh, my dear Olivia, Manny can't fly right now. The high altitude and lower oxygen on a plane would cause his body even more stress."

I felt so helpless. Sal did, too. Ironically, Manny was

doing well at that moment, and he was the only one in the room not crying.

Finally, I consented to the transfusion. Sal was relieved, although I knew he was concerned for Manny's safety, too. He left for awhile and I knew he was observing the preparations, making sure the needle was sterile, and checking the blood as best as he could without being a nuisance.

"It will only take a couple of hours," Sal explained. "Then we can probably go home."

Because Manny was already sleepy and on pain medication, he barely flinched when the needle was poked into his arm. I sat with him and watched the bag of blood trickle through the tube and into his arm, blood that was full of life-giving oxygen and healthy red blood cells. I prayed it would help.

Sal left for a half hour to find some food for us. Hospitals in Africa don't serve meals. Unless a patient has a friend or family member bring in something to eat, one could go for days without food, making the healing process even more arduous.

As soon as the blood transfusion was complete, Sal made plans to get Manny discharged. I knew he wanted us out of that hospital as quickly as possible.

Within a week, Manny was walking. The blood transfusion really boosted his energy, and he seemed so much perkier. He smiled and giggled and attempted to say dada, which of course Sal loved.

Jesse called a few days after we got home. His graduation was coming up in a few weeks, but there was no way we could make it to the ceremony. I congratulated him and filled him in on the success of the blood transfusion, then spoke to Adam for a few minutes. He had a bad cold and was sneezing and coughing, but he assured me it was only a cold.

Manny only had a couple of minor episodes of coughing over the summer. It was nothing that required antibiotics, and I was grateful. I almost forgot we had a sick baby on the inside. Even Sal seemed to relax with each good passing day, although he was still not back to taking overnight trips.

The days continued to fly by, and I treasured each one. Manny was now a feisty toddler who was learning to assert himself and test the waters with his parents. Sal loved to play hide and seek almost as much as Manny did.

The Rollofsons came to visit in late October, and it was wonderful to have guests in the house. They hadn't seen Manny since he was a few months old and marveled at the changes in his personality. Most 15 month olds go through a phase where they are afraid of strangers, but not Manny. He took to the Rollofsons with delight and they loved it. Mrs. Rollofson especially lavished attention on him as though he were a true grandchild.

The Rollofsons stayed with us for five days before preparing to head to the southern part of Uganda. On the morning of their departure, I awoke to find Sal and Dr. Rollofson deep in conversation at the kitchen table. They were speaking in hushed tones and I knew it had something to do with Manny's health. I sat down next to Sal and he put his hand over mine on the table.

"Dear, Dr. Rollofson thinks we should take Manny to the States for further evaluation. They have sickle cell experts and regimens that are not available to us here."

I nodded, secretly a bit relieved because I had been hoping for something like this to happen. As much as Sal loved and cared for Manny to the best of his knowledge, I knew there had to be new and better treatment options available in America. Sal greatly respected Dr. Rollofson's opinion.

"I'd suggest that you come to England, dear," Dr. Rollofson explained. "But with us making preparations to go into the jungle for a few months, it's best that you go to the US soon. And since Emmanuel is already an American citizen, the hospital admittance process should be easier there."

Mrs. Rollofson walked into the kitchen with Manny in her arms. "Look at this little sunshine!" she exclaimed fondly. She sang to him softly as he clapped his hands. I hopped up to help them find something for breakfast.

"When do you think we ought to go?" I asked. "Perhaps at Christmas time? Or maybe that would be a little crowded at the airports. Perhaps earlier in December?"

"Now, dear," said Sal. "We should take him soon. I've already looked up flight information and we can get flights this Thursday."

As I turned around to set a bowl on the table, Manny suddenly cried out and arched his back in pain. Dr. Rollofson stood up and caught him as he nearly wrenched his way out of Mrs. Rollofson's arms. Dr. Rollofson took Manny to the couch and laid him down gently. Sal rushed to his side as they tried to pinpoint the source of sudden discomfort. As Dr. Rollofson gently prodded his fingers across Manny's abdomen, the toddler writhed in pain. It was his spleen. The left side of his abdomen was swollen.

Without realizing it, I had started to cry. Mrs. Rollofson put her arm around me and said, "There, there, dear," over and over. Things had been going so well with Manny that I had almost convinced myself he had somehow outgrown the disease. But that was not true.

Sal put Manny on antibiotics again with the hope that his spleen would calm down enough for the long trip to America. He made arrangements at a hospital in Minnesota that had sickle cell specialists on hand and told me he had already made plans with Jesse for us to stay at his apartment. I don't know how or when he did it, but Sal really was amazing.

It would be chilly in Minnesota in November, but I didn't have many warm clothes for Manny. We'd have to shop when we arrived. If he was doing well enough, perhaps we could fit in a quick a trip to the Mall of America before the hospital appointments Sal had lined up. Manny might like all the sights and sounds.

The flight to London was uneventful, other than a screaming baby seated two rows behind us. Manny didn't cry at all. He sat on my lap or Sal's for the entire flight. I noticed his feet beginning to swell by the end of the flight, and I massaged them ever so gently.

We stayed in a hotel near the airport overnight. In the rush to pack, I had forgotten that our luggage would be kept at the airport overnight. My only carry-on was a diaper bag with some disposable diapers that Mrs. Rollofson was kind enough to bring over. The hotel had toothbrushes and combs at the front desk, and I enjoyed the amenities of a modern country.

The room had two twin beds pushed next to each other. It was an odd set-up, one I had never seen before, but Sal assured me it was very European. Since one of the beds was next to the wall, we put Manny on that one so he wouldn't crawl out.

Manny woke up crying in the night, completely inconsolable. He was so distraught that I feared we might get kicked out of the hotel. Sal gave him some pain medication and that eventually calmed him down.

Early morning came all too soon. I was so glad Sal had the sense to arrange for a wake up call or else we might have slept right through our flight. I hated to wake up Manny from his deep sleep, but we had to get back to Heathrow and through security.

Almost as soon as the Boeing 777 took off, Manny started to cough and cry. It was going to be a long day. Two hours into the flight, he hadn't let up. He coughed so hard that some of the passengers around us looked alarmed and gave us dirty looks. The woman to my right kept sighing and crossing her arms on her chest. Sal tried to assure those around us that Manny's condition wasn't contagious, but I heard mumblings about Africans bringing over their diseases. It's a good thing I was too tired to fight it.

Halfway across the Atlantic, Manny had a stroke. The sickle cells must have blocked the blood flow to his brain. It was the most frightening moment of my life, but thankfully Sal was able to remain calm. The right side of Manny's poor little body flopped around and I held onto him for dear life, wishing my healthy energy could flow through him somehow. Another doctor on board was summoned to help by the flight attendants, but there was really nothing we could do except pray it would pass quickly without causing further harm to his already weak body. The doctor wanted to take Manny from me, but I refused to let go.

Manny slept for the remainder of the flight. His breathing had become very labored and raspy. I worried about the oxygen levels on the plane and about the possible damage the stroke had done to his brain.

A senior flight attendant came to speak with Sal to decide if we needed to land somewhere on the east coast. But Sal and the other doctor decided it would be best to keep going. If we landed, we didn't know where to go or if anywhere was equipped to care for a sickle cell patient. By the time we raced around, we could already be landing in Minnesota and on our way to where they were expecting us and already had Manny's records. Sal requested the use of an on-board phone to call ahead to the hospital in Minneapolis. He let them know we'd be coming tonight and not in two days. They told Sal they'd have an ambulance waiting for us at the airport as soon as we cleared customs.

CHAPTER THIRTY-ONE

I was usually quite excited to see the cityscape of Minneapolis out an airplane window, but this time I was filled with dread. The last time I had been here, it was to give birth to Manny. And now we were here to save his life. The stroke had changed things.

The flight attendants were kind enough to ask passengers to stay seated so we could get off the plane first. The woman who had sighed so heavily when Manny was crying actually gave me a hug as we got out of our seats and said, "Good luck, dear."

Emergency personnel were waiting for us on the other side of customs. Manny had regained some movement, enough to throw a few punches and kicks as they attempted to strap him onto a gurney. Sal climbed up behind me into the ambulance. The door was still open while the EMTs were getting Manny situated and filling in paperwork, and suddenly I decided to hop back outside for a minute. My black sweater-covered arm would be perfect. I held it up so the falling snowflakes could land on it. Then I hustled back inside and went right over to Manny's face. I tried to get him to look.

"Do you see the snowflakes, Manny? This is snow, darling," I whispered. "Take a peek, my love." He was so groggy that I'm not sure he really saw them before they melted into my sleeve.

As we traveled to the hospital, I realized we hadn't picked up our luggage. One of the EMTs kindly offered me his phone so I could call Jesse. He wasn't home and I dreaded leaving a semi-coherent voicemail in my sleep-deprived stupor. I explained that we were arriving a few days earlier than expected and that we would be going straight to the hospital, not to his apartment. Then I described our luggage and asked if he could go and pick it up from the airport. Jesse was such a dear friend that I knew he'd follow through.

It was snowing quite heavily on the way to the hospital. The ambulance driver didn't put on the siren because we weren't rushing to get to the hospital, and I was glad. The roads were slippery enough without adding the element of speed. There weren't windows in the back of the ambulance, but we could feel the vehicle slipping every now and then. Sal wasn't used to snow and he gripped my arm firmly.

The radio came on in the ambulance and we could hear reports of crashes happening on the highways throughout the city.

"People need to stay home," remarked the EMT named Jay who was seated nearest to me. "We're supposed to get ten inches of snow by midnight, followed by rain. These temps are hovering around the freezing point."

Another call came in of a five-car pile up.

"Change the route, pal," Jay called up to the front. "That latest crash is about a quarter mile up the highway from here." But it was too late for the driver to make the nearest exit ramp. Traffic slowed to a crawl as vehicles carefully made their way around the scene of the accident.

I peeked up through the front window and saw a van that had been flipped onto its roof. Two smaller cars were spun around and now faced the opposite direction of the flow of traffic. A fourth vehicle was nearly cut in half, and a semi was jackknifed through two lanes of the highway. We'd be fortunate to get through this area before police had it blocked off.

But we made it through with only a minor delay. I wondered if people who had been in the accident were expecting this ambulance to stop for them.

After arriving at the hospital, Manny was admitted to a room right away and two doctors with whom Sal had been corresponding met us there. I excused myself after a few minutes and stepped out into the hallway. The combination of medical terminology being tossed back and forth with a severe lack of sleep was making my head swim.

A nurse at the nurse's station directed me to a phone that I could use. I tried calling Jesse again and this time he answered. He had gotten my message and was en route to the airport to pick up our luggage, but there was an accident blocking his route and he'd been sitting in his car on the highway for twenty minutes.

"Oh, Jesse, I'm so sorry," I said. "Can you skip it and turn off somewhere? Maybe the airlines can deliver our bags to your place tomorrow?"

"No worries, Liv, I'm seriously about a mile from the airport," he replied. "I wish I could be at the hospital with you right now. But I've called Adam and he should be there soon. I'll take a back route to the hospital on side streets after I get your bags."

Just then I felt a hand on my shoulder. "Adam!" I cried out.

I said goodbye to Jesse and turned around to hug my dear friend. Sometimes the best thing in the world is a simple hug from someone who knows you so well that you don't need to say a word because they already understand.

After filling Adam in on the latest with Manny, we walked down the hall to Manny's room. Sal was coming out the door just as we approached. He and Adam had never met. As I prepared to make brief introductions, the men decided this was no time for small pleasantries and they hugged each other through tears.

Sal explained that the doctors wanted to take a scan of Manny's brain to see what damage, if any, the stroke had done. They were also discussing the possible removal of his spleen but would take it one step at a time. Right now, Manny was resting comfortably while an IV administered medication to ease his pain and prevent further infection. He wasn't on oxygen at the moment, but it was ready to go. A blood transfusion wasn't out of the question, either.

I took Adam into the room so he could peek at Manny more closely. He walked right over to the hospital crib and reached through the bars.

"Hey, little man," he said softly while caressing Manny's fingers. "You're getting to be so big, buddy." Adam's voice cracked as he spoke. He stood there for a few minutes just watching the sleeping baby while Sal and I did the same on the other side of the crib.

Adam finally looked up at me, his eyes brimming with tears. He started to say something, but at that moment a doctor walked into the room. Adam motioned that he was going to step out into the hallway so we could discuss things with the doctor, and I nodded.

Sal and I decided we weren't going to leave the hospital. For one thing, it was an inconvenience to expect Jesse or Adam to drive us back and forth, especially with the bad weather. And for another thing, we didn't want to leave Manny. We planned that one or the other of us would always be by his side whenever possible.

It was a toss-up as to which one of us was more exhausted at that point, but I insisted Sal get some rest first. The chairs in Manny's room weren't very comfortable, so Sal went to find a couch in the family waiting room down the hallway.

Adam and I were sitting and talking in Manny's room when Jesse showed up about an hour later. I had been asking Adam about himself to distract myself from the problems with my son. Adam had new health problems of his own. He had lost weight since I had last seen him and he told me his medication was giving him some unwanted side effects, but he didn't go into detail.

Jesse entered with a smile but wasn't quite his usually spunky self. It's hard enough to walk into a hospital room, but when the patient is so tiny, it's even more difficult.

"Oh, Manny!" Jesse exclaimed a little too loudly, causing the baby to stir slightly. I stood up and met him when he was halfway into the room. Another hug, more crying. I was becoming an expert at this.

After about ten minutes of talking softly over Manny's bed, Jesse's phone beeped. He got a very concerned look on his face and bit his lower lip as he read the text message silently.

"What is it, Jess?" I asked.

"It's from Stanley. He was on his way over here and got a call from a friend whose family was in a bad car accident. He's going to meet them now and will come up here later."

"Oh, dear," I said. More tragedy. This early major winter storm of the season had caught everyone off guard.

My eyelids were getting heavy and Manny seemed peaceful for the time being. I told the guys I was going to wake up Sal and make a switch so I could rest for awhile. But Jesse and Adam insisted that I leave Sal sleeping and said they would stay with Manny.

"Promise you'll wake me up if anything changes," I insisted. "Anything. If his heart rate changes, I want to know. If he wakes up, get me immediately."

"Liv, you're ten paces down the hallway. We'll get you if anything changes."

I found an empty couch near Sal and was sound asleep within thirty seconds.

I awoke about an hour later to find Adam gently shaking my shoulder. "It's time for Manny's brain scan," he said softly. I nodded and tapped Sal.

The four of us followed along as Manny was taken down two floors to radiology. We sat in a small nearby waiting room that was painted a dark green. The chairs were made of stiff black vinyl. It wasn't going to be a comfortable place if we had to wait for very long.

"Why don't you go and find something to eat, dear," suggested Sal. "I'll meet you back up at the room in awhile. They said this could take thirty minutes or so."

I wanted to stay, but I didn't want to argue with Sal. He probably wanted to discuss things with the doctors that he didn't want me to hear, and frankly, I was glad to not know everything. At least being ignorant meant I could remain hopeful.

Adam said he'd come with me, and Jesse offered to stay with Sal. The cafeteria was nearly deserted at this late hour and the food stations were closed, but coffee and a few assorted pastries were still available.

Adam and I sat down at a shiny, silver table with our snacks, the only people in the seating area except for someone who looked like a first year resident. Adam walked over to grab some napkins from the condiment station, then motioned that he was going to duck into the restroom quickly.

I lifted the paperboard cup to my lips and inhaled the rich, deep aroma of freshly brewed coffee.

"Olivia? Is that you?"

I'd know that voice anywhere. Michael.

Slowly I lifted my eyes as Michael made his way across the room toward me.

"Gosh, it's been a long time," he said. "You look great."

I knew he was lying and just trying to be kind. I had gotten about two hours of sleep in the past two days and had cried my eyes out more times than I could count. But I didn't feel like arguing, even half-heartedly. He pulled out a chair across from me and sat down.

"Hey, Michael," I said softly. "Are you on call tonight?" It hadn't occurred to me that I might run into him here at the hospital.

"I wish that's why I was here," he replied. "No, I'm here because Ellen and the girls were in an accident this evening. I'm just grabbing some coffee for Stanley and me. I needed to walk for a few minutes."

That was the accident in Stanley's text.

"Oh, Michael, I'm so sorry. How bad was it?"

"Ellen's femur was shattered, so she's in surgery for that right now. She was picking up Christina after school when a school bus skidded right into her car on the ice and pinned her behind the bumper. Christina and Ronnie were already strapped in, so they're okay other than being a little shaken up. Thank God. Christina had a collar bone break that just healed. But Ellen had been leaning over to put our youngest in the car seat when the bus slammed into her."

"Maggie?" I asked.

Michael gave me a quizzical look and nodded. He probably wondered how I knew his youngest daughter's name. He would have had no idea that I was on the other side of the birthing suite's door when Jesse took Manny out into the hallway for photos with Maggie and Michael on the day of the babies' birth.

"Is she…is Maggie going to be okay?" I asked hesitantly.

Michael teared up. "The doctor part of me says yes, she'll be okay. But the daddy side of me is flipping out."

"Broken bones?" I asked.

"Oddly enough, no broken bones for Maggie," explained Michael. "But she suffered some head trauma. Her face hit against the headrest of the front seat pretty hard during the impact. She's gonna have two black eyes, that's for sure, and who knows what else. Knocked out a front tooth. And it had finally come in all the way last week."

"Wow, that's tough," I said, instinctively reaching my hand across the table to squeeze his. He placed his other hand on top of mine and looked into my eyes. Oddly enough, it didn't feel awkward to look back at him. In fact, it felt just right.

"Oh, Liv, I'm so sorry about everything," Michael said tenderly. "I didn't handle things well after my brother died. You were so good to me and I really stomped all over your heart."

I couldn't argue with that.

"I just can't express enough how sorry I am for breaking your heart. Mine was already so broken and I couldn't see clearly enough to think of any other options."

"It's okay, Michael," I assured him. "Really."

"No, it's not," he said. "I really was a monster. Can you ever forgive me? I've thought about you so many times over the past years. But I stayed away because I heard you had a new life and I didn't want to hold you back in any way. And I really do love Ellen and the girls."

"Oh, Michael, I forgave you a long time ago. I had to," I replied. I remembered so clearly the day Sal picked me up from the internet cafe and we ended up on the patio in the dark, burning my list of heartaches in the candle. "I have a wonderful husband now. I really have moved on."

"Oh. I'm so glad." He sounded relieved. "I used to ask Stanley about you every now and then, but he told me to proceed with my new life and never gave me any details."

"Didn't Jesse ever tell you anything?" I asked.

"Jesse?" Michael asked, sounding surprised. "Have you stayed in touch with Jesse all this time?"

Oh my goodness, Jesse really hadn't said a word to Michael about me. He promised he wouldn't, but with his trips to Uganda and my months-long stay at his apartment, I was amazed that such a big talker could keep my secrets. I loved him dearly for it.

Right then Adam walked over to the table.

"Adam, this is Michael," I said, introducing the men. "Michael, Adam." They shook hands.

"I think I remember you from the Guatemala team meetings a few years ago," said Michael. Adam nodded.

"So is this your husband, Olivia?" Michael asked. Adam

232

snorted a little too loudly. I would have kicked him under different circumstances.

"Umm, no," I explained. "My husband's name is Sal. He's with our son right now." Then turning to Adam, I asked if he had gotten a text from Jesse about Manny yet. Adam shook his head.

"So, why are you here at the hospital at 3 AM?" Michael asked.

"It's our son. He's got some serious complications with sickle cell disease."

"Sickle cell?" Michael asked a bit incredulously. "But..."

"My husband is Ugandan," I explained, digging around in my purse for a family photo. I slid it across the table and Michael drank it in. "This was on Manny's first birthday this summer. He's almost 16 months now."

"Your son is so close to the same age as my daughter, Maggie. When's his birthday?"

"July 23."

Michael's eyes widened inquisitively just as Adam's phone beeped with a message.

"Manny's done with the scan and they're wheeling him back to his room now," said Adam.

I pushed the chair out and stood up to go. Michael stood up, too. He shook Adam's hand again, then stepped toward me. As he pulled me in for a hug, he bent down and kissed the top of my head. Just like he used to.

CHAPTER THIRTY-TWO

Manny's scan showed some damage to his brain, but we wouldn't get more detailed information than that until sometime in the morning when the doctors were scheduled to arrive and discuss the next move. Hopefully, they lived close to the hospital. News reports said the total snowfall accumulation so far was 11 inches of snow, but the temperature had risen to 33 degrees. Any further precipitation would come in the form of sleet or freezing rain.

I tried to encourage Jesse and Adam to go home and get some decent sleep, but with the roads so bad, they decided to stay. I was wide awake, not sure if I was more wired from the coffee or the unexpected meeting with Michael. I offered to sit with Manny and encouraged the three men to catch some winks in the waiting room. Sal looked so exhausted. He loved to be able to help people with his medical knowledge, but there was nothing he could do for his own son right now and that pained him.

A nurse came in to check on Manny about 45 minutes later. I must have dozed off because her presence startled me.

"Has he been coughing?" she asked me. "Struggling to breathe in the last few minutes? His pulse ox level is dropping on my monitor. The doctor may want to get him on oxygen now." She left to call the doctor, telling me she'd be right back.

I stood up and peeked down at Manny. He was indeed struggling to breathe, beginning to gasp like a fish out of water. I felt so helpless. He was already on IV antibiotics because of an infection in his lungs.

"Oh, my darling, " I cooed to him, brushing my fingers gently across his forehead. He felt warm. "I love you, Emmanuel James. My sweet, sweet boy."

I knew they had Manny medicated to ease his pain, but I desperately longed for him to wake up and look up at me with those big brown eyes. I realized I was breathing slowly and deeply as I watched him, as if somehow he might be able to mimic me and relax.

Sal entered the room.

"I can't sleep," he said. "I want to help Manny so badly, with everything in me." Sal stopped talking and listened to Manny gasping for a deep breath. He looked alarmed.

"The nurse will be right back. She's getting approval for oxygen," I explained. Sal nodded and put his arm around me.

Suddenly Manny's wheezing increased dramatically and he began to thrash about. He was having a seizure. I knew that was a possible complication from sickle cell, just like the stroke was, but I never expected it to happen here in the hospital.

Sal shouted out the door and two nurses came running. It all happened so quickly. Suddenly, Jesse was there, hustling me out the door as a doctor was entering.

I sat with Jesse and Adam for what seemed like hours, but in reality it was probably about twenty minutes. Where was Sal? He must have found a way to stay in the room. He eventually worked his way to the waiting room and found us there.

Sal looked numb, but the blank stare on his face was about to crack. This amazing and wonderful doctor-husband of mine, who was always calm in a desperate situation, fell apart.

Manny was in a coma. The stress of the seizure following the recent stroke was too much for his brain to handle. The sickle-shaped cells apparently had gathered in the small blood vessels in his brain, causing a clot. That was happening in his lungs, too. They were going to give him a blood transfusion to see if that might help. But Sal was not optimistic.

"Could we have done anything differently?" I cried. "What if we had come to America earlier? What if I had remembered to get the follow-up blood test after Manny was born? What if I had agreed to that blood transfusion sooner?"

I wept bitterly. We all did. Nobody really wanted to answer those questions because their answers wouldn't change anything now, and they might not have changed anything in the past.

We were interrupted in our sadness when Stanley found us the waiting room. Jesse explained everything to him as best he could, and Stanley sat down and cried with us.

When we were finally allowed to go back to see Manny, the feeling in his room had changed. His breathing wasn't quite so labored, and therefore his body was more relaxed. It was somehow peaceful standing there, watching him sleep now. Would he ever wake up? That was another question I didn't want an answer for right then.

Adam eventually announced that he needed to go home and take the dose of anti-retroviral medication that he had missed the night before. He promised to come back within a couple of hours. He looked exhausted and I wondered if it was because of his illness, or if perhaps I looked that exhausted, too.

The snow had stopped hours earlier and plows would have cleared the roads by now. Jesse offered to go with Adam, but first he asked if Sal and I wanted him to stay. I assured Jesse we'd be okay and thanked him profusely.

"Want anything out of your suitcases, or should I take them home?" Jesse asked. I had completely forgotten that our luggage was in his trunk.

"Take it home," I said. "It's too much to drag it all in here and I don't feel like digging through your trunk in a parking ramp in the cold. But could you please look in the side pouch of the big, green bag and get Manny's little purple giraffe?" Jesse had bought it at the hospital gift shop when Manny was a newborn and it had become a cherished toy.

Jesse winked. Right then I wished everyone could have a Jesse in their life.

After the guys left, Sal and I needed to have a heart to heart talk about Manny. Things were progressing so quickly. I knew it was unlikely he'd be going home with us to Uganda and that it was only a matter of time before the sickle cells destroyed his body. Why, oh why was I about to lose another person so dear to me?

Sal wanted to talk to me about donating Manny's body for research. The thought horrified me and I couldn't imagine my little boy being cut apart and picked at by medical students. Sal was a doctor—of course that's what he'd think was a good idea. I got so mad at him that I left the room, but only for a few minutes. If there was a way that something good could come out of something bad, then I wanted that. If studying how the disease affected Manny's body would enable one other child's life to be spared of this ugliness, then I wanted that.

The sickle-shaped cells in Manny's blood were damaging his organs, so we couldn't donate any of them. It would have to be his whole body for research. I shuddered at the thought of returning to Uganda without him.

"I have ever been to Uganda," squeaked a little voice. "Have you?"

I turned around to see Manny's purple giraffe peeking through the doorway. Jesse.

"Excuse me. I have ever been to Uganda. Have you?" he asked in a silly voice that had first come to life when Manny was a newborn.

The phrase "I have ever been to Uganda" was one the kids at Okusuubira used to say to visitors. They heard people asking each other, "Have you ever been to Uganda?" and somehow turned the words around to come up with this silly saying that they thought was perfectly correct. In fact, one of the children had spelled it out with shells on a piece of wood and presented it to Jesse as a going-away gift on his last trip. It had become a fun joke between us.

The smallest smile crossed my lips as I walked to the door to retrieve the giraffe. But Jesse wouldn't let go. He walked softly over to Manny's bed and made the little giraffe say something to Manny that I couldn't quite hear. Then he tucked the giraffe under Manny's tiny little arm, being careful to lift wires and tubes out of the way.

Soon after Jesse left again for home, Stanley came up to the room. He had just been to see Ellen. She was heavily medicated due to the pain of having her leg broken in two different places, but she was expected to make a full recovery. There would be much physical therapy down the road.

I wanted to ask how Maggie was doing, but we were interrupted by another doctor making rounds. As Sal started in with a thousand questions, I stepped out into the hallway with Stanley.

"Michael said you two caught up in the cafeteria," he said. I nodded. "That meant a lot to him, Olivia." I nodded again.

Closure is a weird thing. I liked it. It felt like I had closure on that chapter of life with Michael since we had talked. I had moved on when I went to Africa, it was true, but now it felt like a circle was completed.

I spent the next couple of hours sleeping in a chair next to Manny, holding his hand. I wasn't sure if we had to do a big "pull the plug" moment similar to what I had experienced with both my father and Ronnie. I trusted Sal to let me know what, if anything, we would need to do. In the meantime, I wanted to spend every moment we had left together touching my baby, trying desperately to let him know how much he was loved.

I sang the snowflake song softly to Manny and I was sure he squeezed my hand during the song, just a little bit firmer grip with those tiny fingers. He truly was a one-of-a-kind, precious, beautiful child. As much as I was going to hate to say goodbye to him, I wouldn't have traded any of those days of his life we spent together. Even the bad days. If my heart hurt, that meant I could still feel. I didn't ever want to stop feeling.

CHAPTER THIRTY-THREE

Later that evening, Sal asked me to go down to the cafeteria and find him a sandwich. It was obvious that he knew something I didn't.

"Can you tell if he's about to have another seizure?" I asked. "Is it almost time? Why do you want me to go?"

Sal assured me he didn't know anything, but it was just a feeling he had. His instincts were usually right. I still wasn't sure if I wanted to be there with Manny or if I'd rather not see him struggling at the end. What a decision to have to make. Would it make me a bad mother if I preferred not to be there? I knew Sal wouldn't think so.

"Can I wait til Jesse and Adam get back?" I asked. Sal consented. That would give me more time to decide if I really wanted to be there with Manny or not.

Of course the guys arrived moments later, making the decision easier for me.

I kissed my sweet little boy's forehead and whispered a prayer of thanks for the short time I had been privileged to be his mother. Jesse and Adam took a moment to say goodbye to Manny, each in their own special way. Then I kissed Sal on the cheek and stepped out of the room with my two dearest friends.

By the time we reached the end of the hallway, monitors at the nurses' station started beeping loudly and there was a flurry of activity at Manny's door. We stepped onto the elevator and I didn't look back. I couldn't. I wanted my last memories of Manny to be of his peaceful sleeping face. Jesse and Adam each took one of my hands as I shut my eyes. The doors closed behind us with a slight shudder.

The cafeteria was bustling with activity, and I felt hungry for the first time in days. Ravenous actually. We got in line and I chose turkey with mashed potatoes, gravy, and green bean casserole. I probably wouldn't be able to eat a bite due to the enormous lump that had taken up residence in my throat, but it was strangely satisfying to watch comfort food being scooped onto my plate. Could a meal somehow fill the void that had already begun to penetrate so deeply within me?

"Thanksgiving isn't for a few more days, Liv," teased Jesse. He asked for the identical meal while Adam got a plate of steamed broccoli and pears.

We sat down at a corner table. Adam went back to get some napkins, and while he was gone, I asked Jesse if everything was okay. Well, besides everything with Manny. Adam had been extra quiet since their return.

"He got into an argument with his old man on the phone," explained Jesse. "His parents tried to call him last night when we were here, but his phone battery had died. When he didn't answer by midnight, they panicked. Sent the police to my apartment and had my landlord let them in. His parents seem to think he's going to drop dead of AIDS someday soon. They are really freaked out, as in 'control-freaked' out."

Adam came up to the table right then and didn't seem to mind that Jesse was sharing his story with me.

"The worst thing about it, Olivia, is that I think they'll be glad when I'm gone,"said Adam sadly. "They won't have to worry about me anymore. They surely won't hang around my room caring for their son like you've been doing for Manny." He hung his head. "My dad thinks he's the expert on everything I should be doing 'cause he's a doctor. But he's an eye doctor, for crying out loud."

"Oh, Adam, I'm so sorry." I didn't know what else to say, but Jesse was used to hearing about the garbage Adam got from his parents. Eager to lighten the already somber mood with a dumb joke, Jesse started to tell one about a birdie going to the hospital for a tweet-ment. Just as he was getting to the punch line, his phone rang. It was Sal.

Jesse looked at me while he was listening to Sal and I knew. Manny was gone. No more gasping for air, no more crying out in pain. His suffering was over.

When Jesse hung up, he said we needed to toast to the little guy. So with eyes brimming with tears, we raised our glass of Coke, bottle of orange juice, and cup of coffee to the memory of Walugembe Emmanuel James, a beautiful, young boy who was dearly loved by his parents, Salvador and Olivia, and his amazing uncles, Adam and Jesse.

Jesse assured me that Sal was okay and had said to finish eating. He needed to fill out some paperwork for the donation process and would call again when he was ready for my signature.

I tried to take a small bite of mashed potatoes, but I couldn't swallow and finally had to spit them out into a napkin. I shoved the plate into the middle of the table and put my head down. I already knew what a broken heart felt like, but this time the pain was even deeper than I remembered.

My child was gone. My own flesh and blood. He symbolized the hope that I had so desperately needed, and now he wasn't here. I felt numb all over. It was like I couldn't even cry anymore, and yet tears slid silently down my cheeks.

A few minutes later, Jesse nudged me and motioned for me to look across the room. I wiped my eyes and slowly propped myself up. Michael was just sitting down with a little girl about 2 1/2 years old who I assumed was little Ronnie. Christina was pulling her wheelchair up to the table with her back to us.

It didn't take long for Michael to spot us. He waved and I waved back. Christina turned around to see whom he was acknowledging and I could see him explaining to her. Immediately, her eyes got wider and she craned her neck to look in our direction. There was a look on her face of surprise...and joy? Was that joy?

Christina's head bobbled as she said something to Michael, and then she started to back her wheelchair out from the table. She was heading our way.

"Olivia!" she squealed as she got closer to our table. "Olivia!" I pushed my chair out in preparation for a hug. There were no pretenses with this child, even if it had been nearly three years since I had last seen her and subsequently disappeared from her life.

Christina and I embraced gently. Within the same hour that I had lost one child so precious to me, I was reconnecting with a child who had once also been very dear.

"Daddy, bring Ronnie over so Olivia can meet her!" Christina shouted to Michael. Then she whispered to me, "I call Uncle Michael Daddy now so Ronnie and

Maggie don't get confused." I smiled at her justification of the title change.

Ronnie was a darling little girl with blond curls and big blue eyes. She resembled Christina, and no one would ever suspect that Michael wasn't her birth father. Ronnie was shy. Although I opened out my hands to her, she clung desperately to Michael's leg and refused to let go.

"How's Maggie?" I asked.

Michael explained that there was no major brain trauma, but that the impact with the seat had severely damaged the cornea on each of Maggie's eyes.

Christina chimed in. "That's the little clear circle that goes over the black dot and the colored part of your eyes."

Michael smiled at Christina and told her she was right and complimented her on remembering what the doctor had said. The cornea does indeed cover the pupil and iris. Michael went on to say that Maggie faced serious visual impairment, as the cornea's main function is to help the eyes focus. And without the protection of that transparent outermost layer of the eye, UV radiation could cause further critical damage.

We chatted a few more minutes before Ronnie started to whine. She wanted to finish the plate of macaroni and cheese that was still sitting at their table.

"We'll catch up again later," said Michael as he was dragged across the room by a feisty blonde. "I want to hear more about how your son is doing. Come on, Christina. We'll see Olivia again."

Christina didn't follow Michael right away.

"You have a son? What's his name?" she asked.

"Emmanuel. We call him Manny," I said as Adam mumbled something in my right ear.

"Manny. I like that. I bet he's cute!" Christina called out as she wheeled across the room.

"What are you mumbling at me, Adam?" I asked him, a bit irritated.

"Corneas don't have blood vessels."

"What?" asked Jesse. "What are you talking about?"

"I said, corneas don't have blood vessels." Adam repeated himself. "Do you know how many hours I spent after school waiting in my dad's office? He had charts plastered all over the walls and I studied the eye inside and out. Blood flows through other parts of the eye, but not the cornea."

"Oh my goodness!" I exclaimed, as what Adam was saying finally sank in. "Do you think they could give Maggie the corneas from Manny's eyes?"

"Get your old man on the phone, Adam!" Jesse commanded.

Adam reluctantly dialed his parents' number. He turned away from us while talking and I could tell the person on the other end of the line was yelling at him. Adam got up and walked to another table to finish the discussion. When he came back, he looked enthusiastic.

"Well, he thought I was the one who wanted to donate my corneas. He had a fit because they contain bodily fluids, which means the HIV virus could be passed along. I finally got him to answer the question, and I was right. No blood vessels in the cornea."

The three of us looked at each other for a minute and then scrambled up from our seats and ran to the elevator. When we arrived at Manny's room, it was empty. I looked around desperately for Sal and yelled his name.

"Honey, your husband is on the phone over here," called a nurse at the station.

Sal was on the line with someone at the hospital. Jesse, Adam, and I caused such a commotion that he excused himself from the phone and said he'd call right back. Breathlessly, we told him about our idea to have Manny's corneas transplanted in Maggie's eyes. They were the same size and the same age, and Sal confirmed that there were no blood vessels in the cornea. There would be no concern about sickle cells getting into her system.

Sal told us it wasn't very likely to be authorized, especially because cornea transplants in small children had a low success rate, but he'd make a few calls. Michael's family would never have to know where the donation came from, but that wasn't the point. We all desperately wanted a part of Manny to live on somehow.

"Go back to the cafeteria," suggested Sal. "I'll find you down there soon."

We returned to the cafeteria and a puzzled Christina came over to our table.

"You disappeared!" she said. "I wanted to ask you to braid my hair like you used to." She handed me a small bag that contained a brush and pony tail holders, a look of pleading in her eyes. Her hair looked like it hadn't been brushed in a few days. Michael probably wasn't used to adding hair duty to the list of other responsibilities that had been thrust upon him since the accident.

"Sure, sweetheart," I replied, taking the brush from her and gently working out the snarls. Jesse went back for a refill on his Coke, and Adam kicked back to check emails on his phone in the chair next to me.

As my hands twisted and pulled each section of hair up and around, I thought about how different this hair was from Manny's. His head had been covered with a thick mass of tiny black curls. Christina's golden curls were more delicate and her hair held a lot of static. Without realizing it, I had started to cry. Michael and Ronnie were walking toward us, almost to the table.

"What's wrong, Livvy?" Christina asked me. "Why are you crying?"

I told her in the most delicate way possible that my baby had died that day.

"I'm glad," she said matter-of-factly.

"What did you say?" asked Michael. "Christina!"

"I said I'm glad Olivia's baby died today."

"Why on earth would you say that, child?" Michael asked her. He was getting visibly upset.

"Well, my daddy never got to meet Ronnie. And I'm sure he would have liked Maggie, too. He missed out on our babies. But now he can play with Olivia's baby. Now they have each other."

She stated it with such confidence that I couldn't help but smile. "Well, there you go," I said. "I'm glad your daddy is already in heaven to welcome my Manny."

Jesse had gotten back with his Coke a few minutes earlier and Adam was looking up from his phone. Sal had also come into the cafeteria and was standing behind me. They were all staring at us, listening to the bizarre exchange of words. But Christina and I were lost in our own conversation, oblivious to anything happening in the rest of the room.

Christina reached up to her neck and pulled a necklace out from where it was tucked underneath her shirt. It was the snowflake necklace I had given her on the night her daddy died.

"I think you need this back," she said, reaching to unclasp it.

I took her hands in mine. "You don't have to do that, sweetie," I said softly. But she was intent.

"I really think you need it now, Olivia. I'm sorry that it isn't the same as when you gave it to me."

I looked closely at the necklace that hung around her neck. The silver snowflake shape was the same, and the tiny diamonds on each arm of the snowflake were still there. But in place of the original blue stone in the center, there was now a pearl. A beautiful, shiny pearl.

"Ronnie took it from my room one day and banged a rock on it. I think she was mad that she wasn't the baby in our family anymore 'cause it was right after Maggie was born."

Christina paused to swallow and catch her breath, unaware that all of the adults in the room were hanging on her every word.

"Mommy and me looked everywhere for the blue stone but we couldn't find it. I cried and cried because it was my special necklace from you. Then my daddy—well, you know, Michael—said we could get a new stone. Do you know why we picked out a pearl?"

My heart was pounding so loudly, I thought surely the others would hear it. What was she going to say about the pearl? That she knew someday she'd run into me on the day my baby died, my precious little pearl from the Pearl of Africa?

"Why did you pick out a pearl, Christina?" I finally asked after realizing she was waiting for me to respond. I was absentmindedly twisting the pearl wedding ring on my finger.

"Because of Maggie. Did you know that the name Margaret means 'pearl'?"

I nearly gasped out loud. How ironic.

"There's another reason, too. Do you want to know?" Christina asked. I nodded eagerly.

"It's because of how pearls are made. Mommy told me that when a grain of sand gets stuck inside of an oyster and bothers it, the oyster squirts stuff at it so it won't hurt so much. That stuff makes bigger and bigger layers around the grain of sand until one day it turns into a shiny pearl. It's magical. Mommy said that could remind me of when I was mad at Ronnie for breaking the necklace. She bugs me now, but someday we'll be friends when she grows up. So the pearl reminds me of both of my sisters."

"That's beautiful, Christina," I said. "Your mommy is very wise."

"Olivia, you need to have the snowflake necklace back. To remind you of your baby Manny. And so you can think of my little sisters and me, too." And then she added quietly, "So you don't forget about us again."

"Oh, my goodness," I said softly. "I've thought about you so many times, Christina. I've never forgotten you." I looked deeply into this precious girl's eyes. "If you're sure about the necklace, I would love it, truly I would. Oh, thank you, sweetheart."

I carefully squeezed Christina's hand as Michael reached behind her to unclasp the necklace. As he placed it around my neck, Sal leaned over and lovingly lifted up my hair in the back. For a brief moment, Michael and Sal stood side by side helping each other arrange the sparkling snowflake around my neck, the beautiful necklace given to me by my father all those years ago. The special, unique, one-of-a-kind snowflake that would forever remind me of my son. The distinctive necklace that now held a pearl in the center, a pearl that would remind me not only of three darling little blonde girls, too, but also of how an oyster squirts shiny stuff at the things that cause it pain so eventually it won't hurt so much.

Made in the USA
Lexington, KY
04 July 2019